Orchid

– ALFRED SCOTT –

http://www.fast-print.net/bookshop

ORCHID
Copyright © Alfred Scott 2016

ISBN 978-178456-310-3

First published 2016 by
FASTPRINT PUBLISHING
Peterborough, England.

ORCHID

**This book is on sale at your local
Waterstones
and also
as a book and an Ebook is available** at
Amazons

Chapter 1

F or many years, you couldn't cultivate it in their house; it was even forbidden to mention its name. His father used to call it "that accursed flower," but his wife loved it so very much, "that orchid flower."

Yet, for the time being, I will say only one thing that their son, who was my best friend, told me:

"When you put the orchid in a flower pot, first it loses its freedom, and then if you don't know how to care for it, it loses its leaves. With its leaves gone, its roots dry up. That way the orchid is condemned to die and it returns to the soil, just as my mother did."

Whenever I visit my friend's grave, no one can take this truth away from me. No one has to tell me what flowers to put on his grave; I choose to cover it with orchids.

I visit the grave almost every day. I stay there for hours talking, gossiping, agonising about life. Sometimes, I can't stop myself laughing, like a child. And sometimes, I cry bitterly. I remember all that we went through, my friend and I. It is impossible to forget.

When I remember his love for me, I have a desire to open his grave and lie near him and be comforted. Once upon a time my friend, too, wanted to open a grave, his mother's grave, and lie next to her to be comforted. But, like me, he didn't do it. If I lay near him to seek comfort, his grave would lose its peace, and I would be breaking my promise to him.

These memories have prematurely aged me. On my lengthy visits to the graveside, I just get exhausted, and when I get home I collapse on my bed. Then, before losing all my strength, I beg God in my prayers to comfort me. If only someone else could take my place to continue what I've begun I would be able to die in peace and be reunited with the spirit of my friend. My mission accomplished, I too would rest in peace.

I don't remember the exact date, but I know that it was a Sunday. I know because I was near the grave, gathering up fallen hazelnut leaves. I had planted a hazelnut tree there to be a home for the squirrels. When my friend was still alive, we had chosen these amiable creatures as our lucky charms.

I had no more energy left to bend down, so I knelt to gather the leaves. I picked them up one by one and put them in the bin liner. Lost in thought, lost in the past, I heard the sound of a car. I tried to lift my head and turn towards it, but my aged body caused a sharp pain in my neck that stopped me.

I had to force myself to stand up. Using all the strength I could muster to straighten first my right and then my left leg, another sharp pain shot through my back. As I put my left hand there, I lost my grip on the bin liner, which being only a quarter full, blew away in the wind.

As the car approached, my pain seemed to ease somewhat little and I managed to move my body towards its sound. I had to retrieve my glasses from my half torn shirt in order to see. Their lenses were dirty and I still couldn't see properly, so I cleaned them on my shirt.

The car approached slowly from the distance and stopped in front of the house. In amazement, I stared at the scene in front of me. I started to walk towards the car and as I did, its doors opened. Five people got out. Three of them were children – two boys and a girl. They looked around but they couldn't see me, hidden as I was in the shade of the hazelnut tree.

But soon, one of the boys must have seen me move and pointing a finger in my direction, alerted his father. In a trice, all eyes were on me. I still didn't know what was going on; I didn't recognise my visitors. I only realised who they were when the boy's father bent down and whispered something to the children. A smile broke out on his face, which passed from child to child.

Beaming with happiness, they ran towards me shouting, "Granddad! Granddad! Granddad!" In spite of my age and the pain, and without thinking, I rushed towards them. The soles of my shoes were ripped, so running in them made me trip and fall.

My visitors were my son and his family, whom I had missed badly for the past forty-two years. Lying on the ground and shaking like a crazy person, I sobbed loudly. Nonetheless, the three children were suddenly hugging and kissing me. My son followed. Crying, he said between sobs, "Forgive me, my dear father." One of the little children wiped away our tears with its tiny hands. We were all overwhelmed with joy. We didn't know what to do next, we were that happy.

I was the most excited one there. Perhaps I wasn't thinking straight, but my whole body was now shaking with happiness.

Time must have passed. My daughter-in-law approached us. Holding my hand she knelt down and looked at me with sorrow, smiling tenderly.

Slowly and with patience, they helped me up, took me home, and sat me down in a chair. I then realised that my energy had all gone. My son sat next to me holding my hand and kissing it.

Wanting to be a part of this reunion, my daughter-in-law bent down and, holding my other hand, said, "It's so great to have an ending like this to pain and sorrow.

"It reminds me of my childhood. My parents were divorced when I was three. Neither of them wanted me. My father's mother raised me, but she could never give me the love that a mother and father could give to their child. In spite of my grandmother's good intentions, she couldn't make me forget my parents.

"My whole aim in life was to be reunited with them. I would send them messages through friends and relatives, begging them to contact me their daughter. I missed them so badly. Finally, years later, one of my relatives said that he knew where they were. The place he took me to was a graveyard. I went first to my mother's grave, then to my father's. Even though they were dead, I was happy. I couldn't be reunited with them, but I could be connected with the soil in which they were buried. Touching this soil, I felt as if they were holding me.

"I know, therefore, exactly what you're feeling at this moment. I live your happiness, because you can now touch each other's bare hands and even breathe, each other's breath, all your tears are worth shedding."

When she had finished, she put her hand on my arm and began to weep. My son and I tried in vain to console her, but she just said, "I need to cry," and continued.

She only stopped and lifted her head up when one of the children approached her asking, "Mummy wouldn't it be better to hug us instead, when you feel like crying?"

"You're right my darling," she replied to the child, finally smiling, and then she stood up and tenderly patted her.

As my son and I were looking at each other, I felt someone tugging my sweater from the back. I turned round and saw the little girl trying to attract my attention. When she saw me looking at her, she held up her hand as if she wanted to salute me: "My name's Miriam, my bro..."

But before she could finish, her brother interrupted. Beaming at me he said: "And my name's Moses and I'm six years old. My brother's name's Jacob and he's fourteen. He's still very shy and he can't speak to anyone, and he's always serious. Miriam's two years and four months old.

"But what I want to tell you is something else, it's a big secret. If you promise never to tell anyone, I will share my secret with you."

I turned my head towards him. "Okay, I promise I won't tell a soul," I laughed.

He became defensive and turned his back to me and started to move away. "I know you'll tell someone... I thought I could trust you; I was so mistaken," he protested.

I lifted him up gently by his shoulders and sat him on my knee. Becoming serious, I looked into his eyes and said, "Honestly, I promise you, I'll never reveal your secret to anyone. This is a granddad's promise."

He too looked deeply into my eyes and held the sides of my moustaches with his hands. He put his forehead against mine saying, "Since you've given me a granddad's promise, I believe you." This time pulling my moustaches even closer to him, he whispered his secret into my ear.

When he had finished, I laughed so much that my cracked lips, which had forgotten how to smile for so long, hurt but I still carried on laughing. His mother came to see why I was laughing so much, why I was having such an outburst of joy.

As soon as I saw her, I lifted my hand and repeated, "Granddad's promise, granddad's promise," as I sat the other two children – who I had surprised with my outburst – on my lap as well.

Although they didn't know why I was so amused, my son and his wife joined me in my laughter. Even though the children didn't laugh, I was very happy. It's impossible to describe that feeling, a feeling that I hadn't experienced in many years.

When Miriam saw that I was still laughing, like her brother, she pulled at my moustaches and said, "You're crying, aren't you?"

But before she could finish, Jacob, who was the quietest and very shy, interrupted her: "He isn't crying; Granddad's tears are tears of joy." Then he started to wipe away my tears. While Miriam and I were looking at each other, he continued, "Granddad's very happy; we've managed to make him happy, and that's why we're all feeling happy."

With these words, he hugged me and the other children did the same. I turned my gaze towards my son whose smiling face had many questions written on it. Still hugging me, Miriam spoke again and this time no one interrupted her: "Who's buried in the garden?"

As she asked this question, her brother wanted to butt in, thinking that he was brighter because was older. I placed a hand in front of his mouth for a second, but then I forgot myself. Looking at my son, I could see that his face was as sad as mine.

Breathing deeply I straightened my back. I looked at them all with deep sorrow and said, "After lunch, I'll tell you the true story about the person who's buried there; it's a very long and a very sad one. But Moses, you mustn't interrupt me like you interrupted your sister."

Moses jumped down from my lap and promised all of us that he wouldn't do that.

A silence descended on the room. Seeing their father's signal to leave, the children each gave me a kiss and ran to their mother. Gently, she gathered her children to her, holding the hands of the two youngest ones as they left the room.

After making sure that the children were out of earshot, my son told me that he had a surprise for me. He took a little box wrapped in a handkerchief from his pocket. The scent of rose oil reached my nostrils. It was the scent that my wife loved the most; I already knew the news I was about to receive. Smiling, he handed me the box. I couldn't hold back the tears. I took the little object with my trembling hands, and, as I untied the knot in the handkerchief, I wiped my cheeks.

I was very careful not to let a teardrop fall onto the handkerchief. Untying the knot calmed me. I opened the lid and saw a letter and a few red rose petals. Seeing the petals made me smile. Underneath the letter were a ring and a photograph of us. All the items were familiar to me. The ring was her engagement ring.

Many years ago, she had said that if this ring was ever to reach me I should know that she still loved me and that her soul was at peace. Now, I was holding the ring that I had given her. I had given her the handkerchief, too, to wipe her tears when her aunty died. Now, it was me who was wiping my tears with the same handkerchief.

Turning towards my son, I held his hands in mine and kissed them, showing my gratitude to him. I told him that I would read the letter after telling them the story. Before I could finish saying what I'd wanted to say, the children came in again, announcing that dinner was ready and pulling me to the table.

The smell was wonderful. It reminded me that I had found my family. Nothing was missing at the table. I sat in my usual place. My son put his chair next to mine and rearranged it so that he could be even closer to me and smiled.

Realising that no one was speaking and all eyes were on me, I put my hands together and started to pray: "I have spent many days and nights praying in tears.

"I am crying again, but this time, I am not alone. I am reunited with my family. Thou took away the one I loved the most, my wife. But Thou hast sent me now my son and my grandchildren, and the one who gave birth to them, his wife. For all of these many years I have missed them, thou hast not given me such a gift until now. With my deepest gratitude, I ask Thee to bless them.

"Let tonight's dinner with my family be the first of many that Thou witnesses. I am old now and thou knowest all my deepest thoughts, but I would like my family to know them too. Please let my family understand the message behind the story that I want to tell them. I pray now with my family and as we say 'amen', please except my prayer.

"As Thou knowest, my son grew up without a father; perhaps he hasn't forgiven me for that yet, but please help him to forgive me if he hasn't. I have always behaved in a way I felt that Thou wanted me to and have done my best not to do anything wrong.

"Please help my grandchildren respect and obey their parents. Please help us in all things always. And please bless this food that it may be good for us. Amen."

I still had tears in my eyes when I ended the prayer. When I looked around, I saw their pale faces staring at the floor as if we had no more hope left. At that moment, a Jewish folksong that my father used to sing came into my mind. As I started singing, first my son, then the children, and then their mother joined me; and the life returned to the table. After the song, we started to eat.

But before I could even tell my daughter-in-law how delicious her food was, I left the table and took my shotgun and ran out of the house; for I had heard the chickens making a terrible racket. I thought the fox was attacking my chickens again. My son and my grandchildren followed me to see what I was going to do.

I was upset, but I managed to walk slowly towards the chicken shed. When I opened the door, I couldn't believe my eyes. A baby squirrel had fallen in and was trying to get out. Seeing that it wasn't the fox, I relaxed.

Holding the squirrel, I called the children. It was the first time in their lives that they had been able to touch such a beautiful creature with their bare hands. As I lifted my head towards the tree above me, I saw the squirrels mother was quite distressed, so after letting the children kiss the animal, I set it free. Within seconds they had vanished.

This episode brought smiles to the children's faces. They told their parents how soft the squirrel's fur had been. My son whispered to me, "Had there been a fox, would you have killed it?" In response, I showed him my rusty shotgun. He shook his head and smiled.

We returned to our dinner. My son started to tell us all about how he'd met his wife and other important events in their lives. Taking this opportunity, I mentioned to my daughter-in-law how delicious the food was.

When dinner was over, I sensed the children's impatience and headed towards the living room. They followed me. I sat in my favourite chair while the children sat cross-legged on the floor in front of me. I could feel their excitement. Once their parents had taken their places next to them, I wanted to start my story. But first, I thought I should tell them about the history of the chair I was sitting in, so I started with that.

"As I wasn't sure if I had done the right thing by returning to the country of my birth, I prayed to God to confirm it to me by giving me a sign. When I entered an antique shop, which wasn't far from the house I had grown up in, I couldn't believe my eyes; it was a tremendous sign. If I hadn't seen it, I would have returned immediately to Switzerland.

"But God wanted to say to me, 'You haven't made a mistake!' I was sure of that when I saw this chair I'm sitting in now there in that shop. This chair is my father's and belonged to his ancestors before him. Everyone who's owned this chair has written his name on it and the names of the members of his family.

"So I wrote mine next to my father's. I'm the twenty-fifth owner of this chair and my son will be the twenty-sixth. I'll tell you an anecdote related to this chair at the end of my story."

Everyone was absolutely still. Telling them that I would be back immediately, I went to my bedroom to get the box I had hidden there many years ago. When I returned, they were all crowded around the chair trying to make out the names on it. Before sitting back in my chair, I bent down and read all the names to them one by one.

After everyone had resumed his place, all eyes were once again on me. Sitting down, I took out the diary that I had hidden in the box and started my story.

I can finally reveal my story, which I wrote in this diary and hid in my drawer. What is written in this diary isn't fiction; it's a true story. When others read my story after my death, they too will be saddened by it. The reality of my life will emerge, they will understand what true love is, and will never put barriers between two people who love each other.

I opened the first page and showed them the orchid I had drawn there myself. Telling them that this story was mainly about such a flower, I began.

Chapter 2

I t was a year and five months before the Second World War broke out. It was August; the weather was hot and oppressive. I'd never liked hot weather, especially in August. But August was still a special month; it had a certain beauty with its multi-coloured flowers and greenery everywhere, and the birds singing melodically.

I thought I was in heaven in our garden. My mother used to feed the birds with bread every day and I always used to help her. The birds were so tame that they would sometimes eat from the palm of my hand. If my mother forgot to feed them, they would all perch on a tree in our garden and start to sing; then my mother would remember and feed them. Because of his work, my father didn't have the time to appreciate the beautiful nature around him but my mother did, and she loved it. Like my mother, I too loved nature.

Because of all that heat, the weather in August could sometimes be suffocating, and, of course, on such occasions, I would get a headache and feel ill. Then I used to walk slowly to the nearby river and splash my face with its cool water. Strolling along the riverbank, stopping occasionally to wet my brow, would make me feel better. It would stop my head aching and it would cool me down.

Obviously, I never left the house without my mother's permission, but no one else used to go where I went. There had once been a cemetery near the river and its gravestones could still be seen, although nobody knew who was buried there. It wasn't a Jewish cemetery. It was impossible to see the inscriptions on the gravestones. Being there never scared me. For years, I used to go there and felt comfortable.

One day like any other in August, I went down to the river to cool myself from the day's heat in the usual way. But that day, I decided to plunge into the water. It did cool my body down, but, to my surprise, it also made my headache worse. I lay on my back under a tree. Possibly because of the headache, I fell asleep. I even dreamt. I still get the shivers when I think of that dream.

In the dream, I heard a bird's screech, which was coming from the top of an immense mountain. Although the mountain was really high, the bird's screeches made me climb it. The climb was a very painful one because I had to get on my hands and knees, and they were soon covered in blood. Once I was at the top of the mountain, the scene before me wasn't what I'd expected to see at all. One of the wings of the bird – a falcon – was trapped under a stone. It looked as if it had no strength left to screech anymore. Its eyes were closed. Cautiously, I released the wing and the falcon flew off, this time screeching with joy.

As it was about to flap its wings above my head to thank me, an eagle flew down, pecked off its head, and threw the lifeless body down at my feet. I watched this in amazement because the eagle was smaller than the falcon. I was very upset by what had happened to the poor falcon and started to cry.

The eagle flew proudly above my head, screeching with joy. Then it approached me and, in a terrifying voice, it spoke: "The ones who think they are strong and free will suddenly end up dying under the claws of the ones who are thought to be weak," and flew off screeching into the sky above.

I stared after it with tears in my eyes. After circling above me a few times, the eagle attacked just as I was about to stroke the dead falcon. The eagle thrust at me powerfully with its talons. I started tumbling down the mountain. However, I woke up before I landed on the ground. Although I knew I'd been dreaming, I couldn't stop my body from trembling.

Still feeling shaky, I stood up, fetched my clothes, and got dressed. As I was about to leave, I saw a squirrel in the forest across the river. Instead of running away, it was staring at me. As all my thoughts were still on my dream, I didn't pay much attention to the squirrel. Turning my back on it, I took a few steps and then turned to look at it again. The squirrel was still staring at me. I was still under the influence of the dream and didn't know what I was doing. I couldn't bear its stares anymore. So I bent down and picked up a little round stone, and with all the force I could muster, I threw it at the squirrel.

The stone landed not far from the squirrel. Rather than being afraid of it, the squirrel picked it up and started to eat it. When I looked upwards I realised that I was under a hazelnut tree. Instead of hurling what I had thought was a little round stone I'd thrown a hazelnut at the squirrel. I'd never intended to harm it anyway – or indeed any other animal. But my dream had affected me so that I didn't know what I was doing.

After eating the nut, the squirrel made its way towards the forest. It stopped briefly to look at me as if it was asking me to follow it. Since I was so intrigued, I decided to do so. When the squirrel saw that I was following, it disappeared into the depths of the forest.

I was left alone in the midst of the tall trees. I looked around me; it was so beautiful, especially the colourful mushrooms that grew on the barks of the trees. That made me forget everything else; although the mushrooms were poisonous, they looked so beautiful that I couldn't take my eyes off of them. They had such an effect on me that instead of turning back and going home, I walked further into the forest.

Then I heard a voice. I walked cautiously towards the voice. Walking closer and closer, nearer and nearer to the voice in the distance, I saw a child. It was a boy. I crept up to him unobserved, and then I sat under a big tree and listened to him.

As he talked, I cried because he was obviously standing by his mother's grave and talking to her: "Mother, I haven't been here for three days, but it seems to me like three years. My hands have started to dry out because I haven't touched the soil on your grave, dearest mother.

"I couldn't even bring you a bunch of orchids. Instead, I've brought you your favourite orchid bulbs. It's the first time I've brought you orchids since you died. My governess brought them when she came to see me for the last time. They aren't very fresh anymore because I hid them from my father, but their leaves are still beautiful."

He continued with his cheek pressed against the earth, "I can almost feel your heart beat. It feels, mother, as if I buried you yesterday, instead of many years ago. I could be lying next to you.

"What you have is an endless happy life, whereas each day without you, I am full of pain and sorrow. Wouldn't it be lovely to be together again reunited. We would never have to be apart again. But we can't. If I did lie next to you now, the grave would become derelict and your name would be forgotten.

"I made a promise to you, and that's another good reason why I can't lie near you, but I know that one day, once my promise has been fulfilled, you will send for me as I wish it. I can't wait for that day my dearest mother. It's very hard to be separated from you, but I'll still come to this earth on your grave. Don't be saddened by my tears; they will fall on this earth so that my scent will linger till the next time I come here."

When he'd finished, he continued crying as he lovingly caressed his mother's grave. My tears too were still flowing. I took a few steps towards him. He was still sobbing and didn't notice me. I took a few more steps towards him. I was now standing beside him. I started to talk to him.

Upon hearing my voice, he jumped in utter surprise. I said, "I know how painful death is. I loved my grandfather as much as you loved your mother. He died in my arms. Before he passed away, he told me that if I loved him, I shouldn't cry for him; but, just like you, I can't help it. Whenever I think of my grandfather my tears start to flow.

"When my grandfather was dying, he told me, 'If you cry for me my dear grandson, your tears, will never dry and you will end up making yourself ill. I haven't chosen to die at this time but it is just the way it is. I have thanked, and still *do* thank God for everything in my life. I know that once He takes me, I will end up in paradise. I also know that I will see there all those who have died before me, whom I love so much.'"

The boy continued staring at me in surprise until I'd finished this speech; and when I told him that my name was Jacob, he seemed even more surprised. Then the boy lowered his head as he looked towards his mother's grave, and, after gently biting his lip, turned towards me with a big smile on his face.

Before running away, he told me that his name was Christian, adding from a distance, "I'll see you here tomorrow at sunrise!" He repeated this information and was gone. After he had left, I felt lonely. I felt as if I'd known him all my life. I stared at the point where he'd disappeared for a long time. I just couldn't turn around and walk away.

As I was thinking, I felt the warm wind. It seemed to tickle my ear, which I liked. I gazed at his mother's grave with sadness. Then I saw further away amongst the weeds a pure white flower. I moved closer to the flower and bent down to caress it. In the midst of all the green, there was just this one white flower. I turned my head towards his mother's grave and decided to pick the flower. It came out easily. I placed it on the grave. Then I touched the earth on it a few times and left.

Deep in thought on the way back, I was very sad. I had overheard the boy promising to cover his mother's grave with orchids. I didn't know what type of flowers orchids were. He had brought dried orchids for the grave, but I hadn't looked at them properly. As it was getting dark, I quickened my pace.

Once home, I wanted to tell my mother all that had happened, but I didn't have the courage. When my father saw how pale I was, he asked me what was wrong. I couldn't answer him. When he repeated the question, I only told him that I'd found a friend. My father ruffled my hair and left the room smiling. My mother did the same.

When I was left alone, I started thinking again and become restless. Even in bed that night, I couldn't sleep; all through the night, I thought of the sad boy.

★ ★ ★

Finally, when I heard the rooster, I got out of bed and quietly left the room. Once I found myself outside, I start to run and when I couldn't run anymore, I walked.

As I approached the graveyard, I saw him. I thought I'd be the first one there, but he'd obviously beaten me to it. When he saw me, he started running towards me. I wanted to run towards him too, but he stopped me with a gesture of his hand. When he reached me, he grabbed my hand and continued to run, pulling me along. In a couple of seconds we were running together.

After that, we were always running together and he was always screaming with joy. I didn't know why he was so happy. One day, as we ran at a steady pace, he said, "Be happy too, because you will soon be as free as a bird, and you will fly!" I still didn't understand what he was trying to tell me. Wasn't I free? Did I need more freedom? Although I couldn't make any sense of what he was saying, I didn't ask him what he meant; I knew that in time I would understand.

He was running very fast. I had never run so fast; neither had I ever had to run for such long way. When we finally stopped, I fell to my knees; I could barely breathe. When Christian saw the state I was in, he started to laugh. Then he approached me and said that we had to train and get fit. Although I could barely get the words out, I asked him why. He responded by covering my mouth with his hand and said that I should learn to be patient, not say any more about it, and that in time, he would reveal it all to me.

After helping me up, we started to walk. "From now on, we won't walk but run," he informed me. After revealing certain other things, he instructed me to keep them a secret. I treasured everything he told me and knew that I would never disclose anything about them to anyone, and I didn't even write them in my diary.

When we came to a mountain, we stopped running. He asked me to look ahead and tell him what I saw. Although I made a big effort, I couldn't see anything. I told him so. He asked me to pay more attention and look again. I still couldn't see anything out of the ordinary. This time holding my hand, he made me get closer to the mountain and asked me to lift my hands up. I did what as I was asked. Then I noticed that he was crying. I looked at him with questioning eyes.

He replied by saying, "Years ago, my mother and I stood at this very spot. My mother held my hand just like I'm holding yours now, but she wasn't crying. I could sense by the way she was smiling that it was her last smile. She tried to tell me everything she knew and said that if I ever I came near here with a friend, I should first take his hand and then uncover the hole that we had filled in with earth." With a smile on his face, he pushed away the earth to reveal a hole. I was very surprised.

Then he said, "As you can see, this is the entrance to a tunnel. My mother told me what to do once we got here. She described you to me, and when and how we would meet. My mother also said that if you walked through this tunnel, in two days you would reach the border with Switzerland; if you ran, it would take much less time. Don't ask me how my mother knew this; I never asked her.

"Of course, if you *did* walk, you wouldn't be able to bear it because the tunnel is very cold and dark. This is one of the reasons why you should train to run. When I walked along the tunnel with my mother, we didn't reach the end. There was another way out somewhere. Don't ask me how my mother managed to get through this opening – although she was very thin of course.

"For many years, this place was our secret, my mother's and mine. I wish this place to be our secret too. You are not to tell anyone, not even your family. You are not to come here alone, only when I tell you to. You will forget all about this place for now. Even when I ask you to come here, you will take extra care not to be followed. Now, we are going to go inside the tunnel."

We went inside. I immediately started to shiver. If I held my finger in front of my eyes, I couldn't see it. The darkness frightened me because it was even blacker than the blackest of nights.

Soon, I felt the cold go right through my bones. I implored him to let me out of the tunnel immediately. He told me that he had said exactly the same thing to his mother and she had trained him to get used to the cold; he would do the same with me. After that, we went back into the warmth and daylight.

As soon as we got out, he went on his knees and started to pray. After his prayer, he asked me not to move and walked some way off. After a very short time, he came back and asked me to give him my hand. When I did, he put a stone into it. I had never seen anything as shiny and I was amazed. His mother had given it to him when they first came to this tunnel. Now he was presenting to me this precious gift that he'd kept for so many years.

I knew that what he'd given me was like a piece of his heart, but I couldn't refuse it. I kept staring at it for a long time. He told me that I was in possession of the most precious gift and that we would never lose touch with each other. My happiness made him even happier.

We heard the birds in the trees settling down for the night, and he said that we should go. We very quickly covered the entrance to the tunnel with some branches we found nearby, and then he prayed silently again.

As we were hurrying away from the mountain, he asked me not to walk home but to run. Then he stood quite close to me with a strange look in his eyes. He pointed to the sky and in a loud voice said, "You are very blessed, my friend!"

When I looked up, I saw a rainbow and started to shout with joy. The rainbow was so beautiful that I couldn't take my eyes off it. When it finally disappeared, I looked to Christian but he wasn't there anymore. Not seeing him there gave me a feeling of deep sadness. I started to walk very slowly towards my house. Feeling very lonely, I kicked at the ground. Suddenly, I thought I heard his voice telling me to run. Thinking he'd come back, I turned round but he wasn't there.

At this point, deep in thought and running, I started to sing a song that I half knew, a song that my father had taught me and one that cheered me. When I reached the river, I threw myself in without even stopping to take off my shoes. After cooling myself down, I sprinted home. I was still singing when I went indoors, but my parents didn't even ask me the reason for my happiness; the fact that I was home and happy was enough for them.

Chapter 3

I t was a Saturday. I always longed for that day with impatience, the day of prayers. In those days, I would cut myself off from the world and only think of God, dedicating that day to the source of all my strength and happiness.

We would put on our best clothes and go to the synagogue. There, we would worship, pray and learn. We would pray and meet friends and relatives we hadn't seen for days. My father always went to chat with people. But I didn't because I didn't have any friends; and I wouldn't talk to our relatives either – I just wasn't daring enough. Although my father never put any pressure on me, my mother was saddened by this fact. I was the first one out of the synagogue as soon as prayers were over. Without looking at anyone, I would head home. I had always behaved like this so now no one thought it was odd.

However, one day, it didn't happen like that. On that day, as I left the synagogue, a surprise was waiting for me. Across the yard, in front of the synagogue, a smiling face was looking at me: it was my friend Christian. With tremendous joy, I started to run towards him. Something always happened whenever I was that happy. And this time was no exception.

Before I could reach him, even before I'd taken more than a few steps from the front of the synagogue, I tripped on a little stone and fell. As soon as I hit the ground, I felt the pain in my right cheek and my elbows. But I was so happy to see him that I didn't mind. Christian came and knelt down next to me.

As our eyes met, I realised that he wanted to laugh. He was stopping himself because he didn't want to upset me. I looked at his face intently, wondering how long it would be before he dissolved into laughter. When I finally realised that he wasn't going to, I started to laugh myself. When he saw me laughing, he too burst into laughter.

Only when I saw my father's shoes did I realise how long we had been laughing; my father was one of those who always left the synagogue last. When we saw him standing there, I immediately stood up and Christian with me. He told my friend that my accident was nothing new and that I always became clumsy when I was very happy. My father also told Christian that he knew how I felt.

I introduced Christian to my father. My friend immediately told us that he'd received a telegram from his grandmother. She had invited him to stay for two weeks' holiday and he wanted me to go with him. I looked at my father imploringly. When he said that he would not only let me go for two weeks but even for a month if my friend wished, I burst into tears. I first hugged Christian and then my father. In response, my father told me that he had been praying for years that I might have a friend. He then left us.

When we were alone, my friend told me that he was taking me without his father's consent and that we should pray that everything would be all right. He then said that he hadn't had much time before visiting his mother's grave to ask her for her blessing. With that, he started to run and as he sprinted, he gasped, "He'll send me a message telling me when I'm to go to my grandmother's. Then he urged me to start running as well and disappeared.

With his departure, I felt as sad and lonely as ever, but as soon as I remembered that we were going to spend many days together, I was happy again. If I'd gone to heaven there and then, I wouldn't have wanted to be without Christian. I loved him so much, that I couldn't put it into writing. Doing as he'd bidden me, I ran all the way home.

I opened the door with all my might and jumped into my mother's lap. I didn't see the sorrow on her face until she'd put me down. When I found myself on the floor, I explained to her that I was very happy because I was going on holiday with my friend, and then I stood up. I went to my room and lay on my bed. I wanted to cry because I was so happy but I couldn't.

Not long after, my mother came in, bent over me, and started kissing my hands. Tears were running down her cheeks. She apologised and said how much she loved me. When she had finished, she hugged me so tight that it felt as if she was going to crush all my bones.

* ★ *

Three days later, very early in the morning, the doorbell rang. I jumped out of bed. My father was already standing there with a smile on his face and a letter in his hand. I grabbed it from him and went back to my room. Without even looking at the envelope, I tore it open. Then I realised that it wasn't from Christian. It was written in Hebrew. My joy vanished.

My father soon came in and said that he had succeeded in teaching me many things, but not in helping me to learn patience. He then took another letter from his pocket and removed the one from my hand, saying that he was sad not to be able to read the address on his Hebrew letter, but that he wished I would become more patient. Then he left the room.

I was ashamed of myself for the way I had behaved towards my father, especially as it wasn't the first time I had acted so rashly. I did try to be patient, but without any success. I didn't even feel like reading the letter from my friend because all I could think of was my father's sad face. While I was in deep thought and clutching the letter in my hand, I became uneasy about a wasp that was trying to come in through the window.

I lay down on the bed, opened the envelope without tearing it, and started to read. Three things were written in the letter. Christian informed me that the holiday would start next Tuesday; that I shouldn't bring too much luggage; and that I should keep on praying. I glanced at the calendar: it was Wednesday. I still had a whole week. While I was wondering how I was going to fill those seven days, I thought I heard him urging me to run. No sooner had this thought occurred to me, than I got up, washed my face in cold water, went outside, and started to run.

I spent half of my days running and the other half contemplating nature. I loved nature; wherever I was.

Spending my days in these occupations, I hadn't realised how quickly the week had passed. By the time I checked the calendar again, it was already Monday. As he'd asked, I prepared just a few things to take with me.

On the Monday, while I was waiting for Tuesday, it seemed to me that a hundred days had passed; it felt as if the clock had stopped. I couldn't stop trembling and became more and more impatient.

My parents were always silent and cautious around me, but they smiled all the time and occasionally caressed my head. They made me happy. If they'd told me tomorrow would come sooner, and if I'd learnt to be patient, perhaps I wouldn't have stayed awake crying the whole night through. But in spite of all their efforts, I didn't sleep at all.

Eventually, morning came. I watched the sunrise from my window. When I heard my parents coming towards my room, I went back to bed and pretended to be asleep. They would have been very sad if they had known that I hadn't been to sleep at all.

I was still pretending to be asleep when they came into my room. They both approached the bed and had kissed my cheeks a few times before I decided to open eyes. My mother didn't notice anything, but my father soon realised that I wasn't asleep. He gave me a present. When I looked at it, I saw that it was the stone my friend had given me at the tunnel. My father had made a hole in it and put it on a chain so that I could wear it around my neck and not lose it. I was amazed to see the stone; I had forgotten all about it. Seeing my amazement, my father told me that all important things must never be forgotten.

Then we heard the noise of a car and we all knew who had arrived. Even before I'd managed to get out of bed, Christian barged in. He had terror on his face and a strange look in his eyes. He wanted to tell me to get ready fast, but he couldn't get the words out of his mouth because he was stammering. When my father saw him like that, he brought him a glass of water and calmed him down. Then my father helped me to get dressed faster. By the time my friend had drunk the water, I was ready.

My father handed me the rucksack they had prepared by putting a few things in it for my trip. My mother kissed me on the cheeks and then my father kissed me on the cheeks. Then Christian immediately pulled me into the waiting car. It moved away at such speed, that I barely heard my parents call, "We love you!"

I was just about to ask my friend what had frightened him so much, when he told me that his prayers had been answered. Apparently, two days previously, his father had told him that he would be going to the station with him, to see him off. That made him very frightened because if his father saw him off, I couldn't have met him there. Since then, he had been on his knees praying a lot.

That morning, he had been amazed to see a letter by his bedside: it was from his father. It said that he had important business to attend to and couldn't go to the station to say goodbye. The thing that had frightened Christian was that this had happened before. Every time his father had said that he had some business and wouldn't be at the station, he had still managed to see him off after all. As we got nearer, the terror on his face grew. Seeing him so frightened, made me frightened too.

My friend kept praying all the way to the station. I couldn't help it and prayed too. If what he had said was right, and his father was there waiting for him, that meant that I couldn't go with him and we wouldn't have been able to see each other anymore. Christian knew this as well.

When we stopped and the driver announced that we were at the railway station, my friend couldn't get out of the car; he was completely paralysed. Eyes closed, he was still praying. As he prayed, he got more mobility in his body; I knew that he was having a vision, but I didn't ask him what it was.

He hadn't brought any clothes or anything else with him, so I grabbed my rucksack and got out of the car. He smiled at me, got out of the car as well, and started to walk quickly, carefully scanning everything around him. As we got nearer to the train we were going to get on, he hastened his pace. He pointed to the carriage we were to get in and asked a porter to help us find the compartment that was written on our tickets.

Taking our tickets and scrutinising them, the porter told us to follow him and led the way. When we reached our compartment, he gave us our tickets back, wished us a good journey, and left. As soon as we entered the compartment, Christian drew all the curtains. As he sat down on one of the beds, he started to shiver and said that he felt very cold. He continued to shake, so I covered him with one of the blankets I found in the compartment.

I could see that in spite of my efforts to warm him up, he was still shivering and feeling very cold. Kind words didn't help either; he was still terrified that his father might appear at any moment, and, deep down, I was too. Nonetheless, he stopped trembling when he heard the train whistle.

As the train started to pull away, he began to laugh. When he was convinced that the train had left the station, he opened all the curtains. He lowered the window and kissed the top of my head. With joy, he bounded out of the compartment. I was left speechless. All I could do was stare out of the half-open window. The memory of his terrified face would never leave me; but then I started to laugh too.

After a very short time, he came back and said that he knew why I was laughing. He also said his mother had warned him to be careful of his father. For the first time, his faith had been shaken a bit; and it was also the first time he had been so frightened of his father.

When I lifted my head, I saw many geese in the sky. It wasn't the first time I had seen these birds flying, but I had never beheld quite such a sight. In the sky, there was a big flock of geese on the wing together. When I pointed out the geese to my friend, he became excited too. He said that it was also the first time he had seen such a spectacle. The sight of them momentarily made us forget what we had just been through.

When the geese had disappeared, I turned towards Christian. He was fast asleep with his head leaning against the window. That made me laugh; but if, like him, I hadn't slept for days, perhaps I too would have slumbered like that. Carefully, I took his head in one hand and his waist with my other hand and laid him on the bed. I covered him up with a blanket asking myself why he cared so much about me.

Two things occurred to me: one was that he loved God, and the other was that he loved his mother. I thought both were perfectly good reasons; I could understand it, except why me, who was I to him? Why should he wish to continue living in fear because of me? I couldn't answer these questions at that time.

I turned my head towards the window; doing my best not to think of anything, I concentrated my gaze on the scenery. The wind caressed my skin.

After a few hours, I grew bored. I looked at my friend who seemed so peaceful. Instead of trying to wake him up, I made every effort not to. While I was looking at him, his lips began to move. He reminded me of my father, who spoke in his sleep, sometimes so loudly that people outside could hear him. Whereas Christian's voice was barely audible; even being so close, I couldn't understand what he was saying. Leaving my place next to the window, I carefully went and sat next to him; but I still couldn't hear anything he was saying.

Thinking that the noise outside was preventing me from hearing what he was saying I got up to close the window. But I was stopped in my tracks when he suddenly let out a scream. Seeing the terror on his face, tears involuntarily began to trickle down my cheeks.

Without a word to me, my friend got up and washed his face, repeating all the while, "Why? Why? " I knew he'd had a nightmare. When he'd finished washing, he came and sat next to me. He said he knew why I was sad and before I could ask him what the matter was, he said to me, "I had a nightmare. I won't tell you about my dream, but I will tell you a story that I remember my mother telling me. She told me this story when I was travelling with her just like I'm travelling with you now, in this very same carriage. As all the tickets had already sold out for this particular carriage, I had to wait a whole week for us to be able to travel in it."

Then Christian asked me if I knew what a swan was. I told him that I knew it was a very beautiful bird but I had never seen one. He tried to describe it to me but he couldn't. After telling me that it was sufficient for me to know that a swan was the most beautiful bird in the world, he began his story.

"Hundreds of years ago, before there were any machines and people lived in peace, there was a tiny village in an unknown place. The people who lived in this tiny village were so kind that they didn't even harm the ants. All sorts of animals and birds lived there because they knew that they were safe. The villagers' favourite birds were the swans.

"Although all the swans were beautiful, one was far, far more beautiful than the others. It was white and had a black line that started on its head and continued to its tail. That made it special and capricious, so much so that it wouldn't allow any male near it. All the birds were jealous of its beauty but they never let it be known. They always behaved politely and considerately towards the beautiful swan. That made the swan think they all loved it.

"As time passed, even the devil couldn't bear it any longer and became jealous of the beautiful swan too. One day, the devil disguised himself as a male swan and went into the village. Not only was he handsome, but he spoke beautifully as well. The villagers liked him a lot and after a very short time living there, he had become famous. But the other beautiful swan didn't pay any attention to him at all. The devil did everything to get her attention; one look from her would have been enough.

"Finally, she did look at him and she madly fell in love. They decided to get married. The devil told her that the place where he came from was even better than this one, and that he also wanted to introduce her to his family. Being so much in love, the beautiful swan accepted his offer and together they flew away. They flew, and flew, and flew for a very long time; they didn't rest even for a little while. She wanted to see this beautiful land where he lived. Whenever she was tired, she would ask him how far it was. The devil always answered that they were nearly there.

"The exceptionally beautiful swan became thinner and thinner, and was finally so exhausted from flying that she ceased to flap her wings and fell from the sky. Her once beautiful feathers were in a terrible state. Nothing was left of her looks; she was no longer beautiful or special. On the contrary, she had become so thin and ugly that no one would have wanted to look at her at all. She then realised how vain she had been.

"Seeing that she had lost all her beauty, the devil laughed and flew down to her. Happy with the result, the devil came out of his disguise and revealed who he really was. Planting his great cloven hoof on her neck, he screamed, 'Swan, swan, through their jealousy, the others have sacrificed you to me!'

"Continuing to laugh, he broke her neck with his hooves and watched her die. Still laughing, he said, 'You are beautiful yet. If the others had not been jealous of you and treated you the way they did, your end would have been different. You are not the first or the last creature I will destroy. Those who are haughty towards others are worse than I.' With these words, the devil vanished and the poor swan died in agony.

★ ★ ★

"Before she met my father, my mother was as beautiful as a swan; but if you had seen her towards the end, you wouldn't have been able to stop crying. I was aware of everything that was happening to my mother, but he was my father. That was how I felt and I was helpless. All I could do was pray. Perhaps one day, my father will feel remorse and stop hating the flowers that she loved, and let me take her beloved orchids to her grave."

My friend had started to cry; I didn't know what to do so I put my arm around his shoulders. I was trying to think of ways in which I could comfort him when I felt his tears on my hand. I said, "Always think of your mother as a swan; don't think of your father as the devil who hurt your mother. Perhaps you'll never be able to forget that your mother was always unhappy while she was alive, but try to think of her being happy in paradise.

"This will make her and those who love you happy as well. At least for a little while, forget about everything. We are going to your grandmother's; and now, do your best to be happy. We are not on this trip to cry.

"Don't fall into the devil's trap! Be strong. Make sure that you don't fall into the devil's net; be strong and tear that net to pieces with your faith. Then tear those pieces to tiny little shreds and let the wind blow them away so that they can't be made into a net to catch you ever again.

"Now I'm with you, and your grandmother is waiting for us. Isn't she like your mother? Smile, please; I miss your smiling face. You will make your grandmother happy, too, with your smiling face. And don't forget that your mother was her child. Your unhappiness will make her unhappy too; as you cry for your mother, she will cry for her daughter.

"Don't start the fire of pain; don't rekindle the half-burnt pieces of wood. You have lost your mother, someone you loved very much; but you aren't alone, you've got your grandmother there, and you've got me here."

I managed to make him smile with my words. Whispering that he was grateful that he had a friend like me, he opened the door of the compartment. I got up too and we went outside.

Chapter 4

The corridor was full of people smoking, so we could hardly breathe in spite of the open windows. As we couldn't reach the windows, we couldn't put our heads out through one of them for some fresh air. Realising what we wanted to do, an old man brought us a stool from somewhere. After thanking him, we climbed onto it. Christian told me to extend my arms and close my eyes, then, with my eyes closed, to feel the wind against my face. I did as he asked. As I felt the wind, I felt emptiness inside. For a split second, I could see into the future.

I became frightened and, opening my eyes, hurried back to the compartment. My friend followed and seeing how frightened I was, told me that he wanted me to see into the future. When I told him I had no such desire, he looked at me sadly. I couldn't bear the look on his face; I closed the curtains on the door and opened the window. I asked him to come and stand next to me at the window.

Christian quickly stood up and after making sure that the curtains were properly drawn on the door, he came and stood next to me. He told me to breathe in the air deeply, and then he stretched his arms out of the window. I inhaled and tried to feel the wind with my eyes closed.

I sensed someone's presence. Immediately, I opened my eyes only to see my friend. Laughing at myself, I closed my eyes again. This time, as well as feeling the wind on my arms, I felt a few drops of water too. Thinking it was raining, I didn't even open my eyes. A few more drops fell onto one of my arms, which started to itch. Wanting to scratch it, I opened my eyes and saw a leg next to my arm. I lifted my eyes and saw someone by the window looking at me. I looked at Christian and saw that he was terrified and couldn't move. I too was frightened. Christian and I looked at the man again. He was a big man with a beard; he was smiling.

As we stood speechless and immobilised with fear, he kept looking at us. When I realised that I could move my body, I attempted to open the door of our compartment, but someone grabbed me by the back of my collar and stopped me. However, immediately, that someone let go of my collar again. I turned to see who had been holding me back just a few seconds ago. I saw the bearded man standing in the middle of our compartment. He was no longer smiling. He had tears in his eyes and, waving his hand, begged me not to open the door. He was also gesturing that he wanted to explain something to us.

I couldn't understand what the bearded man was trying to say. My friend, who was no longer frightened, understood and explained that if I opened the door, the stranger would throw himself out of the window. I crept nearer to him and holding his hand, sat him on one of the beds. I wiped away his tears. He couldn't talk because he was dumb but I could see the fear in his face.

He was so tired and frightened; I could even hear the thumping of his heart. I was wondering what he might be afraid of when there was a knock at the door. Before I could open it, Christian quickly hid the bearded man in our cupboard, pushing him in and shutting the door. Then equally quickly, Christian went into our compartment's toilet and closed the door behind him. I only half opened the door.

Three people were standing there, including the conductor. One of the others pushed the carriage door wide open and asked where my friend was. I said that he was in the toilet. The third man enquired why the curtains were drawn. I responded that we were tired and were getting ready to go to bed. He came in and started to bang on the toilet door, He demanded an answer from my friend, who told him that he was feeling ill and trying to vomit.

As the men insisted that my friend should come out, he did so, instantly vomiting on the third man's shoes, causing him to run out of the carriage immediately. As Christian continued vomiting in the compartment, the smell became too much for the other two men, and they too departed. Before leaving, the conductor looked at me and smiled. When I was sure that they had all gone, I closed the door. All was silent.

The smell was very bad; we scrunched our faces up, staring at the disgusting mess on the floor. As we looked at each other, the bearded man came out of the cupboard laughing. We started to laugh too. He gestured that he wanted a newspaper, so I offered to go and look for one. My friend wanted to come with me. This made my task easier and we quickly searched the train. But when we realised that in this huge train, there wasn't a single newspaper to be found, I started to laugh.

Seeing us, the conductor hurried forwards and asked what we were looking for. When we told him that we were looking for a newspaper, he asked us to follow him. He walked quiet fast and we had to run to keep up. He brought us to a carriage where all the collected rubbish was stored; there were plenty of newspapers here. Seeing that we were very happy, he told us that if we ever had a problem on his train, we should go and find him. We thanked him, collected all the newspapers we wanted, and returned to our compartment.

When we got back, we couldn't believe our eyes, we were speechless. There was no sign of any vomit on the floor; the bearded man had cleaned it all up. We were mortified. When he saw this, he gestured to us that he had sent us out looking for a newspaper so that he could clean up the mess. This only made us even more ashamed of ourselves, our tears falling onto the newspapers.

He couldn't bear to see us crying, so he gave us some tissues decorated with smiling faces that he had drawn on them. My friend, who knew sign language, tried to tell him something. He responded by scribbling on a tissue and passed it to us. It read, "I'm very hungry; if you keep crying you'll soon hear my stomach rumbling." When we read what he had written, we hugged him. For some reason, we liked him.

I took out the food that my mother had prepared and put it in front of him. He laughed when he saw all that food. Putting his hands together he prayed, briefly. After that, he started eating. I was surprised because he ate very slowly and very carefully, making sure not to drop any crumbs on the floor. If I had been that hungry, I would have wolfed it down and there would have been crumbs all over the floor; but his manners didn't surprise Christian. As the bearded man ate, he smiled at us. When he had finished, he regarded us intently. We all stared at each other laughing happily for a long time.

When he realised that we weren't going to stop, he took a piece of paper out of his pocket, wrote a few words on it, and tossed it to us. What he had written made us laugh even harder. It read, "My stomach is ten times bigger than yours; I have to eat like an elephant. Only a mouse would be full with the food you just gave me. I'm still hungry."

After reading that and having another good laugh, I left the compartment again, making for the dining car. Before I had got very far, my friend caught up with me and reminded me to be very careful, whispering that I should only buy children's portions. I smiled at him and continued on my way. Christian returned to our compartment.

The dining car was full. I found a waiter, ordered two children's portions, and waited. In spite of the half-open windows everywhere, all the cigarette smoke bothered me. I could barely breathe and it brought tears to my eyes. The smoke stung so much that teardrops even rolled down my cheeks. I rubbed my eyes vigorously, trying to get rid of the stinging sensation.

The sudden sound of a child's cry made me forget all about my eyes. I turned towards the sound. A small boy carrying a birdcage was approaching his mother saying, "Mother, look! Mother, look!"

Without any apparent feeling for her offspring, his mother put down her coffee cup and turned towards her son. Seeing the birdcage in his hands, she enquired: "Did you manage to kill yet another bird my son?"

When the child heard his mother say that, he cried even louder. Handing the birdcage to her, he said in a deeply hurt voice, "Why do you always think I kill my birds? I don't, they die on their own.

"I love my birds with all my heart, but you've never bothered to teach me how to look after them. You just buy me another bird after the previous one has died. I don't want to always have another bird." He cried still harder. "I want my bird to live for a very long time and I want my bird to love me."

Without a word to her son, his mother summoned the waiter and asked him to dispose of the bird and its cage. The little boy grabbed the cage, lovingly held it tightly to his chest, and began to scream. He soon became the centre of attention and all eyes in the dining car were on him. Everyone felt sympathy for the little boy and his mother became extremely embarrassed. Nonetheless, she bent closely down to her son and very quietly whispered something in his ear. The little boy went pale, immediately stopped screaming, and gave the birdcage to the waiter. The waiter took the dead bird from its cage.

At that moment, I jumped up from my chair and began to plead with the waiter to give me the little dead bird. With a fleeting silent smile, the waiter handed over the bird. I thanked him and then I looked at the bird; it was still alive although it was barely breathing. Happily, I approached the little boy. His mother gave me a withering look and went back to her table, not caring anymore about her son's problems. She proceeded to sip her coffee.

But the little boy looked at me with admiring eyes. After stroking the tiny bird, I caressed the little boy's head. Then I sat on a chair and asked, "If I help your bird to live a little longer, will you return it to the cage?"

The little boy looked straight into my eyes and answered, "No, I won't."

Then I enquired of him, "Can you give me your word that you'll never put any bird in a cage ever again?"

The little boy responded, "I can; I give you my word that I will never put any bird in a cage again."

I told him that God had taught Adam and Eve to love each other, and to love all the birds and all the animals too. Then I smiled at him and stroked the little bird's tiny body. I gently kissed the little bird and continued carefully to stroke its tiny body. At the same time, I silently prayed, asking for the little bird to be healed. Shortly after I had finished my prayer, the little bird began to move. The little boy was happy again; and soon after that, the little bird stood on its tiny legs. By now, the little boy was extremely excited and very happy.

He pulled me over to the window and said, "Release my little bird." I let him kiss the little bird and I kissed it too, and then I let it go out of the window. The little bird happily flapped its wings a few times and then fell to the grass.

When the little boy saw that, he became very sad and asked me, "Why is it that my little bird isn't flying anymore? And why did it land on the grass?"

I ruffled the little boy's hair and said, "While in the cage, your little bird got ill and couldn't fly anymore. And now it can't fly very much. It needs to rest on the grass, but later on, it will fly again."

Just then the waiter came over and informed me that my order was almost ready. I told the little boy that I would see him later and left to go and collect my order. As I passed the little boy's mother, whose table was near to where the little boy and I had been standing, she said quietly to me: "Did you know that the bird would die quite so soon?"

"Yes" I replied, "I knew it was dying."

"Why, then, trouble yourself?" she asked very quietly but extremely cynically.

I too spoke quietly, replying, "The little bird didn't end up dying in a disgusting, smelly rubbish bin, painfully and slowly suffocating. It died flying free in the air."

Then I looked at her with pity, turned on my heel, and went to collect my order. As soon as I had got my food, I left the dining car. One thing was missing but what was it? I tried to think. I realised it was the drinks, so I went back for them. I got the drinks and walked happily towards our compartment. I was truly very happy.

When I opened the door, I immediately saw Christian. He handed me a piece of paper. On it was written 'Marcus'; it was the bearded man's name. I put the food and drinks on the table. Then I saw that my friend was frightened of something; I couldn't tell what it might be, but I felt a chill go right through my body although I didn't know why. When Christian pointed at the drinks, I realised that instead of two bottles, I had bought three. Marcus saw my mistake as well. At that point, the door suddenly burst open.

Someone pushed me and I fell to the floor. Someone else attacked Marcus, but he managed to fend him off. Marcus was terrified and had tears in his eyes. Giving me a sad look, he opened the window and attempted to jump out. But another man ran in and stopped him. One of them had his foot on my chest, stopping me from getting up. Marcus was on the floor, totally powerless, and my friend was crying.

The three men looked at me. It took some time to calm Marcus down. Finally, using his head, Marcus let them know that he had composed himself. They let him stand up. When I saw that they had handcuffs in their hands, using all my force, I escaped from underneath the man's foot. Then I stood up and hugged Marcus. I was now crying. Marcus hugged me too and slipped a piece of paper into my shirt. I started screaming when they handcuffed him. The same man pushed me on the floor again and this time, he planted his foot more firmly on my chest. I couldn't even breathe freely. Then they took Marcus out of the compartment.

Christian hadn't moved; he was quietly crying. But when he'd heard my screams, he'd moved swiftly and attempted to hug Marcus. One of them had held my friend back while asking the other to remove Marcus.

When I saw that Marcus had disappeared from right in front of my eyes, I took hold of the foot of the man who had placed it on my chest and pulled out a chunk of hair from his ankle. He screamed and let go of me. I quickly got up, and jumped on the man who was holding my friend. Again, using all my force, I bit his hand, and he let go of my friend. He turned to me and slapped me so hard that I found myself out in the corridor. As the man was screamed in pain, Christian made a bound towards Marcus. I got up and ran towards Marcus too. I didn't know what my friend was going to do, but I was following him.

Away from us, Marcus was now quieter, but suddenly, he broke free of the three men holding him and ran. We leapt towards Marcus. He turned to face us giving the biggest smile I'd ever seen. But I realised then what he was about to do. When he saw us getting closer, he opened the carriage door and jumped out of the train. Christian started screaming. I was so afraid of making a mistake and losing my friend too that I didn't dare move, thinking that he too might jump out of the train. I held Christian tight and tried to calm him down. Finally, I managed to quieten him. It wasn't easy, but when my friend was calm, he said he that wouldn't leave me.

We realised that a crowd had gathered around us so we slowly made our way back to our compartment. Once inside, I stopped crying. But my friend closed the curtains, sat in a corner, and started to weep. He kept asking God why He allowed people dear to him to be taken away: "Don't keep on taking the ones I love," he beseeched, "Please! This friend here! Please! Give him a long life!" he implored.

Very quickly, I realised that it was me he was talking about. I couldn't say anything, so I just listened and continued to stare at him.

The conversation between two people who were standing in the corridor just outside our compartment took me aback. One said, "You know, the one who jumped out of the train was apparently a Jew who had escaped from an asylum." This was the first time I had heard the word 'Jew' spoken in such a belittling way and I was shocked.

The other replied, "No, he wasn't a Jew. He was in the headlines a few weeks ago. His name was Marcus and he was German. Poor man, but to die like that is better than to die in an asylum. I know what these places are like; still, what a shame."

I was amazed at what I had just heard and became lost in thought. After ending his prayer, when Christian saw that I was deep in contemplation, he came over to me and knelt down beside me.

I was about to say something, but he covered my mouth with his hand and said, "At this moment, we are having an enormous amount of challenges. Don't let this destroy our friendship or our happiness.

"My mother taught me never to question God. I promised that I wouldn't, but that doesn't mean that we shouldn't be determined in life; not only in my life, but in yours too. You're a Jew, and those people chose to talk in such a way right outside our compartment. They could have had their conversation anywhere, but they chose to speak within our earshot.

"The most important thing in life is to obey our Lord and be thankful to Him for everything we have. I know why you are sad. First, you accidentally made a mistake and Marcus died; and then you overheard a conversation that was demeaning to Jewish people. Both of these things have made you very sad. I know how to stop our challenges."

He started to pray. While he was praying, I closed my eyes too and felt warmth inside me. I kept repeating "Amen" so that his prayer would be accepted. When he had finished, I removed from my shirt the letter that Marcus had given me and handed it to my friend. He was surprised and started to laugh. It had an address and stamp on it. We realised that he hadn't managed to post his letter; Christian said he would put it in the letterbox at the railway station.

Later, my friend looked at the envelope again, but this time more carefully and realised that the address wasn't far from his grandmother's house, and that we could take it there by hand. I was very happy to hear this, so I folded the letter in two and put it in my pocket.

★ ★ ★

In order to reach our destination, we had to travel all through the night. We were dog-tired; my eyelids were very heavy and, looking at my smiling friend, I fell asleep.

We slept so deeply that the next morning a train attendant had to awaken us. We were told to get up and get dressed. We got up quickly and dressed even quicker. A uniformed policeman entered our compartment. He smiled and told us that we would be going to the police station to answer a few questions, but there was no need to be frightened.

Christian was nervous. Knowing that the policeman would be waiting for us at the station, he said, "Now my father will learn that we are together. But it's too late; he has no time to separate us, and we are well protected at my grandmother's."

The train came to a halt. While I was gathering my things together, my friend leaned out of the window trying to catch sight of his grandmother. Then I heard him. Instead of shouting, "Grandma! Grandma!" and leaving the train by the door, he climbed through the window. He frightened me by doing that.

I looked out and saw him in the arms of his grandmother. They were near our compartment window. His grandmother looked at me and said that he had always behaved like this. Smiling, I stepped through the door; I preferred it that way.

As I left the train, I saw the policeman standing nearby. When I joined them, Christian's grandmother hugged me too and thanked me for making her grandson so happy. My friend started to tell her about all the things that had happened to us, but she stopped him, saying that we shouldn't make the policeman wait.

So we followed the officer to the police station. My friend's grandmother knew everything that had happened to us; she had been informed while she was on her way to the railway station. Of course, I wasn't surprised to learn that Christian's father knew too, but as he didn't mention it, I didn't either.

Taking advantage of the situation, my friend succeeded in summarising all the events of the train to his grandmother. When he had finished, he started to cry so much so that he was shaking. I thought that I would never see him cry again. But I was mistaken.

Chapter 5

C hristian's behaviour didn't shock his grandmother, who bent down and said, "Let me tell you a real story about your mother. One day, she promised me that she wouldn't cry again. Why do you think was? I will tell you.

"I remember vividly, she was just five. We had a big and spacious garden. So that she wouldn't wander far, we put a wooden fence around it. But somehow, one of the planks had broken, leaving a hole just big enough for her to squeeze through. Your mother took this opportunity to get out of the garden and have a look at the world outside.

"When she saw the beautiful flowers in the grass, she started picking them. But because she was just a little girl, she hadn't noticed the nettles among the flowers and got stung. She threw the flowers down but couldn't stop the itching. Scratching her arms and legs, she saw the blood running down, and started to cry loudly and scream for her mother.

"Because your grandfather and I were in the back garden, we couldn't hear her screams. Seeing her in that state, a lady who was passing asked if she could help her. As she couldn't do anything, she gave your mother a flower from the bunch in her hand. After caressing her head, the lady continued on her way.

That flower made your mother forget everything. She found us at the bottom of the garden. It frightened us, seeing her in that state, but your mother had a big smile on her face, which made her look very beautiful.

"She came up to me and asked the name of the flower in her hand. I had only seen it in books. And when I told her that it was an orchid, she said, 'Mummy, don't worry about my scratches; they hurt a lot, but I forgot all about them when I saw this flower. I love it. I understand that love is a cure for pain. As long as I have people who love me, I will never cry again. I'll always keep this orchid with me to remind me of that.'

"Your grandfather and I were amazed by what she had said. It was unbelievable to hear such words from a five-year-old. I have never forgotten what your mother said."

★ ★ ★

When she had finished the story, Christian's grandmother took a box out of her handbag and gave it to my friend, continuing, "Here's the flower that your mother fell in love with at first sight. For the sake of this flower, forget about what you've just experienced on your train journey.

"When you look at this orchid, don't think about anything or anyone else. Whenever your mother looked at this orchid, she was happy. Be happy too."

Then my friend's grandmother planted a kiss on his forehead. He caressed the orchid and, hugging his grandmother, promised her that whatever happened, he would never cry again.

Actually, after that day, I never saw him cry like that again. I'm sad that I don't have a photo of them hugging each other on that day; nonetheless, that scene has stayed in my mind ever since.

After that, Christian's grandmother reminded us of the policeman and we resumed our walk to the police station. My friend had his eyes firmly on the orchid.

At some point, even though his grandmother nudged him, Christian started to talk to himself: "Mother look, I'm with my grandmother again. This time, you're not with us, but when I look at this orchid she gave me, I feel as if you are walking beside me; when I caress this flower, I feel as if I'm caressing you; and when I smell it, I feel as if it is you I can smell. My grandmother told me a story about you and this flower, and, like you, I've promised not to cry. Today, you, mother, are with me but perhaps I shall soon reach the place where you are."

We were moved by my friend's words. The fact that he wanted to be with his mother made us very sad and thoughtful. His grandmother's face went pale, and we looked at each other in silence. Since I had known him, he had always wanted to be with his mother. If I hadn't entered his life, perhaps he would have gone to be with his mother. I couldn't understand his great love for his mother. My love for my mother wasn't so extreme.

While we were all deep in thought, we found ourselves at the police station. We were ushered into an empty room, and told to sit and wait. Soon, three men entered the room. The most senior policeman sat down and asked us to tell him what had happened.

As Christian was about to start, one of the policemen caught my eye. I looked at him and he asked if I was a Jew. When I confirmed that I was, the senior officer told me to leave the room and wait outside in the outer office. We were all surprised. I looked at my friend and his grandmother, but no one said anything. So I stood up and left the room.

I wondered how he had known that I was a Jew just by looking at me but I couldn't find an answer to my question. Swinging my legs, I thought about what had happened in the train.

Lost in thought, the sound of chains made me look up with a start. A man was sitting across from me on a chair. His wrists and ankles were bound. Two men who were with him chained him to an iron pole and disappeared into the nearest room. I was frightened of the prisoner. He had blood on his clothes.

The policemen raised their voices in the other room. One of them shouted, demanding to know why the man had been brought to the police station; and the other replied just as loudly that it was the nearest station to the scene of the crime. Another officer would come and pick him up, he bellowed.

When I looked at the chained man opposite me, he smiled. He had an innocent look about him. Had I met him outside the station, I would have pitied him. But in spite of such feelings, I couldn't look at him anymore.

Just then, I heard him whisper something. When I looked up again, he pointed to my right. I looked in that direction and saw a bar of chocolate. He wanted it. I picked up the chocolate bar and approached him. Before he could touch me, I threw it at him and went back to my chair. He grabbed the chocolate, quickly unwrapped it, and began to eat it. I began to think about the situation he was in, wondering why he was at the police station.

As if reading my thoughts, he stopped eating and looked at me. Then he said, "I know what you're thinking. You're wondering why I'm here. It's strange that you threw the chocolate at me rather than hand it to me. I know you're afraid of me, and you are right to be afraid. I don't even like myself in this state that I'm in.

"I too was once a young child like you. I had a mother, I had a father, and I had many friends. I might be eating this thrown away chocolate bar with pleasure now, but as a young boy, it was far worse for me. I suffered very much at the hands of my parents; they used to beat me daily.

"When my father was drunk, he would beat my mother. And, trying to protect her, I would be beaten as well. Then when my father was out, wanting to release her anger against her husband, it would be my mother who beat me without mercy. I don't remember a day that I didn't get a beating.

"When he was drunk, my father used to bang my mother's head against the wall to calm himself down. When he was sober, he would say that he couldn't remember anything and blamed it on the drink. "As a result of this abuse, my mother died very young. But I wasn't upset because it meant she couldn't beat me anymore.

"My father wouldn't let me go anywhere and I couldn't understand why that was. I was afraid that something might happen to him. I was actually far more frightened of being left alone than I was of him. I had resigned myself to my fate, saying to myself, 'He is my father, after all, and I do love him very much.'

"I used to pray he'd stop drinking. I wanted a miracle to happen but it didn't. Instead, the more I prayed, the more he drank. After my mother's death, he started to drink even more and beat me even harder. My white body was often purple, and my mind was affected. My friends distanced themselves from me and started to treat me like a crazy person. When I was alone, there was no need for my father to beat me, because I cried anyway.

"I don't know, why I'm telling you all this; I suppose it's so I'll feel better. No one has ever wanted to listen to me until now. Normally, as soon as I open my mouth, people move away from me; and that makes me long to be in the ground.

"Anyway, I'll continue. One day, when my father had had a lot to drink, he came up to me, knelt down, and started to cry. With one hand, he caressed my head. That shocked me and, at the same time, made me very happy. I sighed with relief. I thought that my father was regretting his past behaviour and that my prayers had finally been answered.

"But I was mistaken; my father wasn't caressing my head because of remorse or because he loved me. It was because of something else. I will never forget his first and last tenderness towards me. When he had stopped crying, he tied me to a chair and then he left the room. I had no idea why he had done that. I thought it was just his way of relaxing, so I didn't do anything about it. When he came back with a rope, I realised what he was about to do. I started crying loudly and begged him not to do it, but he shouted at me and stuffed a handkerchief in my mouth, telling me that he was a big sinner. Then he hanged himself.

"I fainted, but not for long. When I came round, I realised that I was still there with my dead father. Three days went by with me tied up and my father hanging there. Because of this, I had a nervous breakdown; I even forgot my own name.

"After some time, the neighbours alerted the police; they hadn't seen me or heard my father for three days. The police and ambulance crew broke down the door. They had a huge shock when they saw me tied up with my father's stinking corpse nearby. I was untied and taken to hospital.

"Neither I nor anyone else could make any sense out of my father's actions. I had long psychiatric treatment in the hospital and they only released me after I had become completely well again.

"The neighbours came up with several ideas about how they could help me, but I refused them all; I wanted to succeed on my own without anyone else's help. For many years, I tried to lead a normal life and forget all about my past. But when I saw parents being kind to their children, I was always reminded of my painful past. That upset me a lot, but it was impossible to avoid these kinds of situations and I forced myself to go on living.

"After working hard and putting some money aside, I rented a house far away from where I had lived before. I was very happy for several months. I began to laugh and even managed to make friends.

"One day, I was looking out of the window and saw that some people were moving in next door. A girl was trying to lift a box that was much too heavy for her. When her father saw that, he went up to her and slapped her so hard that she fell to the ground. I flew out to stop him from hitting her any further. He pushed me out of his way and I fell to the ground as well; he was such a large man. He shouted at me, saying that she was his daughter and he could do whatever he liked with her. He then took a few steps towards her, but he didn't hit her anymore. The poor, frightened girl carried the heavy box into the house.

"This event reminded me of my own past. I imagined that I saw my father everywhere; he was beating me and I was shouting, 'Don't hit me! Don't hit me!' I even began to have nightmares. I hated the night; I didn't want to go to sleep at night.

"During one of these nights, as I was having a nightmare about my father beating me, I was woken up by the sound of someone else shrieking the same words: 'Don't hit me! Don't hit me!' I ran to the window.

A crowd had gathered in front of the house next door. Although, terrible screaming could be heard from inside, no one dared go in or knock on the front door. I lost all reason and, taking a big kitchen knife, ran outside and into the house next door.

"The girl was totally naked and he was lashing her with his belt because she had refused to bring him a bottle of booze. I shouted at him not to hit her any more. He then turned on me, but he hadn't seen the knife I was holding. When he advanced towards me, I ran towards him and stabbed him with the kitchen knife. I don't remember how many times I knifed him, but I continued until I thought all the blood had run out of his body. I was upset that the girl had seen this, but I'd had no choice; if I hadn't killed him, he might have beaten her to death.

"With all that she had been through, the girl was in shock. I wrapped her up in a blanket and took her outside. The police were already there and I gave myself up. They handcuffed me and brought me here.

* * *

When he had finished his story, he lost control and started banging his head against the wall. I couldn't bear stories like that: I was very much shaken by what he had told me and could feel the paleness of my face. I was shaking and unable to focus on my surroundings. Retreating to a corner, I started to talk to myself.

Suddenly, I saw Christian and I jumped up to hug him. My friend took me by the arm and led me outside. We sat on the steps of the police station and he showed me the orchid in the box. Then he talked to me about the flower. As I relaxed, I wanted to describe what had happened and what the man had told me, but as he continued to talk about the orchid, I prayed instead. Then, closing his eyes, my friend joined me in devotion.

This was my prayer: "I am a weak person. First, I witnessed Christian's pain and sorrow, then Marcus's, and now this man's; all this has had added to my own pain.

"I came to have a good time with my friend. But if your aim is to test my faith like you tested the faith of all the prophets, I will bear it; I will bear everything that you test me with.

"My father taught me how to thank Thee and how to be strong like Moses. Whatever happens to me, I will accept my fate. Amen."

I felt better after praying, and got up and started to walk quickly. When I heard Christian's voice full of laughter calling me, I turned towards the sound. With one hand he pointed to his grandmother and with the other to a taxi. Then my friend asked me if I knew where we were going. I shrugged my shoulders and shook my head.

When Christian's grandmother got into the taxi, I ran and climbed in too. My friend got in beside me and started to laugh again. The more I asked him why he was laughing, the more he laughed. He was laughing so much that I started to laugh too. When his grandmother asked us what was so funny, Christian pointed to my head and I realised that there was something on it. Then I felt something crawling in my hair. I was frightened but continued to laugh.

My friend asked his grandmother for a mirror, but she didn't have one. I wanted to remove the creature from my hair, but my friend wouldn't let me. The driver handed him a mirror; he took it happily and showed me the creature: it was a big fat caterpillar. I relaxed, but the caterpillar was moving in a strange way. It would crawl for a few steps, stop and lift its head up, looking to the right and then to the left, and then start all over again. It probably wanted to know where it was. When it reached my forehead, it slid down and fell into my lap. I took it in my palm and we stared at each other.

Christian asked the driver to stop near a tree, which he did. We got out of the car. I looked at the caterpillar in my palm for one last time and said that I was sorry if I had separated it from its family, but it would begin a new life on this tree. Then I put the caterpillar near a hole in the bark of the tree trunk.

But just then a bird swooped out of nowhere, swallowed up the poor caterpillar, and flew away just as swiftly. We couldn't take in what had just happened; we just kept our eyes fixed on the spot where we had last seen the poor caterpillar. Everything happened so fast that we had no time to be surprised. My friend and I both became very sad and returned to the taxi.

Seeing our faces, the driver laughed. When Christian's grandmother asked us what the matter was, we told her. We just repeated what the driver had already told her, that a bird had eaten our caterpillar.

My friend's grandmother was sad for us and caressed our heads; whereas the laughing driver told us that if we were as slow as the caterpillar, we too would lose our very lives. We continued on our way. But I never forgot what the driver said that day; and years later, his prophecy came true.

While I was lost in thought, I remembered Marcus's letter, and took it out of my back pocket and examined the envelope. I felt Christian getting restless. When I looked at him, I saw a serious expression on his face. I asked him when we could deliver the letter but he didn't reply. I repeated the question: again, no answer. I felt a kind of restlessness settling in the car. I kept repeating my question and he kept on ignoring me.

When my friend realised that I wouldn't give up asking him the same question over and over, he grabbed the letter and, looking at me angrily, scrunched it up in his hand. He was biting his lower lip. I too become serious and asked him to give me the letter back. He didn't answer. I asked again for the letter, and when he ignored me again, I lunged at him. Laughing at what I had done, he pushed me down, planted his foot on my chest, and squeezed me against the taxi door. I couldn't move at all; whatever I tried to do to escape was of no use.

With his grandmother looking on passively, Christian looked at me angrily and shouted, "Jacob, please don't aggravate my wounds anymore; I already have enough pain! Don't treat me like a child!

"I know we're both children, but we saw Marcus die on the train and got very upset. What the man at the police station told you also upset you very much. We will see and hear many more things that will upset us.

"Even when I laugh, my heart is crying! As you know, the pain I feel is because I've lost my mother and that makes me feel most days like a dead person inside. I crumble even more when I see and hear things like that.

"Don't burden me with more problems. I can't handle them all; I will collapse. And if that happens, none of us will reach our goals and my mother's story will turn into a lie. We came here to gain more power, not to lose it. This letter will destroy what peace we have"

With that, he opened the window and threw the letter out into the gentle breeze. Seeing this, without thinking, I tugged the door open. In a split second, the driver, who knew what I was going to do, slammed on the brakes. But before he actually managed to stop the vehicle, I had thrown myself out of the taxi.

After a few seconds of somersaults, I found myself at the edge of a field. Blood was pouring out of my legs, arms and forehead. I was in such pain that I thought all my bones were broken. My friend was there in no time. He sat down next to me and sighed.

I said to him, "When someone dies, one must fulfil their last wishes. I want to do that for Marcus. I promised him that even if I lost my life in the attempt, I would do my best."

Tears started running down my cheeks, but I wasn't crying; it was only my eyes that were. Christian was laughing at me. He couldn't believe what I had just done. Looking up at him, I told him that I wasn't interested in this trip anymore and I wanted to go home. My friend asked me if I was serious. When I confirmed that I was, he got up and, saying that his mission had been accomplished, started to walk towards a cornfield.

I had no idea what he was going to do. His bizarre behaviour made me forget my pain and I stood up. Although I kept calling his name, he ignored me. As he walked into the depths of the cornfield, someone saw him. When this person started to shout, I realised that there was danger in the cornfield. My friend's grandmother started to cry. I lost no time in running into the cornfield as well.

I frantically called him, "Christian! Christian!" But there wasn't any reply.

Seeing me walking in the cornfield as well, the other person shouted even louder, "Danger! Danger!"

I too screamed, "Danger! Danger!" and kept on calling, "Christian! Christian!"

Because the corn was a lot taller than I was, I couldn't see my friend but I continued to cry out, "Where are you? Where are you?" As there was no sign of him, I kept stopping and looking around me. When I saw some broken corn stems, I realised which direction he must have taken and started to run.

Finally, I saw him. He was talking to himself and laughing. I knew he was talking to his mother, and that wasn't a good sign. Then I heard someone very nearby shouting, telling me to leave the cornfield, but I was determined not to go without Christian. I had almost reached him when I stumbled and fell. I got up and I started to run once more, but as soon as I leapt forward, I fell again. After this had happened four or five times, my friend had disappeared from view.

I heard Christian's voice. He was very close and was calling out to me. When I reached him, I saw that he was sitting on the ground, a big trap in front of him. Now I knew why that person had warned us so urgently. In fact, he was still looking for us and shouting.

When my friend saw me, he said, "If it wasn't for the vision of my mother, I would have been dead a long time ago. The reason why I'm still alive is because I made a promise to her; I didn't come here for myself. But now you are the one who is keeping me alive. I'm not afraid of death, but I'm afraid of not being able to keep my promise to my mother.

"As you want to go home, my promise has been fulfilled. I can now go to my mother in peace. Like you want to keep your promise to Marcus, I want to keep my promise to my mother. Leave me now; don't stay here with me because I want to be alone when my soul is finally reunited with that of my mother."

In tears, I told him that I was very sorry, I *wasn't* going home, and I didn't want to let his mother down. He made me repeat these assurances a few times, and then he got up and grabbing my hand, started to run. Because of the pain in my legs, I kept stumbling but he kept on pulling me up.

When we were out of the cornfield, Christian told me that the farmer was still very angry. Although he had seen us leave, he continued shouting. When we were far away from both the cornfield and the farmer, my friend gave me a corncob, saying that it would remind me of the promise I made in the cornfield.

When Christian's grandmother saw us, she wiped her tears, then handed me Marcus's scrunched up letter and got back in the taxi with us. Handing my friend the first aid kit, the driver said that this was the most adventurous fare of his life. Christian started to clean the dried blood from my legs. Then he said that if I didn't keep my promise, he would kill himself. When I replied that I might not keep it if I accidentally boiled the corncob and ate it, he reacted by putting a lot of iodine on my wounds, only stopping when my screams became too loud to bear.

When I heard the rooster in my friend's grandmother's garden I relaxed. I was very happy; I opened the car window and introduced myself to the rooster. But it didn't care about making my acquaintance and continued running around the hens. Christian said that his grandmother's rooster didn't like guests. When I asked why, he laughed, saying that whenever there were visitors one of the roosters found itself in a pot. But instead of finding this joke funny, I was saddened.

My friend was laughing so hard that his grandmother joined in too. I opened the car door and tried to get out, but I couldn't manage because of my wounds. Seeing my difficulty, the taxi driver helped me out, sat me on a garden chair, and then left us. A little later, he returned with my corncob and said, "You forgot your promise in the car," and handing it to me, he left again.

Holding the corncob in my hands, I looked at Christian. He said that the letter and the corn should be kept side by side, and he would put them on a shelf next to each other in our bedroom. He then sat next to me and started to recount some of his memories of his grandmother's house. With the soft breeze blowing, I felt my eyelids drooping. His stories were like a lullaby and nothing was going to stop me from falling asleep.

Chapter 6

I slept so well that I didn't wake up until the rooster crowed the next morning. I was thrilled that it was still alive. After I had opened my eyes, I examined my surroundings. I looked like a clown in the short pyjamas that were a size too small; they belonged to Christian. Mine were obviously still in my rucksack and no one had thought to look for them.

I noticed a picture on the wall, but as I couldn't see it properly from my bed I got up to take a closer look. It was high up near the ceiling, so I had to climb on a chair to see it properly. It was a drawing of a lady with an orchid in her right lapel. I knew at once that she was my friend's mother. I had never seen anyone more beautiful than she was. I felt inspired to write about her beauty in my diary, but later I couldn't find the appropriate words.

As I gazed at the picture, I realised that my friend's grandmother had come in and was standing next to me. I turned my head and looked at her sadly. She smiled at me and said, "She was beautiful wasn't she?" I nodded. Then she looked at the wounds on my legs and said, "Go back to bed." I looked at the picture once more and caressed the face in the drawing, and then I went back to bed. As Christian's grandmother put iodine on my legs, I kept on looking at the picture.

When she saw me still looking at the picture, she said, "I know what you are going to ask me first; you are going to ask me when it was drawn. And then you are going to tell me how beautiful she was. Before she died, I use to hang this picture on the wall only on her birthdays; but since she died, I've never moved it from the wall.

"One day, my daughter had come to visit me on her birthday. That birthday, I had a surprise for her. My brother was a famous painter. I asked him to come all the way from America for my daughter's birthday.

My daughter loved me, and seeing her uncle here as well made her very happy. When she learned that my brother had come here just for her birthday, she was so amazed and cried out with joy, and gave her uncle a big smile. He put an orchid in her lapel and started to draw her.

"It took him many days to complete the drawing. The result was so good that I thought I had twin daughters. It looked as if an angel had drawn it rather than a human being. My daughter didn't take the drawing home with her but told me to hang it here on the wall on my happiest day. And that's what I did. Of course, my happiest day was her birthday. Even though I now cry on her birthdays, they are still the happiest days of my life. Then I remember that I have my grandson and I feel better."

As she finished talking, she also finished putting the iodine on my legs. Then she started dabbing it again, but this time on my elbows, and continued with her story.

"After we got married, my husband and I tried for six years to have children. I couldn't conceive and no one could help us. I was upset because my husband was so unhappy. Then we moved to Berlin for his work.

"One day, we were in a coffee shop having breakfast when someone approached us and gave us a tiny book. Its title was *Pray to God and your Wish will be Granted*. It was the true story of a mother whose son had been missing for fifteen years, and after praying, she was reunited with her son.

"As soon as my husband saw the word 'God' he mumbled something to himself and threw the book across the table. I picked it up and started reading it. Neither of us believed in God. But one idea intrigued me, which was that if God hadn't had a son, we wouldn't exist either.

"At that moment, the bells of a nearby church started to chime. A voice inside me told me to go to that church. Even though my husband tried to convince me not to go inside, I did. Because he loved me so very much, he followed me into that church. I was following my inner voice. I didn't know where God was, but once inside the church, I lifted my head up towards the sky and asked, 'Are you really there?'

"Then I saw a coffin. A tearful crowd all dressed in black had gathered around it. My husband, however, was discreetly laughing to himself. I sat down in one of the pews. I was wondering why if there was no God so many people believed in Him. The priest talked about the deceased and read a few verses from the Bible. When I heard the words from the Bible, I was frightened. But I listened to the priest with all my heart. Afraid that he might start believing in God, my husband left the church quietly while I stayed inside.

"After the priest's sermon, they took the coffin out of the church and all the people followed. I was the only one left in the huge church, with an exception of an old lady who was praying far away near the altar. For the first time in my life, I got on my knees to pray; and immediately, I wasn't frightened anymore. I didn't know what to say. Then suddenly, I got excited and managed to utter a few words, which were, 'Please allow me to have a child;' and then I stood up.

"I looked around the church, and then I started to search for a Bible. As I was looking at some old books by the window, I heard a voice asking me if he could help me. It was the priest. When I told him that I was looking for a Bible, he smiled and asked me to wait.

"He quickly came back carrying a Bible and handed it to me. When I asked him how much it cost, he said it was a gift. I thanked him and took a few steps towards the door. But then I turned back; with my head lowered, I asked the priest, 'If I pray, will He allow me to have a child?'

"The priest came up to me smiling and taking the Bible in his hands, said, 'If you read it, you'll see that God heard the Prophet Abraham's prayer and granted it. As long as you pray, from the heart and believe, there is no reason why He shouldn't grant your prayers as well. We are all His children; He loves as all, but we must obey Him in all things.' After that, the priest left.

"When I got home, I opened the Bible and turned straight to the story of the Prophet Abraham. After a few months, I had read the whole Bible. My husband kept mocking me and did everything he could to convince me to stop believing; but his words had the reverse effect: the more he mocked, the stronger my belief became.

"One day, my husband said, 'The doctors can't help every woman to have a child. If you truly believe in God, pray to Him that He will allow you to have a child.' When I heard that from him I had no more doubts.

"I replied, 'If I beg God to allow me to have a child and He does, will you then believe in Him?'

"'Yes,' he smirked.

"I went to my husband and got on my knees. Holding his hands, I said a short prayer. After the prayer, I saw fear in my husband's face. He told me that while I had been praying, he'd felt a strange kind of warmth suffuse his body, which had frightened him. After that incident, he stopped mocking me.

"Of course, one prayer wasn't enough; but after six months of begging God, the amazed doctor announced that I was with child. When I told my husband, without thinking, he knelt down and thanked the Lord.

"Not long after, he prepared a little booklet called *Faith in God* and started to hand it out to his friends. When he started to invite his non-religious friends to become believers, many of them disappeared from our lives, as did mine. In his prayers, my husband wanted a daughter. It happened: I gave a birth to a baby daughter, and she was so beautiful.

"Not long after our daughter's sixth birthday, my husband died. But he died a Christian, which made me very happy. I gave him a Christian burial. I loved him very much, and I still do; often, I shed tears when I think of him.

"I raised my daughter with lots of love, care and attention. Then she met that accursed man. I was against the marriage, but when I saw how much she loved him, I gave my consent. Before that, I had secretly asked him not to marry her, but he tearfully assured me that he loved her very much.

"I lost half of my heart when my husband died, and I lost the other half when my daughter married him. I was without a heart for many years. But with time, I healed, especially when my grandson came along, who gave me a reason to live. After he lost his mother, he couldn't open up to anyone except me and that made me very sad.

"My grandson used to talk to me a lot, but I knew he needed a friend of his own age. A few weeks ago, I received a letter from him. He wrote about you, saying that you had listened to his stories and problems, and had even cried while he was talking to you.

"The fact that you've promised to make sure his mother's grave will always have orchids on it has made him very happy. He loves his mother so much that if it weren't for you, he would have opened her grave and buried himself alive. You are keeping him in this world.

If anything happened to him, my heart would break; and you would not only lose him, but you would lose me too."

I knew why she had told me this story. I promised her that I would never make the same mistake again, and told her that in the cornfield, I had promised her grandson as well. Then I hugged her. She returned the hug in a way that made me realise the extent of her gratitude to me for keeping her grandson alive. As I told her how much I loved her grandson, she noticed that I was still sleepy. After kissing my forehead, she put my head on the pillow and left me. Because I was really feeling very tired, after changing into my own pyjamas, I fell instantly asleep again.

* * *

I awoke from a deep sleep with a soft touch to my cheek. I tried twice to brush it away, but couldn't; something was tickling my cheek. Then I was wide awake. I opened my eyes and saw Christian smiling at me. He was holding the biggest chick I had ever seen. He placed it on my chest.

Holding the chick, I sat up in bed and saw that it wasn't an ordinary baby chicken but another kind of bird. When my friend realised that I didn't know what it was, he informed me that it was a cygnet; then he told me that a cygnet was a baby swan.

Mesmerised by its beauty, I heard its mother calling and the cygnet responding. I wanted to release it, but Christian wouldn't let me. Hearing her baby, the swan came into the room and saw her offspring struggling in my hands. As I admired the swan's beauty, it didn't lose any time in attacking me. I stood up on the bed and lifted the cygnet in the air. Because the swan couldn't reach her baby, it bit my leg. But in spite of the other wounds I already had, the swan didn't hurt me much; it didn't have any teeth. I even liked its bites and they made me laugh.

When she realised that she couldn't get her baby released by biting me, the angry swan lunged at me with her beak hard in the stomach. I fell on the bed in pain and let go of the cygnet. Seeing this, the swan bit me on the ear. My friend fell on the bed laughing. The freed cygnet went to its mother, who lifted her head high, gave me one last look, and left the room.

It was the first time I had seen a swan. It was unlike any other bird. It was very beautiful, just as my friend's mother was; and Christian's mother was unlike any other woman I had seen before.

I couldn't laugh or cry because of my pain. Hearing her grandson's mirth, my friend's grandmother came in and asked what we were laughing about. Unfortunately, I was incapable of answering her because of the pain in my stomach and Christian because he was laughing so hard. When my pain had eased off, I started laughing as well.

Although my friend's grandmother didn't know why, we were laughing so much that she began to laugh as well. Between guffaws, he tried his best to tell her what had happened. As she managed to understand the story, she laughed even louder and tears even ran down her cheeks. Finally, we all felt our stomachs aching and calmed down.

When I felt that I could get up, I went to get the letter. As I was just about to pick it up, I saw the corncob next to it and thought better. Silence fell in the room. Christian's face became sad. He got up and went to the window. I looked at his grandmother, saying that I only wanted to look at the address to find out if she knew where it was. She said that her daughter had known this area very well and that her grandson knew it even better; then she caressed my head and left the room. Seeing the very unhappy state my friend was in, I went up to him and apologised.

Christian was calm but I could sense the anger inside him. He said, "Marcus is long dead; it doesn't matter whether we deliver it today or tomorrow, or a few days later. We two are the most important people here. I could have come here alone but there is reason why I brought you with me.

"Don't make me repeat the same things again and again. In the name of our Creator, I promise you when the time comes to deliver this letter I will remind you of it. Please act as I do. Accept things the way they are because I pray and act according to the signs I receive. We have very little time left to reach our goal.

"The time we have here with my grandmother is very short; we won't reach our goal if we do other things first. My goal for you is that you should run for very long distances, and for you to become a very fast runner without getting tired so quickly. Remember, we are here for only two weeks. The most important thing is that you must run so fast that no dog will be able to keep up with you.

"All of this is so that we can realise the vision my mother had for us. She told me everything, including your description and your destiny. Forget everything else and just think about making my mother's soul happy."

He had such a sad expression on his face that I couldn't bear it any longer and started to cry. He wiped away my tears and told me that my weeping was making him sadder. I asked him what I could do to cheer him up. He said that I shouldn't worry about him, but that I should try to make myself happy. Then grabbing me by the hand and pulled me outside from the house without giving me any more time to think, he started to run. As he was pulling me hard, I had no choice but to run with him.

This wasn't the first time my friend had run so fast that all my previous training proved to be inadequate. My face grew red and I felt a pain on my right side; and my pyjamas were rubbing against my legs with every move I made, which caused me further pain. But I had to continue running. We ran for a very long way; all the time, he held my hand and didn't listen to my protests.

Despite falling a few times and getting up again with Christian's help, we continued to run. He told me that I should try to control my breathing as I ran but even if I collapsed altogether, he would pull me along. Finally, I did collapse. He continued to pull me along as he had promised until he got so tired that he couldn't pull me anymore. When he was totally exhausted, he stopped.

My friend lay down on the grass beneath a big tree. I lay down next to him. It was a walnut tree we were under. As I was looking up at the tree, I saw a walnut falling in the direction of my face. I had neither the strength nor the time to move my head, so I closed my eyes and waited. Of course, it fell right in the middle of my forehead.

Christian heard me say "Ouch," and started to pull me again. As soon as we moved, lots of walnuts fell down. Some had fallen on my friend too, and he rubbed his head while I did the same. We stopped when we lifted our heads and saw two squirrels playing in the branches of the walnut tree. Without making a noise, we gazed at them. Suddenly, more squirrels appeared and made for the foot of the tree, where they started to gather up the walnuts. We were immobile like that tree; we had never seen so many squirrels together in our lives, not even in our dreams.

Seeing their friends arrive, the first two squirrels we had seen also came down and started to gather walnuts. When they had collected all the walnuts, nearly all the squirrels left. But one stayed behind, and instead of being frightened of us, it repeatedly approached us. We were amazed because it wasn't a domestic animal. The squirrel sniffed our feet and stood up on its hind legs; then, after a good look at us, it left. We were astonished and had no words to describe what had just happened or what we felt. I was so impressed that I thought I had been to heaven.

When everything grew silent again, Christian grabbed me by the hand and we resumed running. Just as I was thinking that he wasn't running as fast as before, he accelerated and my wounds started to hurt again. After a long time like this, and in spite of me telling him that we should stop, I was very tired, and I needed to rest, he still kept running.

Long after that, realising that I was on the verge of collapsing again, he let go of my hand and I fell down. He carried on running. It seemed that he didn't know the meaning of exhaustion. As I was lying down on the grass trying to catch my breath, I heard a dog and sat up. I had been bitten by a dog a long time ago, so I was very nervous about being bitten again.

Quickly, I turned my head towards the sound of barking; a big dog was running towards me. I knew it was impossible to run away so, putting my hands in front of my face, I waited for the dog to bite me.

Then I heard two different sounds. One was that of the dog approaching, and the other was my own heart beating. After a very short time, I could hear other dogs approaching as well. I thought the time had come for my last prayer. But when the first dog reached me, it stopped barking and began to make whimpering noises instead.

I summoned all my courage and looked directly at the dog. I saw that it had a kind look in its eyes. Then I knew that it wouldn't hurt me, although I was still frightened. Seeing me looking at it, the dog came right up to me. The other dogs, which by now were nearby too, carried on barking; I didn't yet have the courage to look at all of them. I sat on the ground motionless. I let the first dog lick my cheeks. Even though my brain was telling me that this dog wouldn't harm me, I was still frightened and listening to my heartbeat. The other dogs followed the example of the first one and they all started to lick my hands.

The licking of my hands made me ticklish. After that, they started licking my face. Although it must have looked very funny, I couldn't open my eyes, but I was laughing. Dogs normally disgusted me, but I was pleased with these ones' behaviour.

My fear totally vanished when I heard Christian's voice. Then I heard another voice in the distance calling the dogs. Wiping my face, I stood up. When I turned round, I saw my friend waving to me and standing next to a tall, burly shepherd. As the dogs disappeared, a flock of sheep with their lambs came and surrounded me.

Christian, who was laughing very hard, kept on waving to me. Next to him, the shepherd waved to me as well. Walking slowly towards them, I stroked the sheep. When I reached them, the smiling shepherd introduced himself and gave me a hug. He then told me how much he loved my friend.

However, I could hardly breathe for the shepherd smelt like the sheep. I liked the smell of sheep well enough, but not the smell of sheep on the shepherd. Christian noticed my face growing red and saved my embarrassment by asking the shepherd to tell us how he had saved his sheep from the wolves.

The three of us sat down on the grass, but just as the shepherd was about to begin his story, he noticed that the sheep were beginning to stray. Saying that he would tell us the story another time, he began to run towards them. Christian started to laugh again and told me that this shepherd never tired of telling his story; in spite of his advanced age, he had the heart of a child.

Then my friend smiled and picked a few daisies, which he handed to me. I was taken aback by this act. Noticing this, he said, "I know you're surprised and wondering whether a boy can give flowers to another boy. But the act of giving flowers simply means that the recipient is as innocent as a flower, and his or her heart is as pure and lovely as a flower.

You can give these to my grandmother along with a hug and she will appreciate them."

I bent my head as I wondered what to say. After giving it some serious thought, I looked up and was about to speak but found myself tongue-tied. Christian laughed as he waited for me to say something. As I couldn't think of anything, I stood up, grabbed his hand, and started to run.

My friend laughed as he ran. He knew what I was going to be faced with shortly; and very soon I began to feel the pain on my right side. I stopped running and touched the place where it was hurting. Christian said that this discomfort would soon pass and I would feel no pain when I was running; I would be able to run like him. Then he decided not to push me anymore for the time being and said we could walk home.

On the way, we talked about the adventures we'd had and managed to laugh in spite of their upsetting nature. Of course, we both avoided talking about the incident with Marcus. When we arrived at the house, I dodged past Christian and went indoors first. His grandmother was sitting on a chair reading a book. When I asked her what kind of book she was reading, she said it was the Holy Bible.

I gave her the flowers and told her that I loved her just as if I was truly her grandson as well. After placing a kiss on my forehead, she asked me to look at her face. When I did, I saw tears in her eyes. She said that she had dreamt of her dead daughter. In her dream, the girl had smiled happily as she said, "I've sent you a second child, who will keep Christian alive."

As I felt my friend's presence behind me, I turned around. He didn't have tears in his eyes; he was smiling. His grandmother asked us to sit next to her and, placing me on her right and Christian on her left, she started to read from the Bible a story about Jesus.

As she began, I ran out and got the stone my friend had given me at the tunnel, and my father had put on a chain so that I could wear it around my neck. My running to get the stone made Christian fidget. But I sat down again and listened to the reading very happily and very carefully because it was the first time I had been read to from the Bible. I didn't even ask a single question. My father had always taught me never to interrupt when someone was reading aloud or telling a story, and I didn't.

When my friend's grandmother had finished the whole story, she kissed me on my forehead and kissed Christian on his forehead, and then she left. After his grandmother had gone, I asked my friend to clarify the things about Jesus that I hadn't been able to understand, and he explained them to me in such a way that I never forgot them.

Chapter 7

Days passed and all we did was run. As my holy day was Saturday and for Christian, it was Sunday, we didn't run on those days. I prayed on Saturday the way my father had taught me that I should when I was unable to go to a synagogue; whereas my friend and his grandmother went to church on Sunday. I went with them and found the sermons very interesting and enjoyable.

After training day after day, I realised that the pain on my side when I ran a lot had disappeared. I could run as fast as Christian and even cover the same distance as him without getting tired. Seeing that I had managed to accomplish all this in such a short space of time, my friend next made me run uphill; and I sometimes had to jog with a rucksack full of stones on my back. I never complained but as I accomplished each of his tasks, he always came up with another one.

Then when Christian said that he had a surprise for me, I immediately thought of Marcus's letter and looked in that direction. When he saw that look, he lost his enthusiasm and his joy. He came to me and, getting on his knees, held my head with both of his hands.

After looking at me for a long time, he said, "I won't get angry with you; I can never be angry with you again. I'll treat you the way my mother treated me, and

I'll teach you the way she taught me. Let me tell you a story that she told me.

"One day, she saw her dream orchids in the flower shop window, but she couldn't afford them. As she had no money to buy the orchids, she walked many miles every day and stood at the same spot in front of the flower shop window, and gazed at them for hours.

"That lasted for a few months. Finally, my grandmother gave her some money and told her to go and buy some of those orchids that she loved to look at so very much. Hoping to realise her dream, my mother went eagerly to the flower shop. She knew she could only afford one pot of orchids; nevertheless, she was very happy, as she would have been with just one orchid petal. But when she arrived at the shop where she had spent months staring at the flowers, she was faced with a sad surprise.

"The flower shop that had stood there for many years was now closed because its owner had died. Instead of becoming upset and sad, she considered ehrself grateful for the opportunity to look at those beautiful flowers for so long, and started to walk back towards her house, smiling and singing.

"Seeing a bridal car speeding along the road, she stopped to let it pass. But instead of continuing on its way, the car stopped right beside her, and the groom leant out and gave her a bunch of orchids, saying, 'Smiling suits you.'

My mother was amazed, and didn't know how to thank him. She could hardly believe that she was holding a bunch of orchids.

"After telling me this story, my mother asked me never to rush things and learn to be patient.

"I've always followed her advice and always been rewarded. So I'm telling you this: before I get an answer to my prayers, we won't deliver that letter.

"But when the time comes, no one will stop us from delivering it. I want you to be as strong as a poplar, but not as fragile as a new shoot."

My weakness was my impatience and I was aware of it. I tried very hard to be patient; I continually prayed but I never succeeded. This wasn't the first time that the subject of Marcus had come up. We both knew that I had no patience, but there was nothing my friend could do about it. All he could do was give me advice when I made a mistake. On the other hand, *he* always had a lot of patience with me, and he wanted me to be the same; he wanted to help me acquire that kind of patience as well.

★ ★ ★

I awoke very early the next morning with Christian repeatedly calling, "Wake up, wake up," but as I was still very tired, I couldn't even open my eyes. As usual, I felt as if there was a heavy weight on my eyelids. Feeling that tired, I had no desire to wake up. Taking no notice of my feelings, my friend started to shout at me while laughing at the same. I finally gave in to his persistence and began to think about getting up.

However, I hadn't yet opened my eyes, so I didn't see him throwing something at my head. I was still feeling tired, but with great difficulty, I opened my eyes. He continued to throw things at me. He was standing by the door with a grin on his face. I saw a crumpled up piece of paper at my feet. I picked it up and read what was written on it: "Follow me." My eyes were finally wide open, but my friend had already gone; so I quickly got dressed and ran outside.

There was no sign of him. I saw scraps of paper strewn all along the road, so I started to follow this trail. It was enjoyable following the pieces of paper along the road like that. Making sure to pick up all the scraps, singing all the while, and wondering what the surprise might be, I continued to follow the paper trail until I reached a small forest. I slowed down. In the forest, there was a certain tree. I went up to the tree and I saw a piece of paper stuck on its trunk. It read: "Stop and be quiet!" So I obeyed.

I could hear a chorus of birds singing. I was fascinated by all their different songs. Then I heard Christian's voice telling me almost in a whisper to prepare to enter paradise. He was standing near the tree trunk. I went and stood next to him. He said that we should now walk very softly and quietly. We advanced slowly. He told me that because in this forest no one knew the names of these birds, and no one bothered to find out where they had originally come from, they called them 'birds of paradise'. In spite of hearing so many birds, when I looked up into the trees, I couldn't see a single one.

We finally arrived at the spot in the forest that Christian wanted to show me. I was so amazed by the scene before me that I was speechless. It was spectacular. Right in front of me, there was a little lake and directly above it there was a small waterfall surrounded by hundreds of swans. My friend told me that this place hadn't changed for many decades; and that the first time he had been there was with his mother when he had been just three.

I knew he was speaking to me but I didn't register anything he was saying; I was mesmerised by the swans. When he realised this, he stopped talking. I didn't know what to do or how to feel; I had never seen so many swans together – nor have I since. They were washing their feathers, drinking from the waterfall, and communicating with one another.

I stole a quick look at Christian; he nodded in the direction of the swans. This time, after making a pleasant sound, they all flew away. Their flapping wings made a noise that disturbed the other birds, which then all started to sing at once. I couldn't believe that so many different birds could live together in such a small forest. It seemed to me that the other birds were communicating something to the swans while they were flying around.

The place became quiet after all the swans had left, and the little birds settled down again and went back to their branches. My friend ran to the waterfall, took off most of his clothes, and dived into the shallow lake. His chattering teeth told me that the water was very cold. He wanted me to dive in as well. He kept trying to convince me to get in, saying that the water couldn't harm me. I refused to go into that cold water until I saw the very sad expression on his face and he entreated me, "Please!"

I gave in and started to get undressed, but then the thought of that freezing water stopped me; it looked so cold that it made me change my mind, so I put my clothes back on. Christian was still insistent but I was firm in my resolve.

My friend's expression became even sadder as he said, "It isn't me who wants you to come into the water; it's my mother. She wants you to become hardened to this cold water; please do as she wishes."

Hearing this and seeing the expression on his face made me undress all over again. When I was about to put my foot in, he stopped me and said that I should dive in instead. After giving it some thought, I threw myself into the water. It was so cold that I felt I had frozen and attempted to get out immediately. Grabbing me by the shoulders, he ducked me in the freezing water. I thought I was in an icy Siberian lake. The more I tried to come up for air, the deeper he pushed me. When I was totally breathless, I was finally allowed to regain the surface; but as soon as I had filled my lungs, he plunged me under again.

After giving me a quizzical look, Christian said that he had forgotten to ask if I knew how to swim. I told him that my father had taught me at a very early age. I then noticed that he was looking at my chest where I wore the stone that his mother had given him. He touched it, and after ducking me a few more times, climbed out of the lake with a smile on his face. Taking advantage of my freedom, I jumped out of the water and found myself happily on the dry and warm shore. But I lost my joy when he said that I shouldn't be so relieved, for we would come here for a swim after each run.

We got dressed and had taken a few steps away from the lake when my friend asked me to run back to the waterfall and have a look. I didn't take any notice of him and continued to walk slowly away. Then he took me by the shoulders and turned me round; although the view was breath-taking, I wasn't overjoyed.

The thought of going back to that freezing water every time we had been for a run made me shiver; I didn't like the idea at all. If anyone else had seen this beautiful scene, they would have spent hours standing and gazing at it, but all I could think of was how to get away as quickly as possible. As I looked at the water, not only I could feel my body chill, but it even seemed that there was ice in my stomach.

Then I realised what Christian wanted to show me; it was the small rainbow over the waterfall. When he saw that I wasn't interested, he grabbed my hand and started to run back to his grandmother's house. I told him to let go because I could run just as fast as he could. He released me and increased his speed; so did I for I didn't want him to run faster than me.

When my friend realised that I was keeping up with him, he said that we now had to run faster. He started to run so swiftly that I had no way of keeping up with him; he was like the wind. I didn't want to be left behind, but all my efforts to catch up were in vain and he quickly disappeared from view. I jogged back to his grandmother's house on my own, and he got there way ahead of me.

Chapter 8

Early one morning, in order to wake me up, Christian suddenly shook me vigorously. This was a big mistake. I wasn't used to being shaken; no one in my family woke me up like that, but I had neglected to tell him this. His action frightened me so much that as I jumped up, our heads hit each other and he fell off my bed.

Holding my head, I fell back on the pillow. It was so painful that I couldn't even scream. My friend was in the same state. Slumped on the floor, wriggling like a worm, he told me that he could feel a bump on his head; whereas I could only see thousands of stars.

In spite of all the pain he was in, Christian held on to the corncob that he had boiled for us, saying, "Let's halve it." Forgetting my pain, I took the corn and was about to take a bite when he stopped me. Looking at me he said that we would eat after a prayer.

I didn't listen to all of my friend's prayer, but it began, "The corn we are about to eat is…the promise I gave him about Marcus's letter…!" He then continued with the prayer.

I understood that eating the corncob meant that we would deliver Marcus's letter today. When my friend had finished his prayer, I tried to eat my half very quickly. Seeing how impatient I was, Christian said that

I was the first person to make him laugh so early in the morning.

But I wasn't laughing; all I wanted to do was eat my corn as quickly as possible. But perhaps because it wasn't fresh, it kept making me choke so that I couldn't eat as fast as I would have liked. I finally finished it and got dressed. Shortly after, my friend also ate his half of the corncob.

When I was dressed, my friend told me to wait outside for him. I picked up Marcus's later and went outdoors. Soon after, I saw him come out but he passed right me, walked further down the garden, knelt down, and started to pray again. Only when I had got quite near did he realise that I was there.

Christian opened his eyes and seeing the stone that his mother had given him still around my neck, he started to call, "My mother! My mother! My dear mother, I miss you my mother," and stroked the stone.

Then we started to run. I don't know how far we ran, but we didn't stop until we saw the sunrise. We were on a hill. I used to do the same sort of thing in my village, but this view was different. The sun was still the same but the scenery wasn't: the mountains were higher and the trees were taller; and they had leaves of many different colours. The sky with its soft clouds was also filled with powerful hues. It was a wonderful sight to see.

However, my friend wasn't interested in the view at all; he was preoccupied with the time factor. When he said that although he could understand my fascination with the view, we didn't have time to stop and admire it, I resumed running. But I kept my eyes on the rising sun until its rays were much too strong for me to look at it directly.

As we ran, we talked about what had happened that morning. my friend told me that he had a bruise on his forehead; and I responded by saying that not only did I have a bruise, but my forehead was also swollen and hurt so much that I couldn't even touch it.

As I spoke, I noticed that Christian had stopped, so I did too. I looked in the direction he was pointing. In the distance, we could see some tiny black creatures moving around in the road, but we were too far away to make them out properly. Speculating as to what they might be, we continued running. For now we, had no answers to our questions.

As we got nearer, what we saw surprised us so much that we had to stop and sit down. For about four or five metres along the road, there were hundreds of thousands of ants carrying wheat from one field to another; each ant carried one grain.

Continuing on our journey meant that we would have to trample on a great many ants, but we didn't want to do that. I stood up and plunged into one of the fields and started collecting ears of wheat. As there weren't very many, I had to go right into the middle of the field. My friend followed my example. Then when we had enough ears of wheat, we used them to redirect some of the ants to the right and some of them to the left, clearing a way for us to pass down the middle of the road.

On reaching the other side, we asked the ants to forgive us if we had harmed any of them at all and resumed our run. Although I was now managing to keep up with my friend, I still felt the pain in my side.

When the sun was directly above our heads, we realised that we had been running for a very long time, for it was now midday. After we had been sweating for some time, a village appeared in the distance. Christian slowed down and started to walk. Then he said that although he had known the way so far, we would have to ask directions to Marcus's house.

We met a few people on the road into the village, who smiled at us but were reluctant to talk. Nonetheless, as we reached the outskirts of the village, all at once we saw a yellow house standing before us. I couldn't believe my eyes; shaking my head, I followed Christian. This yellow house was the bakery.

As we approached the village bakery, the smell of fresh-baked bread reached our noses. My friend could even hear my stomach rumbling. I told him that it wasn't my fault; faced with this fantastic smell, my nose was alerting my stomach.

We entered the bakery and saw an old man sitting on a chair smiling. Christian showed him the envelope and asked if he knew the whereabouts of the addressee. The old man stared at us, but didn't say anything. My friend gave me a look and then repeated his question: still no answer. I wondered if the old man was dead but Christian said that a dead person wouldn't move his eyelids and smile. He then asked him the question again, but louder this time.

A little door opened and a woman came in. She said that the old man was blind and deaf. We felt very sorry him and realised that he hadn't been smiling at us. We showed the envelope to the woman and asked her about the address on it. Seeing the envelope, her expression changed and, almost whimpering, she started to tell us how to get there.

Then she saw me sniffing the air like a dog and gave me one of the loaves she was holding. I took it readily. Feeling Christian's gaze on me, I thanked the woman and left the bakery. He hadn't prevented me from taking the loaf, so as soon as I was outside, I broke it into pieces and started to eat it. Because it had been baked in a large wood-fuelled oven, it was very tasty.

Eating my bread, I stared at the yellow-walled bakery. Truly, it was the first time I had seen a house painted such a colour. While I was in a kind of daze looking at the brightly painted house, someone came and put a ladder up against the wall and started to paint it blue. I was so surprised that I started to choke on a piece of bread.

When my friend heard my spluttering he ran out of the shop. In between coughs, I managed to tell him that the house was now being painted blue. The painter heard me and said that it was he who had painted the house yellow three days ago. Since then, everybody had made so much fun of him that he had decided to repaint it another colour. Then he continued with his work. Christian gave me a look and I knew what it meant.

The address we were supposed to find wasn't very far away so we decided to walk. I wanted to give my friend half of the loaf but he refused it. Nonetheless, when he realised that I was going to eat his half without offering it to him again, he grabbed the remainder of the loaf from my hand, broke it into smaller pieces, and placed them on the side of the road. It took a while to understand that Christian was worried that I might put on weight; and then I wouldn't be able to enter the tunnel again. He was right: it was already a tight squeeze.

All became silent. I was thinking and wondering what would become of me.

A huge house interrupted my thoughts. Looking at it intently, we smiled at each other. I was very happy to be there because of the promise I had made Marcus, although I had no idea why Christian was happy as well. I ran up to the big gate, only to be accosted by three large dogs that barked savagely. I was so frightened that I froze in my tracks. I took a few steps backwards and started to tremble in terror. While keeping his gaze steadily on me, my friend approached the dogs and then called to me to follow.

At first I refused, but Christian asked me to trust him, so I did. I sat next to him and looked at the dogs. He told me that in order to calm them down, I mustn't show any fear. Despite his assurance, I knew that if he hadn't been there, I could never have gone near those dogs. While he was talking, a woman came out through the garden gate. We both stood up.

Without saying a word, my friend showed her the envelope. When she saw Marcus's handwriting, she closed her eyes and sighed, and then opened the garden gate. Realising that I was afraid of her dogs, she quietly ordered them to go away.

Making sure that all three dogs had gone, I cautiously went through the garden gate. When we were in the garden, the woman closed the gate behind us, and we all sat down on garden chairs under a tree surrounded by rose bushes. She asked Christian how he had managed to calm her savage dogs. He told her that his father had taught him how to treat such animals at the age of three.

After telling the woman all about our adventure with Marcus, my friend gave her Marcus's letter. Almost immediately, tears sprang to her eyes, which she wiped away with a handkerchief to stop them rolling down her cheeks.

She put the letter on the grass at the foot of her chair and asked, "Do you hear that nightingale?"

Without waiting for a reply, she continued, "You know, many years ago, I was having a rest like this among the roses; the nightingale had transported me to another world with its song; but when it stopped singing, I opened my eyes. It had flown away because a young man holding a bunch of red roses was standing there.

"I looked at the young man absent-mindedly. Then I felt something fall on my cheek. I wiped it off with my hand and saw that it was blood. Seeing the blood frightened me, so I sat up. The young man knelt down next to me and gave me the roses. He said that seeing how beautiful I was, he hadn't been able to resist picking the roses for me in spite of all the thorns that had scratched his hands.

"The young man then sat down and I sat next to him. He said that I was more beautiful than the flowers. That young man stole my heart with his lovely words. I was very young but I still fell instantly in love with him. I even forgot the beautiful roses all around me.

"After courting for a long time, we got married. We were so happy. We were always together; we couldn't live without each other. We even wished to remain childless so that our love wouldn't be shared.

"After working tirelessly for years, we became very rich; we even had servants and a gardener. We realised that we were getting on and decided to have a child, but we were still wary of having children. One night when we were both drunk, I conceived. As the months went by, we made clothes and prepared many other things for our baby. We were still afraid of having a child, although, in another way, we couldn't wait to have our baby. As we didn't know which it was going to be, we made clothes for both a boy and a girl.

"At last, the long awaited day arrived. I gave birth in hospital and there was a surprise: we had twins. We were even more surprised when they turned out to be a girl and a boy: there were clothes for both of them.

"The years went by, but our love didn't diminish. We told each other all our secrets. But that was wrong, for we weren't aware that some secrets must be buried within ourselves, and aren't to be shared. We didn't realise this because we felt so secure in our love for each other.

"Every year, we had a big birthday celebration for the children. It was the same on their fifth birthday. The living room was full of people and everyone had a drink. I used to stand on a stool and propose a toast to the children. I did the same that year, but because I was drunk, I accidentally proposed the toast to the servants. Silence fell upon the crowd; and they were the wrong crowd to make such a mistake in front of.

"Instead of correcting my mistake, I repeated myself. No one took a drink, but I drained my glass. All the servants had their heads down and no one moved. My husband came to me and after giving me an angry look, proposed a toast to the children and everyone had a drink. He whispered that I was drunk and that I should go and have a rest, but I refused.

"Holding my arm, he tried to steer me towards my bedroom, but I repeated that I wasn't drunk and insisted that I wanted to stay in the living room. I managed to free myself. When he attempted to take army arm again, I shouted that I didn't want him to hold it, and that the best thing for him would be to tell us all about his father.

"Without a moment's thought, he slapped me so hard that I fell on the floor and immediately sobered up. Then he tried to kick me, but the people around us stopped him.

"You see, my husband, didn't know who his father was; it was a secret he had shared with me. He also told me that his classmates at school used to bully him about it, making him crazy with fury.

"The party ended. When our guests started to leave, I was afraid that my husband would beat me when we were alone. I begged my closest friends to stay and not leave me with him but no one listened. I took my children to my bedroom and waited. I expected him to come and beat me, yet when he came in, it was the opposite. He told me that it was all over between us, but that I should stay in the house and raise the children. He then left the room.

"From that day, my love was replaced by fear and because of this, I couldn't even think of leaving him. And for the sake of the children as well, I decided to accept his offer.

"I never had another drink, but he drank more than ever, shouting at me and the children every night. Nonetheless, he decided not to touch them, for as far as he was concerned, they belonged to me alone. They cried every day because their father no longer loved them; and they used to have tantrums, and sit without talking to anyone. Seeing the children like this, he blamed me and drank still more.

"For a long time, I tried to heal our children by giving them all my time and attention. I tried so hard to make up for the love that they were no longer receiving from their father. They actually needed his love just as much as mine but he didn't change his attitude towards them. Yet neither did the children change their attitude towards their father; they still yearned for his love.

"When the twins grew up, they started to drink too, and became like their father. I couldn't help them, but neither could I leave them. One night, when all three of them were drunk, I was in my bedroom thinking about my fate when I heard raised voices coming from the landing, near the stairs that led down to the ground floor. I opened the door and saw the children dangling their father over the banister by his arms and laughing. Before I could say, 'Don't!' they let go of him.

"He lay there apparently lifeless at the bottom of the stairs, but I knew he still was alive for he was breathing. I ran to him. My son looked at me and said, 'You loved our father, and we loved him too.' They slowly approached him; both children briefly caressed his head and then left.

"I immediately called an ambulance and they took him to hospital. I stayed with him until he came round from the coma. By the time they discharged him, he was better, but he couldn't talk, and he had lost his mind as well. I saw him after they had moved him to an asylum. I visited him a few times there, but when they told me he was getting better, I didn't go anymore.

"I looked after our children, but they got worse and worse, and I never succeeded in making them happy again; yet the only medicine they needed was their father's love. As long as they lacked that, no one could help them. So as a result of my husband sharing his secret with me, we both lost so much; we lost everything. That mistake led to our destruction. Marcus was my husband and that was my life with him."

★ ★ ★

As soon as the woman had finished her story, we noticed the twins at the garden gate. They came over to their mother, and, with unbearable pain in their voices, they sobbed that they couldn't believe their father was dead. They said that they had always lived in the hope that he would love them again one day, but now that hope was gone. Then they knelt down and started to cry; "all we wanted from him was his love," they wept.

The woman was crying as well but at the same time she tried to comfort them. She took the letter from the foot of her chair and gave it to her children. They grabbed it and after tearing the envelope apart, read it. When they had finished, they seemed to go berserk, crumpling the letter up and throwing it among the rose bushes. They then turned and ran into the house.

Christian and I were terrified and trembling. As the twins were disappearing into the house, their mother asked us to leave immediately. I went to the rose bush and tried to pick up the letter. I had just managed to avoid the thorns, when I felt my friend's hand on my shoulder. I turned towards him but before I could say anything he pulled me away mercilessly. The thorns scratched my arms from the elbows all the way down to my fingers. In spite of my screams, he kept on tugging me with all his might, seemingly unconcerned about the pain I was in.

As soon as we were out of the garden, my friend told me to run. I tried to tell him about my arms, but he wasn't interested. I had been so very curious about the contents of Marcus's letter ever since he had entrusted it to me, but now I would never find out what was written in it.

We were still quite close to the house when we heard a commotion from that direction. We stopped running and turned towards it. We saw the twins at a first floor window; they were screaming but we couldn't hear what they were saying. We only caught their last words: "Father, we will be reunited with you!" and each placed a rope each around the other's neck.

We realised what they were about to do, but before I could even close my eyes they had hanged themselves. I felt dizzy and passed out. When I came round, I was lying under a tree and Christian was on his knees praying. There was no blood on my arms; he had cleaned it up.

After my friend had finished praying, I asked him how long had I been lying there. He replied, "Ask the last ant on the road." As I watched the final ant indeed leaving the road, I realised where we were and started laughing. So did Christian, before telling me that while I had been unconscious, he had counted all the ants. When I asked him how many there were, he said that he would tell me after I had counted all the leaves on the tree above. I stood up saying, "Let's go home." My friend saw that it was getting dark and stood up too, and we headed home.

As we walked, I tried to forget what we had seen, and thought that a good laugh would help me do this. But it wasn't possible; I kept on hearing the twins' last words in my ears. Against my will, tears started rolling down my face.

Seeing the state I was in, Christian said, "I know why you're crying: we both saw the individual deaths of Marcus and his children; and we heard the story of his life. That should stop us making the same mistakes in our lives. These lessons are also taught to help our characters become like steel.

"I know that my own father doesn't love me; I've known it for a long time. If he does, he's never shown it. You could say that his attitude towards me is even worse than the way Marcus behaved towards his children. I don't remember him ever even ruffling my hair affectionately, but whenever he saw a child in the street he would treat it with kindness. I used to pretend that I was one of those children.

"But I never thought of harming him for all that. My mother gave me so much love that it helped me come to terms with the fact that my father didn't love me at all. She taught me how not to crumble when things went badly, and I never have; she taught me how to be humble, and how to forgive.

"Although I know how much my father dislikes me, I've never thought of killing myself. Following my mother's advice, I've managed to stay alive. She also taught me how to keep my promises, and how always to speak the truth. She raised me as a Christian; and I want to teach you all that she taught me.

"Actually you are luckier than me. In the future, you will hear, see and be faced with even worse things than this. If you hadn't experienced all our previous trials, you would now crumble very quickly. Remember these events and learn from them; learn to be strong and not to cry."

My friend had finished talking, but I carried on crying. The harder I tried to stop, the more I cried. Seeing this, he grinned and said that he knew how to stop my tears and, grabbing my hand, he started to run. He ran as fast as he could, and as I had no choice but to run with him, my tears soon dried in the onrushing breeze.

When we arrived at Christian's grandmother's home, I was pale and breathless. The state we were both in made her smile. I sat at her feet, put my head in her lap, and began to cry all over again. But instead of trying to stop me, she caressed my head and started to sing to me softly. Then she told me that years ago she had done the same thing to her daughter when she had cried in her lap.

I don't remember how long I cried, but I do remember my swollen eyes. In between sobs, I told her everything that had happened to us. She gave me the same advice as her grandson had. I carried on crying, saying that I was weak; but perhaps time would change that, I added.

When I finally started shivering, she carried me to bed. After covering me up with a blanket, she wiped my wet cheeks, gave me a kiss on the forehead, and left the room. I hid my face in the pillow and continued to cry.

Chapter 9

Next morning, I was awoken by the stiffness in my legs. I looked out of the window and saw that it was daylight. As I was massaging my legs, I realised that my eyes were still heavy and fell asleep again.

Next time, drops of water falling on my cheeks woke me up. When I opened my eyes, I saw Christian holding a glass of water at some distance from my bed. Dipping his fingers into the water, he was flicking droplets at my face. I invited my friend to come nearer, if he dared. Pointing to his head, he said that he wasn't going to make that mistake again. He then grabbed my blanket and pulling it further and further away, announced that he had a surprise for me. Fully awake now, I leapt out of bed and started to laugh.

Christian asked me if I was aware how long we had been at his grandmother's house. When I shrugged my shoulders, he asked how long I guessed it was; when should we be getting ready to leave? Getting the same answer from me, he sighed and, coming nearer, informed me that we had been there for thirteen days, and that we were therefore supposed to leave in two.

I went pale and asked him if this was the surprise. He laughed and said that he was just reminding me of the facts. Nonetheless, after a dream about his mother, my friend had decided to extend our stay for another two weeks. But before I could say anything, he started to tell me about his dream.

He had been walking along a straight road, singing to himself. Suddenly, the sky had grown dark and it had started to thunder. He had stopped, but could see that a few steps ahead, the sky was clear and sunny. As he had continued on his way, his mother had appeared and told him not to go any further. But because he was afraid of the dark skies and thunder, he hadn't listened to his mother. He had taken one more step and this time, she had given him an orchid. The gift had woken him.

Previously, Christian had always dreamt that it was he who gave orchids to his mother and never the other way round, and he took this as sign that we should prolong our holiday. Usually, when he told a story about his mother, he would become pale and tearful, but this time he kept smiling – I didn't ask why.

Before he left the bedroom, my friend said that it would be a good idea if we went to the post office to send our parents telegrams informing them that we had changed our plans.

I got up and dressed quickly. With each movement, I felt every single muscle in my body aching. But Christian's grandmother wasn't in the house to console me about it.

When I saw my friend outside, I thought of surprising him by opening the door and dashing out at top speed. I thought this was a great idea. I opened the door very quickly and darted out, but before I could get very far, I fell to the ground. I was lying there thinking, "No harm done," when Christian came up to me with an amazed expression on his face, and asked me what on earth I was trying to do.

When I told him, my friend said, "Come on then, catch me if you can;" and he ran away from me very quickly. I got to my feet and, with a lot of pain, began to follow him. He would sprint, then slow down till I nearly caught up with him, and then he would take off again. He did this again and again. Each time I drew near, I asked Christian where his grandmother was, but he always ignored me. Because I kept on repeating my question, in the end, he increased his speed and disappeared from view. In spite of all my efforts, I couldn't catch up with him.

I grew aware that I was alone, and that all was very quiet. Marcus's twins flashed into my mind, and I collapsed. Christian suddenly appeared, very quickly cradling my head to prevent it hitting the ground. Lying there, I took a few deep breaths and then explained why I had collapsed.

With a sad expression on his face, my friend said, "My mother once told me that many years ago, there was young couple living in this village. My mother was about eleven then. She remembered their wedding. Fifteen months later they had a baby girl. They were very happy. However, because they had a child, they become arrogant and behaved like royalty. They boasted to everyone.

"Each year they had a birthday party for their daughter, but one year the little girl died. They were devastated. They were so distraught that instead of burying their little daughter, they wanted to embalm her so that they could keep her in the house and look at her every day. But the woman's family was against the idea, so they had to bury their daughter in the ground after all. Ten days after their little girl's death, the hair of both husband and wife had turned grey and they had wrinkled faces.

"A few years later, they had another daughter, but she died a few weeks later. This time, their hair turned completely white. All their days were spent at the cemetery. They only talked to each other and distanced themselves from everyone else.

"Some years after that, they had a son, but he died too. Then she was pregnant again; this time the baby was stillborn. In spite of their youth, the couple were totally exhausted and started behaving oddly. At first, their neighbours tried to help them, but they soon realised that they were beyond help. My mother noticed that the couple no longer visited the cemetery.

"Days passed and still no one had seen them. People started to gossip that they had gone out of their minds and were refusing to leave the house. But my mother didn't care about rumours spread by gossip, and decided to go and see them. The woman opened the door with a smile on her face, which astonished my mother, and she asked the woman what had made her happy again. The woman said that it was very simple, and, smiling, explained the reason why.

"'When our first daughter died, we grieved so much that instead of burying her, we wanted to embalm her.

And I kept on moaning about how unfair life was. Before long, our second child died too; then my third child and the fourth also passed away. I decided that God didn't exist; by then, I had lost all my faith.

"'One day I fell asleep at the cemetery. When I woke up, I saw a hedgehog at my side. Its stomach was open and you could see its intestines. But it was still alive; it was blinking and I even saw tears. Taking advantage of its situation, flies were feasting on its stomach. Seeing it like that, I chased the flies away. I placed the hedgehog in my lap and gently stroked it. I knew it was dying, but my caresses helped it die peacefully; it passed away looking at me. I buried the little hedgehog next to my first daughter.

"'Before I covered it up, I looked at it carefully. I thought of myself as that little hedgehog. If I carried on living in the past, pretending that I was dead while I was still among the living, the bad memories would eat me up inside, like the flies ate the little hedgehog. Then I covered it up with earth. I stood up and said goodbye to my children and the hedgehog.

"'When I got home, I humbled myself and knelt down. I asked my husband if he wanted to pray with me and he said he would. We began to believe again. Then I did a lot of crying.

"'From then on, I prayed every day, several times a day. We took the photographs of our children down from the walls and no longer talked to each other about them all the time. We felt as we had when we first got married.

"'My past behaviour taught me that if you dwell on bad times and give up hope, life becomes a living hell. If we hadn't made amends, we could have never been reunited with our children. We would have ended up in hell, away from our children, who are in heaven. By praying, we saved ourselves.'

"Not long after the woman had told her story to my mother, the couple left the village and moved far away. Some years later, my mother received a letter from her. She wrote that they had four sons and two daughters; and a remarkable thing had happened: she had given birth to twins three times."

★ ★ ★

Christian went on, "I wanted to pass on to you what my mother told me because I want to help you develop a strong character; you must become so strong that no one will be able to break you. I don't know if I will succeed, but I won't give up trying. I've promised my mother that I won't give up training you.

"I'm a mortal who is tired of living, in need of his father's love, and desperately missing his mother; but because I made a promise to her, I'm doing my best to live. You can't be with me if you don't try to change yourself. That woman changed and you can too.

"My place is next to my mother in heaven: heaven is full of orchids. If you end up somewhere else, I won't have a friend in heaven. I'll be with my mother but I'll still need a friend.

"Even if, later, you find it hard to go on, you will succeed because I want you to live; and you must live for me."

When my friend had finished, I looked at him and said that I would try to do as he asked. We got up and resumed our run. Smiling as he ran, he kept on an eye on me. I thought, "He struggles with me and I struggle with my thoughts;" and because of that, I had many headaches.

He grew quiet again. Instead of thinking, I wanted to have a conversation, but he insisted that I should be quiet and listen to the crickets instead. So I tried to rest my brain while listening to the crickets.

As we crested a hill, I pointed at a tortoise that was slowly crossing the road. The tortoise's pace made us laugh; but Christian's joy didn't last long. We both heard a car approaching at speed. Without thinking, he ran towards the tortoise. I couldn't understand what he was doing; I didn't grasp things quickly. As he darted into the middle of the road, I just stood there, wondering what he was going to do.

When I finally saw the speeding car, instead of running to help my friend, I just cowered by the side of the road with nothing more than the urge to scream – but no sound came out of my throat. Christian reached the tortoise, and snatched it up, stroking its head and talking to it. But he had no time to save himself. Thinking the car was going to hit him, I continued desperately trying to scream a warning to my friend, but still no sound came out. Feeling helpless, I dropped to the ground and closed my eyes waiting for the car to hit him.

First I heard the sound of breaks, and then there was a loud crash. I didn't want to open my eyes and see Christian's crushed body. But when calm had returned, I heard my friend's voice. I opened my eyes and I saw him smiling at the tortoise and kissing it. I stood up, ran to him, and hugged him, grateful that he had managed to stay alive. He whispered in my ear, "Nothing can happen to me; I'm living for you don't forget."

Tears had started running down my cheeks. He pushed me away, and asked me to wipe my tears and look at the tortoise. But instead of doing that, I looked at the three little tortoises that were approaching the bigger one. When they came nearer, I picked up the three little tortoises.

Instead of shouting at us, the driver of the car came out sighing and said that Christian had been very brave. His behaviour had reminded the driver of an event in his boyhood. He sat down next to me at the side of the road, and took one of the tortoises from my hand and stroked it. Sighing again, he told us his story.

"My father was born and raised in America. My mother was German and met him on a visit to America. When they got married, my father came over to live in Germany with my mother. He had always wanted to live in Europe and was able to realise his dream thanks to my mother. But he had wanted to live in Paris. When he fell in love with my mother, he said that he didn't mind living in another European city; but they spent their honeymoon in Paris, at a hotel overlooking the Eiffel Tower.

"My father never returned to America, but when I was growing up, he was always telling me stories about it.

"Many years later, when I lost my family, I wanted to see my father's birthplace, so I went to America. I was mesmerised by the beauty of the mountains and the forests. I tracked down his relatives and visited them; everything was great.

"One day, I decided to go for a walk. I was very happy to discover a railway in the town near where I was staying. When I was a child, my sister and I used to play with stones on the railway tracks. To remind myself of those happy days, I started to walk on the railway track. As I walked along the track, I played with some stones I picked up. I was so lost in my thoughts that I didn't know how far I had walked. Some youths playing in a nearby disused factory brought me back to the present and the need to find out where I was.

"Although I looked all around me, I couldn't see anything I recognised. As I didn't want to go back the same way I had come, I made my way over to the youths to ask them where I was. Realising the horrific game they were playing, I ran towards them. One of them saw me and started to approach. When he got quiet close, without any warning, he threw a stone at me. As it hit me on the head, I fell to the ground.

"Their game consisted of tying a black man to a tree and throwing stones at him; similar ones to the one that I had been hit with. Seeing double, I crawled towards the black man. The one who had thrown the stone came up and started kicking me. I carried on crawling for I had no strength to stand up.

"The more I crawled, the harder he kicked. Another one came and joined in. In spite of all the kicking, I managed to reach the black man. Holding on to him, I stood up, hugged him, and begged the youths to stop stoning him.

"Then they all came and started hitting me. 'Why do you want to help this Negro?' one of them whispered in my ear.

"I wiped the blood from my cheek and, using the same hand, smeared the blood on the black man's already bloody cheek. Then I put my hand close to his face and said, 'Let me see you separate our blood.' The one who had whispered in my ear looked at me with hatred in his face. After touching my cheek with his knife, he and his friends left.

"Later in the hospital, the doctor told me that what I had done was good, but if I did it again, he believed that I might lose my life. I asked the doctor, 'How is the black man doing?' And I was told that he had died.

"This tortoise that you are holding reminded me of that black man. The only difference is that you have managed to save your tortoise and I didn't the black man."

When he had finished his story, the kind man went back to his car but he couldn't start it. We both stood up and after placing the whole tortoise family in a safe place on the other side of the road, we went over to him. He tried a few more times, but the car still failed to start.

The man was upset and told us that he would have to walk to the nearest village to get a mechanic. Christian said, "I'll start your car." That surprised the man, but my friend insisted. I too was surprised. Smiling, Christian asked me to kneel down with him, so I did. The man approached us and asked what we were going to do?

"We're going to pray," replied Christian.

That made the man laugh, but when he saw the serious expression on my friend's face he said, "Okay, okay," and went to sit on a rock.

Christian knelt down next to me and held my hand. His prayer was very short. He then told the man to go and try it now. With a grin on his face, the man did so, but the car didn't start. He tried again but nothing happened. He then mockingly made noises like a car starting. He said that he would have to fetch a mechanic after all.

My friend insisted that instead of mocking us, the man should have faith and pray with us for the car to start. The man looked at him, smiled and knelt down. We both held his hands. After another short prayer, Christian told him to try again.

Taking his time, the man went over to his car and looking at my friend, said, "Maybe the angels repaired it while we had our eyes closed."

"Yes, I felt their presence," Christian responded.

"You know, the one thing I really hate is praying; actually, I don't believe in God at all," he said.

"We do," said my friend.

With a smile on his face, the man turned the key and the car started. "Oh my God!" he exclaimed loudly.

"Yes! Only God can make miracles happen," laughed Christian.

The man gave us a friendly glance. "Not believing is a habit with me," he said, "and, whatever happens, you'll never convince me of God's existence. There's a scientific reason for it," he informed us.

He offered to give us a lift. "We're very grateful," said my friend. "We're going to the post office," Christian informed him as we got into the car. Then my friend tried to convince him to become a believer – I don't know why he did that or what his motive was.

"Perhaps you're right in not believing," Christian said. "It's just that my mother always used to talk about religion. She did so from when I was very young; so I grew up in that kind of environment. My father was also raised to believe but later, he began to lose his faith. And when my mother died, he lost what little he had left; so now he is non-believer like you.

"My father feels that he has no problems now and that he is better off; I, on the other hand, can't stop believibng. I lead a life full of problems just like my mother did, and I too wanted to become a non-believer like my father; but my mother died with her faith unshaken, and that stopped me.

"I feel that if I stop believing, I will never be reunited with my mother because she is in heaven. I love my mother dearly and I want nothing more than to be with her. If you don't believe in God, and if you lose someone that you love who is a believer, you won't be with them when you die."

"Your mother raised you well," the man laughed. He was so happy that his car had started that, in no time at all, he had brought us to the post office. He told us how happy he was to have met us, and that he was grateful that our prayers had started his car. He then congratulated my friend on his ability to speak the way he did in spite of his young age. The man then dropped us off and sped away. I thought it was true that Christian did have a way with words.

We then went into the post office to send our telegrams to our parents. However, I had a question in my head. I wondered if my friend was personally committed to God, or if it was because his mother had believed, or whether there was yet another reason for his faith. So I asked him.

He looked at me with sadness in his face and said, "No, it isn't because my mother was a believer or that she raised me with His love that I found religion; it's that I really want to be in heaven with her.

"If you want to convince someone, first you have to know what's going on in their heart. When I looked at that man's face, I saw my father's face. My father loved my mother very much. And this man too was separated from the person he loved, and that turned him into a non-believer."

Sometimes, I couldn't understand my friend. It appeared to me that he had an answer for everything. In that way, he was especially blessed. I was learning new things from him every day.

As soon as we left the post office, we started running. On the way, Christian told me about some books he had read. He knew all about the authors and their lives. When he asked me what I had read, I admitted that I'd only read the Torah. He asked me to tell him what I had read from the Torah, but I didn't know what to say because I couldn't remember anything.

I had been blessed with a high IQ: I could remember conversations I had had with people and the details of events I had witnessed long ago; but, for some reason, I couldn't remember anything at all from the Torah, even though I had read it five times all the way through.

We continued chatting and laughing. At some point, I realised that we were following a different path from the one we had taken on our way to the post office. I had a vague idea where we were, but I wasn't quite sure until we passed the big old tree on the way to the icy lake.

As I realised where we were headed, I froze inside and went pale. My friend laughed when he saw my reaction. He said that swimming in the lake was one of the reasons he had extended our holiday, for from now on, we were coming here twice a day. I froze still further: not counting Saturdays and Sundays, we were going to go swimming exactly twenty times. This was too much to ask of me, but I had no choice.

When we got there, I dived straight in with all my clothes on. Christian followed immediately. I felt the cold water seep into my bones. I had no idea why we were there. Whenever I asked him, all he would say was, "My mother told me to do it," and he pretended not to know how I felt or how cold I really was. But I was sure there was a reason for it, and he knew that reason.

We spent hours in the water that day. It was so cold that I couldn't talk, my teeth were chattering so much. We didn't get out until our bodies were totally numb. Then we realised that it hadn't been a good idea to go for a swim with our clothes on because the wind didn't help us to warm up at all; we felt as though we were still in the icy water.

My friend took my trembling hand and, after telling me that we shouldn't go swimming fully clothed ever again, we started to run. I suggested that he shouldn't have simply copied me in diving into the lake.

Although we ran without stopping, the wind didn't dry our clothes, and we entered Christian's grandmother's house shivering. She gave us dry things and made us sit by the fire. Once we were warmed up, my friend's beloved grandmother gave him an orchid in a flowerpot. He was immediately oblivious to everything else around him. Muttering to himself, he left the room.

My friend's grandmother sighed heavily and said, "I've witnessed the same scene for many years now. He behaves exactly like his mother, who used to have the same reaction to the sight of orchids; he reminds me so much of her; the way he behaves and talks, it's just like watching her.

"In my prayers, I beg God not to take this young boy. My daughter was taken before me. I beg that my grandson should live for many more years after I've gone, but I know he's desperate to be reunited with his mother; and what I've observed tells me otherwise.

"If Christian carries on like this, before long, he *will* be reunited with his mother. Nothing can make him forget her, nothing at all. I feel so sorry for him; I know I've made him happy, but I can never replace his mother, and that makes me very sad."

With these words, my friend's Grandmother left with tears in her eyes. I was dog tired and wanted to go to bed, but the warmth of the fire kept me in my place. I contemplated our friendship; I was fond of Christian and, fearful of what his grandmother had said, hoped we would always be together. I didn't want to think of a life without my friend. And with this thought, I fell asleep.

Chapter 10

Next morning, I was woken up by the sun shining through the window. There was no one around. I wondered why Christian hadn't come to wake me up. Then I saw the calendar: it was Saturday. I smiled. At the same time, I felt something move on my forehead. I was just about to touch it, when I heard Christian's voice outside the bedroom window telling me not to move. I stopped dead and remained motionless. I knew there was a creature on my head because it was itching so much that it was becoming unbearable.

Christian ran to me but he was petrified and didn't know what to do. Then he called his grandmother. When she saw me, she too became anxious and told me not to move. She tried to think what to do next. I had no idea what this creature was, but their faces made me laugh.

However, when I dared to turn my head slowly towards the blanket, I saw an open jar of honey. The jar was upside down and the honey was covered with bees. I was allergic to them. If I had been stung, my body would have swollen up very quickly; I would have to be taken immediately to hospital or I would die. They both knew of my acute allergy, as I had mentioned it in passing a few days previously.

Finally, my friend's Grandmother decided to start a fire in the stove and, very carefully, removed a loose piece of fabric from an armchair. After thoroughly soaking it in water, she threw the fabric into the fire, leaving the stove door open. Then she and her grandson left the room, leaving me in it. The billowing smoke disturbed the bees and not long after, they started buzzing around. They were looking for way out. When they saw the bedroom door open, they all flew out, with the exception of those that were stuck in the honey.

Seeing them in that situation made me laugh and with that, my fear disappeared. But when the smoke had disturbed them sufficiently, they managed to free themselves from the honey and they too flew out. When the room was free of bees, I was just about to stand up when I felt another one moving on my head.

Carefully, I moved towards the smoke. As it wafted towards the bee, instead of leaving the room, it angrily flew to my hand; that made me laugh again. As I made my way slowly towards the door, I lifted my hand and looked at it. Then that bee flew off as well. If I had been a bee I too wouldn't have wanted to leave the honey.

Christian and his grandmother relaxed when they saw me outside. I looked at them crossly, but when they said, "We too are allergic to bees," I started to laugh and they laughed with me. After a while, my friend's grandmother went back inside to check the room. Instead of putting the fire out, she dismantled the stove and brought it outside. Christian and I looked at each other in amazement and collapsed in hysterics. I always laughed with my friend – after losing him I hardly ever laughed any more.

Seeing us in hysterics, Christian's grandmother put her hands on her hips and, after giving as a look, she went inside the house. She came back with my clothes, which I put on. Then she told us to follow her. We went to the back of the house.

There were two things there leaning against the coop and covered with plastic sheeting. Smiling at us, she uncovered them. They were two bicycles! Christian was so happy that he started screaming with joy, and hugging and kissing his grandmother.

My friend's grandmother told me that one day, her daughter had come home with these two bicycles. When she had asked her why she had brought two bicycles being an only child, her daughter had replied, "Wait and see, one day you'll need them both."

Declaring that now she understood her daughter's explanation, my friend's grandmother told us to go for a ride while she cleaned the house; and we proudly set off on our new bicycles.

Christian pedalled fast, shouting with joy. I made every effort to catch up with him, but every time I got close, he accelerated and increased the distance between us. It was just the same as it had been with the running, only now we were riding bicycles. While I was doing my best to keep up with him, all at once, he stopped. When I caught up, he said that we would now ride slowly.

My friend wanted to show me the places where he and his mother used to go for a stroll. He shared his memories with me as we rode slowly along. It was very rare that I saw him like this, and seeing him so happy relaxed me.

When the road came to an end Christian said, "That's it." He had no memory of anywhere beyond this point. We stopped, and shortly afterwards, he started laughing and changed direction.

I continued to follow my friend. He was talking to himself again, oblivious to the fact that I was there. As I had seen him like this before after he had seen orchids, I knew that he was communing with his mother.

When we came to the top of a hill, Christian left his bicycle and started running. I stopped to see where he had gone. I too left my bicycle on the roadside and walked over the brow of the hill.

With relief, I saw my friend running in the middle of a field not far away. But then I noticed that he was dashing here and there, stretching his hands out as if someone was holding them. His mother was dead, but he carried on daydreaming about her, pretending, playing games and having conversations.

I was so engrossed in watching him that I hadn't realised it was getting dark. Then I saw a crow settling on a nearby tree and realised that night was falling. But Christian was so happy that I didn't want to disturb him.

Suddenly, my friend ran further away, heading towards the forest. When I saw that, I got scared and ran after him. I stopped at the edge of the forest. The darkness frightened me; the advancing nightfall and the empty field behind me frightened me even more. I couldn't go into the forest or turn around and go back either; so I closed my eyes and prayed. This made me feel better.

Then I heard Christian's voice; he was right in front of me, smiling. So that I might follow him quickly, he ordered me to run. I looked up and noticed that the stars had not yet appeared. Rather than remain there alone, I decided to cautiously follow him. In spite of all my questions, he wouldn't tell me where we were going.

When we came to a small clearing in the forest, I found myself buried up to my ankles in dry leaves. I stood there and looked around. Among all the trees, a pine stood tall and straight in front of me. Christian was on his knees at the foot of that tree clearing the pine needles away. I went and started helping him. Because they were so dry, the more we cleared, the more needles replaced them. I kept on asking him what we were doing, but he didn't reply.

Finally, when we had cleared all the needles, we were faced with a gravestone. I realised that I was standing on a grave. The stone was covered with moss. I was a little frightened of being there; I had never been in a graveyard at night before. Because of the moss all over the stone, we couldn't see anything written there. We started clearing away the moss; that was easy.

Then we noticed that the stone was upside down and needed to be righted before we could read what was inscribed on it. We looked at each other questioningly and placed our hands under the stone. Using all our force, we tried to lift it. I couldn't understand why my friend was so obsessed with this grave.

Unfortunately, not only were we unable to lift the stone, we couldn't even move it. We tried again and again but got nowhere. Finally, we admitted our powerlessness, but then I saw more than ten squirrels in the pine tree.

I nudged Christian with my hand and pointed at the squirrels; that was a surprise for him too. Our hands under the stone and our eyes on the squirrels, we noticed that one of them was staring at us, turning its head from left to right; I was amazed at that and started to laugh.

I looked at my friend, imitating the squirrel, and he too started to laugh. Roaring with laughter, he even lay down on the pine needles in his mirth. I told him that the squirrel was right in shaking its head: there was no way that we could move this stone. In spite of our noisy laughter, the squirrels didn't move.

I wanted to make Christian laugh even more, so I stood up and started to jump up and down on the gravestone saying, "This grave is so strong, no one can break it down."

My friend was so happy that he too stood up and started to jump up and down. But we probably jumped too vigorously, for we soon heard some cracking noises coming from the gravestone. We stopped but the cracking continued. We were just about to get off when the sounds dramatically increased.

We looked at each other and closed our eyes; we knew what was about to happen. As the gravestone broke, we found ourselves in the grave. I was terrified because I could see that I was now inside the grave itself! I saw the fear on Christian's face as well. As the gravestone had broken, it had righted itself. My friend was agitated and frantically clearing the moss away.

Once we had cleaned it up, we could see two letters of the deceased's name and surname. Because Christian was very bright, he only needed to look at it once. With a smile on his face, he tried to get out of the grave. We were small had to help each other. I got him out first and then he helped me with the aid of a thick branch.

As I lifted my head, I saw the same squirrel looking at me and shaking its head again. I pointed out the squirrel to my friend. Suddenly it disappeared. I was astonished when I noticed the same squirrel sitting on another branch of the pine tree still watching us. I never forgot the shaking of that squirrel's head.

The moment the squirrel left, we heard the baying of wolves. Now, I knew why the squirrel had been shaking its head. My friend grew pale and told me to run. I reassured him that the wolves were far away, but he said that they were very near and we must leave before they scented us, adding that they hunted in packs. He grabbed my hand and we started to run.

When I asked Christian why the grave had been so important to him, he told me that he didn't have time to explain it to me now; and for the time being, I should just concentrate on my breathing. It was very quiet; the only thing we could hear was the sound of our footfalls and breathing.

We came to the hill and my friend told me to sit down, regard the forest in silence, and listen to the sounds of nature all around us. Then he said, "Most people are afraid of the night, because it's dark. They don't want nightfall to come. Actually, when they see the darkness, it frightens them. Some people, when they tell a story, they always make bad things happen at night.

"As you can see, the ones who describe the night as terrifying are wrong. When darkness comes, the world is immersed in silence and this helps as to rest our minds. If you lend an ear to the sound of nature, you can hear all sorts of animals at night. You'll be transported to another land.

"Look at the moon and especially the stars that ordain the sky. You can see that there is infinity in that. The night's not there to scare us but to help us rest. I love the night – isn't it beautiful?"

By the time Christian had finished, he had succeeded in making me think about something I had never contemplated before. I absent-mindedly looked at the forest and considered what he had just said. Seeing me lost in thought, he stood up. I stood up too and we went to get our bicycles, and made our way back to the house.

Back in his grandmother's garden, my friend happily rode his bicycle around me in circles. I kept asking him why he was so happy but he didn't want to tell me and just continued with his game. Realising that I wouldn't get an answer from him, I tried to stop him circling me.

As soon as she saw us, Christian's grandmother ran out of the house towards us. She had been very worried. My friend threw his bicycle down and ran towards her. His grandmother kept on repeating how concerned she had been. When Christian reached her, to pacify her, he put his hand on her mouth and then started to dance with her. Although I was puzzled, I was very happy looking at them. Still on my bike and laughing, I wiped away tears of joy from my face.

My friend looked in my direction and called me over. I put my bicycle down and joined them. They put me in the middle and danced around me. Suddenly, Christian said that he had seen his mother's image. She was standing on the grave but had soon disappeared. When his grandmother heard that, she stopped dancing and asked him to repeat himself.

When my friend took a deep breath, I knew what he was going to do. I sat down and put my hands over my ears. He proceeded to tell her everything. In spite of having my hands over my ears, I heard all he said. He even told her the man's last name as we had read it on the gravestone. His grandmother was extremely excited and asked him to repeat everything again. After he had told her yet again, she screamed with joy. I still had my hands over my ears.

Christian's grandmother ran into the house. She was so happy that in spite of tripping, she managed not to fall. As she went indoors, I heard her cry out with happiness. Shortly after, I went in too. She was sitting in a chair with a book writing a name in it. I was really puzzled by it all and had no idea what was going on. When she saw my confusion, she called me to come and sit next to her, and gave me the book to look at.

The names of many people were written in the book, along with the dates of their deaths. The dates went back hundreds of years – three, perhaps four, centuries. I had no idea what they represented. Seeing this, she opened the last page and showed me her own name. Then I knew what they meant. My friend's grandmother confirmed it when she told me that her ancestors' names and deaths were all recorded in the book; she had now unearthed more information about where she had come from.

I told her that my father had a similar record, but he didn't have as many names as she did; and our ancestors' names were written on a chair instead of in a book. She grew excited on hearing this and started telling me all about her ancestors. But unfortunately, I was extremely tired and half way through her account, I fell asleep next to her on the floor.

Chapter 11

N ext morning, I awoke well tucked up in bed. I opened my eyes but it was impossible to lift my head for a while. When I was able to get up,

I went to find Christian's grandmother. She was where I had last seen her the night before. My friend was there too. When they saw me, they announced that we had to go back to the grave because they needed to confirm the date on it.

I felt very tired and gave them an imploring look. But they both said, "We don't want to go there either, but we must double-check the date."

As I had slept fully clothed, I said, "Let's go, then."

We all went outside. I sat on a chair, leaning my head heavily on the back of it; I was trying to get some sun. When Christian came over, I opened my eyes and looked at him. His eyes were red because of lack of sleep. He said that he was going to the fountain to wash his face and left yawning.

My friend's grandmother joined me and sat on a garden chair. I closed my eyes again, but she was determinedly trying to tell me something in spite of her yawning: after talking the whole night through, they had decided that we had to go back to the grave.

Soon after that, I heard her snoring, which I found very amusing. I opened my eyes and looked at her: head turned sideways and mouth wide open, she was snoring heavily. The book was still grasped firmly in her hands. Carefully, I took it from her and opened it.

The first date of death was at the beginning of 1600 and the last at the end of 1900. Not all the intervening deaths of her ancestors had been recorded of course; she had only filled in the ones that she had information about, but I was still very impressed. I thought it was such a good idea to learn all about our ancestors.

Quite suddenly, I noticed that Christian hadn't returned from the fountain. After carefully placing the book back in his grandmother's hands, I went to look for him. What I saw made me laugh. With his head on the little fountain, my friend was fast asleep. I regarded him for a bit and then approached him. Slowly, I lifted his arm and put it around my shoulders and laid him on the grass next to the fountain. Then I dropped down next to him and after watching him for a while, I fell asleep too.

A terrific commotion woke me up: someone was shouting. Still half asleep, I couldn't see who it was. When I managed to fully open my eyes, I saw the shepherd from the mountain whose dogs had barked at me. Christian was hugging him. His grandmother was excitedly repeating, "We're going together! We're going together!"

The poor man had no idea where we were going; he was just laughing. I stood up and asked, "Are you ready to visit the dead?"

He stopped laughing and anxiously enquired, "What dead? I came here to cut wood, not to visit the dead."

I tried to explain, but my friend's grandmother interrupted and told the shepherd our plan. She said that we needed him.

"Let me cut my wood and you go," he suggested.

"Please don't make me beg," she said.

"You know I'm frightened of graves," he rejoined.

"We're going there in daylight," she replied, "and we can't manage without you."

She implored him, but he was adamant. Taking up his axe, the shepherd started to leave. But she knew his weakness; she sat on the ground and started to cry. At first, I thought she was shamming, but when he saw tears rolling down her cheeks, he stopped, sighed and turned heavily towards us, and knelt down and started to pray. Seeing this, my friend's grandmother happily wiped her tears. I realised then that she had actually been crying.

The shepherd said that he would come with us not because of her tears, but because Christian's grandmother had saved his wife and daughter many years ago. But he was already perspiring with fear. I heard him say to her, "Let's go, before I regret my decision." My friend and his grandmother immediately prepared to leave.

The shepherd looked at me. Gripping the axe with both hands and using all his might, he sliced a thick piece of wood in two; he said he felt better after that. He then threw his arm around my shoulders and started to walk briskly, and I walked alongside him following the other two. I could feel his hand trembling.

I wondered why the shepherd was so frightened of graveyards; after all, he was such a big, strong man. I nearly asked him, but seeing the fear on his face made me change my mind. His lips were trembling, and drops of sweat were running down his face. We were still a long way from the graveyard, and I was worried that once we were there, he might have a heart attack.

I slowed down; he responded by squeezing my arm and started talking to me: "I know what you're thinking and that you're wondering how a big man like me, who could even fight a bear, is so frightened of an old grave where there are some old bones belonging to some dead person. Perhaps you aren't laughing at me; maybe you pity me instead. But *I* think the worst of myself; I don't even deserve to be called a coward.

"Once, during the coldest month, when wild animals go hungry, I went deer hunting and met five starving wolves. They didn't let me take one more step before attacking me. They bit my legs and my arms and my back, but they didn't harm me more than that, and then they left me.

"I enjoy fighting with wolves and I always use my bare hands. In the end, seeing the wolves' red blood on the white snow gives me strength. Before embarking on my hunting trips every year, I always hope to see the wolves and it always happens.

"I'm never frightened of wild animals; however I'm very frightened of graveyards. If there's a cemetery on my way, I never hesitate to add a couple of miles or more to go around it. No one has ever seen a dead person rising from a grave, but I'm still terrified of them. If I stop talking now, no doubt, you'll ask why; so before you ask, I'd better tell you.

"My family and I used to go to France to visit my grandmother every year. When I was five years old, we went again. She was a lovely woman who used to play with me. She would give me sweets and chocolates, and tell me stories while I ate them. She would never spare any expense for me. I was my father's only child and she was his mother; she used to grant me my every wish, she loved me so very much.

"One day, thinking that I was old enough, my grandmother sat me on her lap and, after giving me the usual sweets and chocolates, told me that today, she had some special stories for me. She said that I could now listen to them and they would make me courageous and fearless. But she was wrong, for I was only five years old.

"She started to tell me some different stories that she knew I hadn't heard before. There were all sorts about witches, ghosts, dead people rising from their graves, and fascinating things like that. When she first told them to me, I wasn't frightened, but then she started telling them to me every night, and I began to dream about them.

"A few days later, I told my parents that I was frightened of the stories, but they didn't take any notice of me. My grandmother said that I would get used to them and be fearless in the end. Once again, she was wrong: instead of becoming fearless, I became more fearful. I could no longer sleep in the dark; it frightened me.

"I told my parents once more, but once again, my grandmother convinced them that the stories were good for me, and continued with them. As she was more than eighty years old, she probably didn't appreciate the fear of a five-year-old child. I tried to tell my parents yet again, but their response was to pretend to be dead, and, seeing me so frightened, they just laughed. I still can't understand why they behaved like that.

"As a boy, my father had listened to these stories as well, but they had had no bad effect on him. But I wasn't my father; he shouldn't have compared himself to me. Parents must treat their children as individuals and not like a copy of themselves.

"Instead of telling me scary stories to make me fearless, they should have told me stories about nature and how to love it; about the animals, the birds, the trees and such things. Then I might have been a different kind of person today. This is the reason I became a shepherd. I thought if I spent time with the beauty of nature, I would overcome my fears.

"When I was single, I used to sleep in the stable because I was afraid to be alone. People used to laugh at my fear. But I haven't overcome it and I still live with it today. Isn't that a sad thing?

"Nonetheless, even if my heart stops in the graveyard, I will still go and help your friend's grandmother because I owe her. I don't want to, but because of this debt, I must.

"I've already told you some things about my life; let me tell you some more.

"Many years ago, my wife was pregnant. We were so happy that we were going to have a baby. We counted the days before the arrival; the more we counted, the faster the days went by. But instead of having labour pains after nine months like other women, my wife started getting them at seven months. When that happened, I didn't know what to do, I kept walking around her, and when I saw how much pain she was in, I started to cry. I thought she was going to die.

"In spite of all the pain, my wife was able to ask me to go and get Christian's grandmother. I didn't hear at first, but when she shouted, I jumped and went to get your friend's grandmother. When she opened the door. I couldn't utter a word, I was crying so much. Without hesitating, she ran past me towards my house. I followed her.

"When your friend's grandmother saw that my wife was in labour, she started laughing. She said that it was the first time she had seen a man crying because his wife was in labour. I told her that I thought she was going to die. Your friend's grandmother told me that my wife wasn't the first or the last woman to give birth at seven months, and continued laughing. Then she told me to stop crying and help her instead. What could I do? I knew I was acting like a child.

"Soon afterwards, my wife gave a birth to a baby daughter. I was so very happy. But Christian's grandmother wasn't. I don't know how she knew, but while giving birth to our baby daughter, my wife had lost a lot of vital nutrients. Your friend's grandmother asked me to leave the room, but I refused. She shook her head and placed my baby daughter in my arms.

"Then she gave my wife something that came out of her womb, which I found repulsive, and told her to eat it. When my wife ate it all, I felt ill. Being grateful that I was a man, I gave my baby daughter back to your friend's grandmother and went outside. She followed me soon after and told me that my wife needed all the love I could give her, and that I should go back indoors. She said that she had saved my wife's life and had saved my daughter's life as well. Then she started to walk back to her house.

"When I looked down at where she had been standing, I saw blood. I ran to catch up with your friend's grandmother and touched her on the shoulder. She turned around and told me that if I didn't go back immediately and give my wife the love and support she needed now, she would be affected and I could lose her forever.

"Your friend's grandmother had no shoes on, and while running to my house, she had cut her feet on some glass. But in spite of the pain she was in, she had saved my wife and daughter's lives.

"How can I forget all that Christian's grandmother did for my family? Even if I were to give her my life, it wouldn't be enough because she saved both my wife and my daughter. I love my wife and my daughter so much; I can't imagine my life without them."

★ ★ ★

I was really touched by what the shepherd had told me and felt sorry for him. Then his breathing became very fast, and that brought me back to the present. His fear was making him sweat again. As he wiped his face, he kept on asking me how far we had to go before we arrived at the graveyard. The last time he asked, I saw that we were on the hill before the forest. I pointed to it and my expression said it all. He had no time to wipe his face again.

Before I could put my arm down, I heard Christian telling his grandmother that the grave was in the forest. We joined them. Apart from the shepherd, we all happily looked at the forest.

Suddenly, we sensed that someone was missing. When we turned to see who it was, a curious scene met our eyes: we were very sad to see the big shepherd on his knees, his face pale and sweating like a river. We looked at each other and felt guilty.

My friend's grandmother went to him and caressed his head as if he were her child. She told him that she didn't want any harm to come to him and asked him to go back. Then the three of us started to walk towards the forest, Christian's grandmother was very upset and kept muttering to herself that we couldn't manage without the shepherd. We walked on in silence.

We were a few steps away from the forest when we heard a loud voice and turned around. We knew straight away to whom the voice belonged: we were very happy to see the shepherd standing on the hill. After shouting that he wouldn't leave us, he started to run down the hill.

My friend and I jumped up and down with joy. When the shepherd had got nearer, instead of stopping, he continued running into the forest. We kept asking him to stop but he didn't. We knew that if he had stopped, he wouldn't have been able to go in there; his fear made him run with all his might into the forest.

Christian and I were worried that the shepherd might get lost so we ran after him, but as he was far stronger than us, we couldn't reach him and he was out of sight very quickly. We had no other choice but to stop and wait for my friend's grandmother. She caught up with us and asked what had happened to the poor shepherd; she was confused. We shrugged our shoulders in acknowledgement that we too didn't know.

Calling the shepherd by his name, Christian's grandmother looked around; and then his voice came from somewhere nearby. We walked towards it. Now we could hear him better but we couldn't see him. He told us to look up, so we did. Then we saw him: he was in a tree, way up near the top, sitting on a thin branch and crying. I had no idea how this flimsy branch could support his weight.

The shepherd called down, "I'll tell you something that I've never told anyone before. When I was seven years old, I had a friend that I was very fond of. He was about my age and we were together every day; we were inseparable.

"One day, I saw him looking very sad and crying, so I asked him what the matter was. At first, he didn't want to tell me but after I'd insisted, he opened up. His parents were having an argument, when his mother had screamed at his father saying, that it was because of him that their son had cancer. He was very sad when he told me that he had cancer and would die. Although he had been to see doctors, at first he hadn't known that he'd got cancer. His parents had hidden the truth from him for years. His treatment was very painful and he couldn't bear it any longer.

"As he couldn't take his own life, he asked me to help him. He wanted me to take him unawares and kill him painlessly. I was shocked by his request, and couldn't be his friend anymore. He continued coming to my house and asking my parents for me but I refused to see him. My parents couldn't understand why I was no longer his friend; I hadn't told them the reason.

"However, a few months later he begged me to play with him for the last time; he was crying so hard that I agreed. We went to our usual place. He removed his T-shirt and asked me to look at him. I could only do so once for I could see his ribs. He told me that his death was coming very slowly and painfully. He didn't ask me to kill him like before; he just said that he had very little time left. When he asked me to spend that time with him, I agreed and resumed seeing him. Every time I met him, I felt awful, for he was slowly losing his strength and suffering terribly while just waiting to die.

"I brought my friend to the forest. That strengthened him, and I thought he would get better. But I gave up on the idea when I saw him the next day: he looked very ill again. After thinking quietly, I took him into the woods and he became better again. Then I realised why.

"After climbing a tree, I asked him to join me. He did. The tree I'd climbed was a very tall one with thin branches. He had no idea what I intended, but when we were close to the top, I stopped and asked him to climb nearer. He was very excited, and that was the last time I saw him smile. Then he put his right foot on a branch, which promptly snapped; both it and he fell to the ground. I've never forgotten the smile he had on his face. I closed my eyes until he hit the ground.

"When I opened my eyes, he was lying on the ground below looking up at me with a smile on his face. I jumped up and down on the equally thin branch I was standing on, but it wouldn't break. Realising that it never would, I climbed down and, still crying, sprinted to his house.

"His parents were arguing again. I told them that their son had fallen from a tree. But the expression on their faces was one of amazement rather than sorrow.

"Since that day, I've always climbed trees and found a thin branch to jump up and down on. Nothing ever happens."

★ ★ ★

When the shepherd had finished his story, he climbed down from the tree and asked us where the grave was. The three of us were shocked by what we'd heard, and couldn't speak.

We resumed walking and before long, we came to the grave. The shepherd had already gone pale and was sweating again, his body shaking. My friend's grandmother smiled when she saw the grave, and knelt down by it silently.

As I was wandering about, I noticed another grave, and became very excited and happy. Without a sound, I started to make my way towards Christian, to tell him of the surprise. I was very close to the others, when I fell into a hole and found myself chest-deep in leaves.

My friend and his grandmother gave me a look and then turned back to the grave. The shepherd was so afraid that he didn't even look in my direction. When I saw that they weren't bothering to help me, I screamed that I was being pulled down. They all looked at me and I faked being sucked under. Then they looked at each other and instead of coming to help me, they ran away. Seeing that, made me chuckle and that stopped them in their tracks. With serious expressions on their faces, they said that it was no laughing matter, and came over to help me.

Christian offered me his hand. As I was about to grasp it, I saw the fear in his face and started to laugh again. However, my jolly mood was short-lived, as I soon felt something touch my leg. I was so terrified that I jumped out of the hole and started to run away. I told the others to run as well. They thought I was joking again and didn't move, laughing instead. When I felt I was at a safe distance, I stopped and I tried to indicate the hole with my trembling finger.

Mute with fear, I couldn't scream. My friend's grandmother, seeing genuine terror on my face, advanced towards the hole. She saw the leaves move. Her eyes opened wide and she pointed first to the others, then at the hole, and then ran for it. My friend saw the hole and he ran too.

When the shepherd too saw the leaves moving, he passed out. I was frightened even as I saw them running away. But Christian's grandmother passed me at such a comically sprightly pace for an old lady that I forgot my fears and started to laugh.

However, I soon began to run again. In spite of her age, my friend's grandmother easily kept up with us. I was running so fast that even a dead person rising from the grave wouldn't have been able to catch me. Even when I got out of the forest, I carried on running.

I heard Christian calling me so I stopped. At first, I could only see him but his grandmother soon joined him. She could hardly breathe but was doing her best to tell him something. She was exhausted and could go no further; she sat down slowly. I approached them.

We all looked at each other. I was just about to say something, but my friend's grandmother spoke instead: we had left the poor shepherd alone in the forest. Christian's grandmother said that she was afraid that something bad might happen to him and we would have to go back. None of us moved.

As we were beginning to argue about what we should do next, we heard the shepherd's screams: "Help! Help! Help!" I was more frightened now, so I jumped up only thinking of running further away. But as we heard the shepherd imploring again and again, we then started to hurry back to the forest; we were running straight back to the source of all our terror.

What we saw was quite amusing and our fears were soon replaced by laughter. The shepherd was on the ground face down with rabbits scurrying all over his back. I then realised what we had been frightened of. As we approached him, the rabbits disappeared into the hole I had fallen into. The shepherd was still screaming, "Help! Help!"

Without thinking, I sat down on his back. As soon as he felt my weight on top of him, he got so frightened that he leapt up screaming and ran for it. His sudden movement sent me flying into the air and then just as quickly back down to earth. I then had the audacity to laugh. When he heard my voice he stopped, turned around, and saw me.

He came over, sat down and started to cry, saying that it wasn't a good joke. But after a while, he started to laugh between his tears. I thought he was right actually: of course, it wasn't a good joke; I shouldn't have played it; I had been completely thoughtless, and I hadn't for one moment stopped to consider his feelings.

Christian and his grandmother weren't laughing either. They said they were very sorry for all the things that had happened to the poor shepherd. I felt so ashamed; I had made him worse than he already was. I hugged him and said that I was very sorry for all of the things I had done, and begged him to forgive me. Without answering, he quickly got to his feet, went over to the grave, and started to clear away the leaves. When we saw what he was doing, we helped him too.

I had learnt a very important lesson: a careless act could lead to a lifetime of regret. I never found out if the shepherd had forgiven me, although I think he did then and there.

The other tombstone was broken. My friend and I first looked at the stone and then at the shepherd. After giving us a look, he put his hands under the stone and attempted to lift it. We were pleased to see that it was moving, but then it slipped from his grasp and fell back into place, which disappointed us.

The shepherd tried again but this time, he fell on top of the stone and cut his lip a little. As the stone was covered in moss he finding it hard to get a good grip on it. He became annoyed with himself, stood up, and started wandering around. He returned with a big log and told me to place it under the stone as soon as he lifted it. I tried to pick up the log, but it was very heavy and I had to let it fall; it was impossible for me to lift it any distance.

I asked Christian to help me. When we were ready, the shepherd lifted the stone and we pushed the log underneath it. He tried to push the log further but it broke. He fell on top of it and cut his lip again, which started to bleed this time. He pressed his finger to his lip to stop the bleeding. I went over to him and asked why tombstones were so heavy. He said that they weren't so very heavy; it was the moss that had prevented him from getting a good grip on the stone.

Suddenly, we heard a noise that frightened me. Removing his finger from his lip, the shepherd stood up and held me by my collar. As the noise came nearer, I grew more fearful. Then we saw a bear running towards us! The shepherd lifted me up by my collar and threw me towards Christian, telling us to lie on the ground.

Then the shepherd went to confront the bear. We didn't have any time to think, never mind react. Thinking that we were about to die, I started to pray. Christian's grandmother held us both and prayed too. I felt her love and that made me feel better. The shepherd was still standing in front of the bear. With his head slightly bent and his eyes slightly closed he was waiting to die.

He was right. What chance did he have faced by a huge, injured wild bear? Growling, the animal lifted its paws to attack the shepherd. I closed my eyes and hid myself in my friend's grandmother's arms. As we were waiting for the bear to kill first the shepherd and then us, we heard the sound of several gunshots.

The bear gave out a great holler and fell to the ground. When I looked up, I saw its lifeless body lying on top of the poor shepherd, with its eyes wide open staring at me. I noticed that the bear had tears in its eyes. The poor shepherd had fainted again and didn't move.

When I realised that it was all over, I approached the bear. Christian and his grandmother joined me, doing their best to remove the bear from the shepherd's back. I wiped the tears from its eyes and closed them; then I stroked its head.

Meanwhile, four people had approached us. They were laughing, very pleased with themselves because they had shot the bear. When one of them saw me stroking it, he laughed even louder. One of the others told him to rescue the shepherd instead of laughing at me.

All together, the four men turned the bear onto its side. Then they threw some cold water over the shepherd's face, which brought him round. Extremely jittery, he went and sat beneath a tree. My friend and his grandmother tried to calm him down; I continued to stroke the bear.

All time, the four men continued to laugh and celebrate their big kill, toasting it with numerous nips from their hip flasks. Finally, the eldest told the rest of them to be quiet and go and sit down somewhere else and rest. A silence fell among them.

The eldest man came and sat next to me, and asked what I was thinking about. Continuing to stroke the bear, I said, "This is one of nature's creatures, so beautiful, who until a few minutes ago was alive; and now it's lying in front of us lifeless.

"Look at its fur isn't it soft? And the colour of it: isn't it beautiful? What a shame; it never harmed anyone, and now it'll be turned into a fur coat for some rich person. It's all the fault of such people. If the rich didn't want to wear furs, we wouldn't have to kill bears; and they could feed many poor people with the money they use to buy their fur coats.

"Like the bears, people kill foxes for their fur too, which is another very sad thing. This is what upsets me. I wait for the day when someone finally puts an end to this killing; but unfortunately, while the rich are encouraged to decorate themselves with animal furs, they will carry on buying them, and creatures like this poor animal will continue to be killed."

"You're right," the eldest man said. "I too have a son about your age. I taught him not to be a hunter, but to love animals. I feel very sorry too about the animals I kill and beg for forgiveness before I pull the trigger.

"But now let me tell you about something that happened to me. I fought in the Great War. At one point, in order to save my life, I had to pretend to be dead; I lay among the dead. I got up after the guns had stopped firing. When I looked around me, I saw hundreds of thousands of dead and wounded. The ground was no longer brown but red. The cries of the wounded were deafening.

"Seeing so many dead and wounded, I took some bloody soil in my hand and lifted it to the sky and said, 'It's for this lifeless soil that so many are lying dead!' It wasn't God's fault that people were killing each other; it was the fault of those who didn't value others' lives.

"After wandering alone for a few days, I went back to my unit. They didn't even let me rest a little before sending me back to the front. I fought for days. The amount of blood and death I saw made me have a nervous breakdown. I was sent to hospital.

"By the time I'd recovered, the war had ended. During the many months I spent in hospital, I saw hundreds of soldiers come and go.

Many of them had been so badly affected by the war that they never recovered. Nobody was sorry for them either.

"So what I want to tell you is that an innocent man who dies in the war is worth a thousand bears to me." After these words, he ruffled my hair and then went to skin the bear.

Several years later, I saw all that the man had told me with my own eyes.

After listening to this story, I went over to Christian, and saw that my friends had been working on the gravestone and were about to cover up the grave. The other hunters had helped Christian and his grandmother while I had been talking to the eldest man. My friend said that it was time to go home. I looked at the bear one last time and said goodbye to the hunters; but no one replied.

I turned towards home and spoke to my friend. I told him all the things the hunter had told me, but he said he'd heard it all before and I shouldn't worry about it. I tried to argue that the hunter had been right, but Christian interrupted me, saying that it wasn't for us to decide who was right and who was wrong. From the way he said it, I gathered that anyone who had done anything, good or bad, always thought they were right.

Then my friend said: "In fact, I think all animals are innocent, but not all men." With these words he turned his attention to his grandmother. I thought Christian was right; it was actually impossible to decide who was right and who was wrong.

My friend told me that he thought his grandmother looked very happy; indeed, she had a big smile on her face. I was totally preoccupied with this observation until I felt a hand on my shoulder; it was that of the shepherd. He was smiling at me; he too looked very happy.

By the time we arrived home, I was utterly exhausted. I went into the living room and stretched out on the sofa.

After telling Christian's grandmother that he didn't owe her anything anymore and that he probably wouldn't be returning for a while, the shepherd left. He didn't even give her time to answer before he was gone. My friend's grandmother knew he was right, but she still sat in her chair with a sad face. I wanted to comfort her, but Christian wouldn't let me.

She took her book of ancestors and wrote down some names that she had lacked for many years. Then she looked at me and thanked me for finding the other grave, where a mother was buried with her baby son. She thought that they might have both died during the birth. Then she knelt and cried.

Before my friend's grandmother could finish her prayer, the doorbell rang. Christian got up to answer it, but his grandmother was faster. She told him that she was very tired and needed to deal quickly with whoever was at the door.

The shepherd was at the door. He was in tears, apologising for what he'd said to her. He said that he'd been very affected by all that had happened and begged for her forgiveness. She smiled and said that he'd done nothing wrong, and, closing the door behind her, she went outside to talk with him some more.

We were left alone in the house. I felt my eyelids getting very heavy, so I too left and went to our bedroom, and fell on the bed.

Christian came into the room and went on his knees besides my bed, asking me to join him. As I had prayed with him before, I knew what to do. I put my hands together and closed my eyes. He started to pray. I liked the beginning of his prayer very much: he had my full attention. But towards the middle of his prayer, my knees started to ache and I wondered when it would come to an end. Unfortunately, I never found out because I fell asleep.

Chapter 12

When I opened my eyes the next morning, as usual, I found myself in bed in my pyjamas, but there didn't seem to be anyone around. Then I saw a piece of paper on my bedside table. I was just about to read what was written on it, when I heard a bicycle bell outside. I quickly read the note: my friends told me not to worry, that they would be back quite soon. Then I heard someone approaching the front door. I managed to get my trousers half on over my pyjamas and ran to the door. But I tripped and fell just before I reached it; I had to open the door with one hand.

It was the postman. He peered into the room and couldn't see me at first but when I lifted my hand saying, "Good morning," then he noticed me. The postman looked down, grinning slightly. He had every reason to smile at me, for I was lying on the floor with my trousers half way up, and with uncombed hair in an awful mess. Without a word, he handed me a letter and went back to his bicycle. As he cycled away, he glanced at me a couple of times then he was gone.

I relaxed and stood up. I got properly dressed and sat down in a chair. The letter was for Christian: his name was written on the envelope. I put it in a place where he would see it.

I was bored because there was no one to talk to. So I went outside and started wandering around; the heat and the silence made me restless. I started kicking the little stones in the garden around. A medium-size pebble hit the chicken shed but didn't make much noise; at any rate, it didn't seem to have bothered the chickens. At first, I thought they weren't there, but then I saw that the door was closed.

This time, I picked up a bigger stone and threw it in their direction. It broke the wood and flew inside. Still, no sound came from the chicken shed. I was curious and went up to it. Then I noticed bloodstains and realised why there was no sound from the chickens. I slowly opened the shed door and saw the chickens all dead on the floor; flies had already invaded the place.

The stench made me feel sick, so I left immediately. I wanted to vomit, but couldn't. I sat on the ground at a considerable distance from the chicken shed and started to wonder what I should do next. The first thing that occurred to me was that this incident was going to upset my friends very much.

It was so hot that I knew that the smell would soon reach the house. Trickling soil through my fingers, I began to think. I looked at the soil and an idea suddenly occurred to me. I lifted my head and saw the shovel next to the woodshed. I picked it up and went to the chicken shed; then I began to shovel soil over the dead chickens. Once they were all covered, the smell disappeared. I closed the chicken shed door and sat down on the ground.

As I was resting, Christian and his grandmother came back. Seeing the sad expression on my face, she came up to me. I pointed to the chicken shed and explained what had happened, and what I had done. She was even more upset than I had thought she would be. Sitting down next to me, she said that she had neglected the chickens for the past three days, and that she was being punished for that. She then thanked me for what I had done.

After briefly caressing my head, my friend's grandmother stood up and began to look around the chicken shed. On seeing the blood stains, she realised that the chickens had been attacked than starving to death. She quickly opened the shed door. When she saw the blood inside, she became even angrier, grumbling to herself about foxes.

Then Christian's grandmother went to the woodshed and returned with a trap, which she intended to place under a little earth close to the chicken shed in order to catch the fox; she started digging. As I knew what she planned to do, I wanted to plead with her not to, but she wouldn't even let me go near her. I was fond of foxes and didn't want any harm to come to them; and I definitely thought that in spite of their actions, they didn't deserve such cruelty. Now I was watching a pair of hands preparing a trap for one of them.

As I watched my friend's grandmother continue with her work, I quietly kept on begging her not to do it but she ignored me. Christian didn't say anything –

not a word – for he wasn't used to interfering with his grandmother's decisions.

This event had affected me badly. When I realised that my friend's grandmother wasn't going to take any notice of anything I said, I decided to leave; but Christian stopped me, putting his hand on my shoulder. I managed to release myself from his grip, but he grabbed me again. This time he held me more tightly. He said that we all liked such animals, but it wasn't a sin to kill them when they harmed others.

However, my friend's reasoning didn't succeed in calming me down. I said that even if they were harmful at times, these animals also had a soul, and lived and breathed just like us. Moreover, as we humans invaded their habitats, what else could they do? They had to attack other animals to eat. With these words, I managed to free myself from his grasp again. Then I took a few steps away from him and went to sit on a large stone.

Christian came over and joined me in silence. Feeling powerless, I fearfully watched his grandmother. When she had finished her work, grumbling to herself about foxes again, she walked briskly away without even looking at us. She quickly returned with a distressed chicken that was flapping its wings as if it knew what was going to happen to it. She tied it by the foot to a peg in the ground next to the trap. The chicken continued frantically clucking and flapping furiously. Having finished all her preparations to catch the poor fox, my friend's grandmother smiled and came over to us, fixing her gaze on me.

Seeing the sad expression on my face, Christian's grandmother took a deep breath and said, "You've probably heard how sly foxes are, but you are evidently not aware of how harmful they can be.

"In fact, they are one of my favourite animals; and chickens are the dumbest birds in the world. Someone once told me years ago, that when they are attacked, instead of screaming all at once, if they remained silent, the fox would only take the nearest chicken and then run away. But because they are so afraid, they scream, and the fox panics and kills them all before taking one to eat.

"This isn't the first time that the fox has attacked my chickens; it has already done so several times this year. Whatever I do to make the chicken shed safe, the fox finds a way to get in and attack them.

"I don't want to harm the foxes – as I said, I like them – but today, my patience ran out. I buy chicks, which grow up to be chickens, because I like to eat them in winter. Unfortunately, every time I start looking forward to a feast, the fox gets them first. I'm sure you appreciate what I've told you; I would never harm any animal if I could help it."

When my friend's grandmother had finished, I was quiet and had nothing to say. I felt that I understood why she had acted as she had now; and I also thought that I knew her better as a result. I looked at her imploringly and hugged her. Laughing, she stood up and took me in her arms. After she had given me a kiss, we all went inside the house. Christian looked surprised by it all.

However, the colour drained completely from my friend's face when he saw the letter waiting for him inside. He told me that it was from his father and probably didn't contain good news. Then he sat down to read it. He read in silence. When he had finished, he told me that his father was letting him extend his holiday by one week. I jumped up and down with joy.

Then Christian asked me how many days there were in a week, not counting Saturday and Sunday. I said that there were five. He told me that we had to go back in three. My joy disappeared instantly. He said that when his father said six days, he meant three. We both knew how I quickly these three days would go. My friend left the house, saying that he wanted to be alone. I was sad and plunged deep into thought. Silence fell over the place.

Christian's grandmother tried to cheer me up, but all her efforts were in vain. I couldn't hear or see her, for I was concerned about Christian and also myself. When she could no longer bear my sad face, she took me by the hand, and led me out of the house and towards the woodshed. Once inside, she let go of my hand. Taking the shotgun that had belonged to her husband, she went outside again and sat on a small mound. I went to sit next to her. She intended to use the shotgun on the fox if it escaped from the trap. She sat in silence.

I saw Christian praying under a tree. Sometimes, he would laugh as if he were enjoying a joke with someone. Even his grandmother noticed his odd behaviour. She said that he was having a conversation with his mother again. I relaxed and smiled. When he had finished his prayer, my friend joined us. He was smiling. Then he turned to his grandmother and said, "I was simply praying; not talking to my mother."

After that, we all waited; indeed, we waited for so long, that it became dark. I made them laugh by turning first to the left, and then to the right while remaining seated. As if it knew the fate that awaited it, the chicken became more and more agitated. This upset me. I thought that even if I prayed, it wouldn't help.

Just then, as if reading my thoughts, my friend told me to pray. Without realising it, I was praying like a Christian, which made his grandmother smile to herself; for she knew that my prayers wouldn't save the fox. And she was right. When Christian told me the fox was coming, I hurriedly finished my prayer and opened my eyes. For the sake of his grandmother, I looked intently at the fox, whose end was near; we were all upset about that. However, his grandmother had the gun ready, her finger on the trigger. But I saw that her fingers were trembling and she was sweating.

The fox wasn't aware of our presence because we were absolutely still and silent. It slowly advanced towards its prey, but I was feeling more and more sorry for the fox. When it was facing the chicken, it stopped and looked at it. The chicken went mad and started running round in circles; it didn't want to end up as anyone's dinner.

Yet, the fox wasn't in a hurry. After it had had a long look at the chicken, it turned his attention to the chicken shed. Then it slowly went for the chicken. The fox thought it was about to get its prey, but I knew that it was only coming closer to its own death.

The fox was a step away from the chicken when it stopped and started to circle the bird. My friend's grandmother was becoming more impatient and trembling more than ever. I was happy that the fox was going to live for a little while longer. But I was wrong. The next moment, the fox decided to go for the chicken and caught its foot in the trap. It screamed, and my tears poured down.

Instead of shouting for joy, Christian's grandmother stood up trembling and went over to the fox. Because it was in such pain, it had bitten the chicken's neck and killed it, but couldn't release it from its mouth. The pain it was in made it utter sounds as if it was crying. It lay on the ground·looking down and shaking. I went over as well and stroked its head; the fox looked at me. I asked my friend's grandmother to kill it quickly so that it wouldn't suffer any longer. Then I turned my back and walked away from the murderous scene.

All this time, Christian hadn't said a word, but he too went and stroked the fox's head, and then he joined me. Taking me by the arm, he wanted to walk on but I didn't move. So he let go of me and went ahead by himself. Instead of hearing a gunshot, I heard my friend's grandmother saying to the fox, "I don't have the heart to kill you." When I looked, I saw that she was on her knees next to the animal stroking it, I was very happy.

When he heard his grandmother talking to the fox, Christian, who hadn't reached the house yet, ran back and released it from the trap.

His grandmother stood up, and immediately struck her gun against a large stone, breaking it. She then threw the weapon in the garden dustbin. She said that having seen that the fox had cubs she had been unable to kill it. I then knew that my prayers had been answered.

My friend's grandmother brought the first aid box from the house and treated the fox's wounds. She told us that it would be better for the animal if we left it, and that it would get better by itself. After stroking its head one more time, we left. The last time we looked, we couldn't see it anywhere. The chicken had disappeared as well. That was one of the happiest moments of my life. After that, we were all silent. Then Christian's grandmother could be heard muttering to herself that next time, she would build a sturdier chicken shed.

The eventful day had affected me greatly, and I was very tired. Changing into my pyjamas, I went to bed but I couldn't sleep. It was the first time the house had been so quiet. I tossed and turned, but the memories of the day stopped me from falling asleep. Through the window, I gazed at the sky and noticed one big especially bright star that seemed to be smiling down. It reminded me of Christian. Staring at the stars, I fell asleep.

Chapter 13

When Christian woke me up the next morning, it was still dark. "We'll live our last three days as if they were three months," he said, and flew out of the door. I knew immediately what he was talking about. We'd spent the previous days mostly in running; and after each run – twice a day – we'd swim for hours in the icy lake that I hated so very much. As the time passed, my body had grown accustomed to the cold water, but – although I didn't want go against my friend's wishes – I didn't understand why we had to swim in it quite so much.

We were both sad that the day of departure was fast approaching, but we pretended to ignore it. Yet, perhaps because we tried to pack as much as possible into those last three days, they flew past like three minutes.

★ ★ ★

The taxi that came to pick Christian and me up seemed like a monster to us. We were both apprehensive and couldn't calm ourselves down. My friend, who was hugging his grandmother, was convinced that he would never see her again and was distraught; he didn't want to leave her. All I could think of was how much he must love her.

When Christian finally stopped hugging his grandmother, it was my turn. I didn't cry, but I embraced her tightly as if I too were saying goodbye for the last time.

My friend jumped out of the taxi, which was about to move off, and hugged his grandmother again, howling, "I don't want to leave you!"

His grandmother kept saying, "You'll be back again."

But he kept repeating, "No, this is the last time we'll ever see each other!"

She picked him up and placed him next to me and told me to hold on to him very tightly; and then she asked the driver to move off very quickly.

Christian was right, though, we never did see his grandmother again.

As soon as the door was closed, the taxi driver drove off at high speed. I held on to my friend tightly. When I looked out of the window, I saw that his grandmother had already gone back into the house. Christian was inconsolable, still repeating that he would never see her again.

My friend didn't stop repeating those same words over and over again during the whole journey to the railway station. By the time we had settled into our compartment, he was totally exhausted. He lay down on the bed and, sobbing all the while, repeated those same words until he finally fell asleep. I felt very sorry for him and I wished I could have helped in some way;

but as it was, I couldn't do anything; all I could do was be patient.

Then after he had dropped off, my friend started to talk in his sleep. I couldn't understand what he was saying, but I was very careful not to wake him up. I covered him with a blanket, but he soon started to sweat and shiver. I became frightened for his wellbeing, so I went to see if I could find a doctor. That at least was easy.

After examining Christian, the doctor said that my friend had had a stressful time and there was nothing to worry about. He then gave him a very small dose of some children's medicine to help him stop shivering and sweating.

I sat next to Christian and, ruffling his hair, watched him sleep. Thanks to the medicine, he slept peacefully. As I regarded him, I thought of all the things that had happened to us on our holiday, but I only wanted to concentrate on the good bits. Although I never forget the bad parts, I tried not to think of them at all.

After a while, I fell asleep as well. But I soon woke up again with my neck hurting so much that I let out a scream, which disturbed my friend. He was confused and tired, and wearily lifted his head to look at me. I then wanted to stand up, but had pins and needles in my legs, and knew that they wouldn't support me. When Christian realised my situation, he started to laugh. He bent down and used one hand to massage my neck and the other to rub the life back into my legs.

But his massage just caused more aches and pains, and each time I groaned, he laughed.

I turned my head towards the window. When my friend declared that it was midnight, I asked him how he knew. He told me that when the Orchid Star was high in the sky this indicated the midnight hour. I'd never heard of the Orchid Star, so I asked him to tell me which one it was. I became so interested that I forgot all about my aches and pains. After looking at Christian's face to determine the direction he was gazing in, I stared at the sky trying to locate the Orchid Star, but I couldn't.

There was only one star in the sky so I asked my friend if that was it, but by the time he'd come close enough to see what I was pointing at, the clouds had covered it up. Therefore, when he asked me which star I meant, I could only point to a part of the sky that the clouds had already obscured. I then realised that he was joking and I laughed.

But he soon became serious again and said, "Look, there it is. I looked and saw that it was the big bright star I had seen from his grandmother's house, which had reminded me of him. "My mother and I named it the Orchid Star," Christian said. I was very surprised at this news. He continued, "Years ago, I gave an orchid to my mother that the servants had given to me, and at that very moment, this star appeared in the sky. My mother said that it was a very rare sight."

I was confused because I had seen it a few days ago at his grandmother's house, when it had looked as if it was smiling at me. I had never told him that I had chosen this star to remind me of him.

We gazed at the star for a long time until it disappeared behind the clouds. Then we looked at each other with the same idea in our heads, to go out into the corridor and explore the train. We opened the door and were pleased to see that no one was about. Christian went first and I followed; we started to walk along the corridor.

With the exception of the snoring passengers, everything was silent. Then suddenly, from further away, we heard the sound of a woman crying out. Taking a deep breath, I told my friend that we should ignore it and go back to our compartment. He turned and said that I was right. But just then, the cries became louder and that made him change his mind. He looked at me and, after saying that he was sorry, proceeded to make his way towards the compartment that the crying was coming from. I knew that if we entered it, this action would affect us both and make us unhappy, but I had no choice other than to follow him.

We made our way very slowly along the corridor and could hear the woman's crying louder as we neared her compartment. The curtains on the door were drawn. Christian knocked softly and asked if we could be of assistance. The crying stopped; then she apologised for disturbing us. Christian quietly reassured her that she wasn't disturbing us but that we wanted to help.

The woman let us in; although I could guess what we might be letting ourselves in for, having come this far, we didn't hesitate on the threshold. Quietly, I begged that this might be the last time we got involved in other people's trouble. As soon as we were inside, she said, "Welcome to the cowshed."

We both looked at her blankly. We didn't find her greeting very funny as we had felt sorry for her. She was very fat. We closed the door and sat down on the bed opposite her. Christian told her that the reason we had come looking for her was that we were concerned about her crying.

Surprisingly, she roared with laughter, and then said, "For many years, my voice united millions. Now, I sound like a cow; but I'm glad that it managed to attract two children." She continued to laugh loudly. I had no inclination that she would soon tell us her sad story.

The woman showed us a photograph, asking who we thought it was a picture of. Without thinking, we both said, "Your daughter." We imagined that she had been crying for her girl; but we were wrong.

She told us that *she* was the lady in the photograph, and then started to tell us her story.

"Long ago, I was a very beautiful woman; even the photograph I've just shown you was only taken three years ago. People could look at me for hours and it still wasn't enough for them; they loved my beauty. And there were always many men around me; I couldn't get away from them.

"I was given a gift, and that was my voice; and my mother taught me how to use that gift. From an early age, I had private tuition, and as a result of all that coaching, I became a world-famous opera singer.

"My mother also taught me to be a firm believer. Privately, I was a devoted Christian and in front of my public, an equally devoted opera singer.

"With my mother's support, I finally made it to the famous Berlin Opera Hall. With that, I took my first step onto the world stage. Famous managers were like octopuses around me, but I choose an unknown good-looking bachelor to manage my career. Soon, I was very well known all over the world.

"With the same speed, however, I started to forget all about religion. I had confidence in my voice and stopped believing that it was God who had blessed me with that beautiful voice. I stopped going to church. By pretending that I didn't have the time, I even stopped reading the Bible. Then I removed all my religious books from the bookshelves in my living room, boxed them up, and put them right at the back of my large garage. I then put other types of books on the shelves.

"As soon as I put the other types of books in my living room, I suddenly had so much spear time that not only did I read them all, but I bought more like them and had to put up more shelves.

"Looking back, I wish I had remained poor. When you are poor, you pray for all that you need all the time, and you never forget Him. But when you are rich, because you can have anything you want, you don't feel the need to pray.

"When my mother noticed what I was doing, she warned me against distancing myself from God. But I was deaf to her advice, and the more she warned me, the richer I got, what with all of the concerts I was giving around the world. I cut myself off from all my religious friends, and exchanged them for non-religious ones. I got married to the manager I had worked with for many years, who was also a non-believer.

"When I did that, my mother finally abandoned me. But that didn't bother me, for I had a husband who loved me; I had my voice, which had made me famous; and I had lots of money, with which I could buy anything I wanted. So I carried on living like that for some time.

"After a few years, we had a son. We were very happy and gave him all our love and attention. Then a year after giving birth, I discovered that I had a cyst that had already eaten half my ovaries. I had an operation. But the cyst came back, and so I had another operation. When my ovaries were removed, I had to give up the idea of having any more children.

"At first, I thought it was just an illness, but now I believe this was my first punishment from God; I was punished because I had forgotten Him and His existence. However, my husband and I now became even more devoted to our son.

"My mother visited me once after my last operation and repeated her advice. I got angry and threw her out of my house. My life was so beautiful that I found God's rules ridiculous.

"But on our sixth wedding anniversary, my husband had a heart attack and died in front of our guests. Because I had loved him so much, within three days I lost half my hair and what was left of it went white.

"While I was still mourning for my husband, my son became extremely ill, but carried on living in spite of the lack of a cure for his illness. All my time was spent looking after him, but my Christian friends distanced themselves from me because they were tired of listening to my problems. Hoping that they would find a cure for my son's illness, I spent all my money on doctors. Meanwhile, my poor son continued to suffer but lived.

"When I was left without any more money for doctors, they stopped coming. My son died. With his death, I lost my fame and my voice. The deaths of my husband and son had a devastating effect on me. I started putting on weight. I put on more and more weight. When I became so heavy that I looked like a cow, I remembered God. I thought that even if everyone else had forgotten me, He wouldn't abandon me. I was so ashamed of myself that I couldn't even go to Him in prayer.

"When I went to see a priest, he told me I had been given me this chance to ask for His forgiveness because He loved me. If He didn't love me or had forgotten about me, He would have simply taken my life. I immediately went on my knees and asked for forgiveness. I understood that people could forget about each other, but God never forgot them.

"Now, I'm travelling home to ask for my mother's forgiveness, and I will do my best to make her happy."

Wanting to comfort the woman, Christian went and sat next to her; she was hurting so very much. My friend told her what his mother had told him: "The only animal in the world whose tail grows after being pulled away is the lizard. You were like the lizard, when you forgot about God. On the other hand, butterflies are so fragile that if just a tiny fibre were to be removed from their wings, they wouldn't be able to fly and they'd die.

"Now that you've repented, you've transformed yourself from a lizard into a butterfly, but if you forget Him again, you will never fly again. My mother always wanted me to be like a butterfly and that is what I'm trying to behave like."

When my friend had finished, I smiled to myself because before leaving anyone, Christian always added his own story to theirs, which made them contemplate his words, giving them a new perspective on their own situation. The woman thanked him and said that from now on, she would try to behave more like a butterfly; and then started to cry again. After we had hugged her, we left.

Back in our compartment, my friend looked at me with a sad expression on his face, and asked me to promise him to do three things when I got home: I was to run; eat less so that I wouldn't get fat; and I was to wash myself in cold water every single day.

He then told me that we probably wouldn't be able to see each other for a long time – days or perhaps even weeks. I was crying as he told me this. The idea of not seeing him once we got home upset me very much.

Chapter 14

T he train whistle woke me up very early the next morning. When I opened my eyes, I saw Christian sitting at the window lost in thought. Seeing him so sad, I went and sat next to him. I was unhappy too. I told him that I was very upset as well, because we wouldn't see each other for a long time. My friend replied that it wasn't this that was making him sad; it was the fact that his father would be waiting for us at the station. That made me smile, and I told him that wasn't important.

Christian then became even more upset and said, "You don't know my father. He never picks anyone up from the station just because he's missed them. Years ago, when he picked my mother up once, he met her with hatred in his eyes rather than affection, because she was wearing a garland of orchids.

"Now, whenever my father goes to pick someone up, he remembers that scene and hates them for just being there. He'll take an instant disliking to you too, and that'll make me feel bad; this is what I'm afraid of."

My friend then went back to staring out of the window. I sat on my bed and I too lapsed into thought: I wondered whether Christian was hiding something from me. Of course he was, but I didn't ask him to tell me what it was. My father used to tell me, "It's better for you if you don't know everything."

As we neared our village, my friend became paler and said that he could almost smell his father. He held my hand very tightly and made an effort not to cry. Sometimes, he looked at me and smiled. His fear grew stronger the nearer we got to the station. Finally, the train slowed down, and we knew that we were almost there. When Christian saw the station, he closed his eyes and sunk to the floor; he was trembling.

Still holding my hand very tightly, I could see my friend's lips moving. I knew he was praying, which was good because I didn't know how else to calm him down. I wanted to cry, but he was in a worse state than I was and that stopped me. I was going to be separated from him. I knew that we would see each other again, but my feelings were telling my brain something else. The last thing I heard him say was "amen."

As Christian finished his prayer, the train came to a halt. I asked my friend if I should now leave him at the station before his father got there. He said that I shouldn't because I wouldn't be able to see him ever again if I did. He also said that his father knew we were together and would want to see me.

We stood up and walked out of the compartment and into the corridor. We then stepped down from the train; and we stood and waited a few feet away from it. I was pleased when I saw that there was no one around. I suggested to my friend that perhaps his father wasn't coming. But he whispered that I shouldn't be so happy, for his father would be here soon. He then told me to count to twenty-seven after the train had left.

Christian continued whispering, reminding me of my three promises: running, not eating a lot so that I wouldn't get fat, and always washing in cold water. I told him that I would keep the promises. After the whistle had been blown, the train pulled out of the station and he started counting.

As my friend said "twenty-seven," we heard his father's voice. Instead of hugging and greeting his son, he complained angrily that every time he came to the station, bad memories of it returned, and that he hated the place. He then glared at me and gripping Christian tightly by the shoulder, they left. Our parting was so sudden that I couldn't hold back the tears. I sat on the ground crying; I couldn't believe that all our adventures had ended so abruptly.

Suddenly, I noticed that my rucksack was missing. I stood up quickly and looked around but soon realised that I had left it on the train. That calmed me down completely. I wasn't worried about my clothes; I had left the special stone in my rucksack. But remorse wasn't going to bring it back.

After another quick look around me, I smiled to myself and started running home. As I ran, I absorbed all the smells of the village, and realised that I had missed it a lot. When I saw my mother in front of our house, I started shouting. She was surprised because she was expecting me a week later. But it was a pleasant surprise for her.

When I jumped up to embrace her, due to her advanced years, she fell over. I fell too, but continued to hug her. She laughed and was happy to see me. Soon, I saw my father, and got up and jumped on him as well; but I didn't manage to knock him over. He lifted me up in his arms and we hugged each other.

I was very impatient to tell them everything that had happened to us but my father stopped me. I persisted in trying to tell my story, but he carried me into the house and sat me in a chair. Then he went to the kitchen and came back with a small glass of water. I quickly gulped it down, but I soon wished I hadn't, as it was so salty that it turned my stomach. As I stood up spluttering, my father knelt down close to me and started to tell *me* a story instead:

"Many years ago, there was an old man who would help anyone and whose advice was appreciated by all. As he didn't want nearby neighbours, he lived alone at the top of a hill. He had such a calm and patient nature that he would think long and hard before deciding to do anything. He lived in a wooden house and was a happy man. Those who knew him called his house the House of Patience.

"One winter's day, seeing the sun shining, in spite of the snow, he left his house to cut wood without his usual coat and gloves to keep him warm. After cutting all the wood he needed, he loaded it onto his donkey and headed back. But because he had left his coat and gloves at home, he grew very cold. His body ached terribly and his hands turned red.

"When he got back to his house, he was in a hurry to light the gas lamp so that he could see better but instead of hanging it up, he put it in the fireplace. Then he bent down to light the fire. He was so cold that in his impatience to get warm, he blew onto the dry wood in the fireplace quickly causing it to ignite. A few sparks landed on his woollen shirt, which started burning. He was so frightened that in shaking his arms trying to put the fire out he hit the gas lamp, which fell over and broke.

"Seeing all the flames around him terrified him even more. Rushing to put the fire out, he fell onto it. He panicked and rolled on the floor, spreading the fire and starting to burn himself. He burned until there was finally nothing left of him. Both he and the House of Patience were reduced to ashes.

"Never forget this, my son: he who acts in haste makes mistakes, and even a minor slip-up can result in his death. I gave you a glass of salty water a moment ago and you rushed to drink it. If there had been poison in it instead of salt you would have died.

"To reach your goals in life, my son, pray and wait. Don't give up, and don't ask for your wishes to be granted too quickly. Wait patiently, and one day your wishes will be granted."

My father left the room and returned with a notebook, which he handed to me. He asked me to write in it all that I wanted to tell him and, in that way, to start my diary. He then ruffled my hair and left, but not before repeating once more his advice.

I took the diary and thought about what my father had said. After putting the date, I started writing in it. As I had a good memory, I had not forgotten any important detail. As I wrote, I felt as though I were living our adventures all over again. Since there were few really joyful days, each word I wrote made me relive the painful times. But if my father hadn't given me the notebook, I wouldn't have written about any of it.

I had no idea then how precious a diary could be; I realised its importance later on as the years went by. And I only dated the good days, leaving the bad ones without a date. I knew this was wrong, but then, I didn't want to remember the dates of those days.

★ ★ ★

Spending all my time in writing, I totally forgot about Christian. Then when I got to the part about the advice he had given to the lady we met on the train, I realised how much I missed him. I stopped writing and started to think about him.

I was staring at a tree whose leaves were gently moving in the breeze. Seeing my mother's shadow on the leaves made me look up. Although I was looking at her, I didn't really see her, for I was deep in my daydream. My mother waved at me and I finally saw her smiling face. She had something in her hand, which she wanted to give me. So giving her my full attention, I saw that she was holding a flowerpot.

I put my diary down and walked slowly towards my mother. I had been too far away to see what kind of flower it was but as I got nearer, I saw that it was an orchid. I was so overjoyed that tears of happiness ran down my cheeks. I started screaming, "An Orchid! An Orchid! And I ran towards her.

When my mother saw me running towards her, she knew that I was going to jump into her arms just like the last time. She didn't have time to put the pot down, so this time, she moved to one side and handed me the orchid. She then turned sideways and closed her eyes. This didn't stop the tears running down my cheeks, but it did make me laugh. For a while, I was crying and laughing at the same time; I couldn't stop myself.

I kissed my mother's hands. Seeing me so happy made her laugh too. The more I looked at the orchid, the more I cried with happiness. It was the happiest I had been for days. I didn't know if I would have been happier if I had been granted a place in Heaven. Indeed, I loved Christian and being away from him even for a second was like a century to me. If I hadn't had the daily occupation of writing my diary, perhaps I would have sunk into such a bad depression that I wouldn't have been able to recognise myself.

My mother pulled me towards her with the pot in my hands. I couldn't keep my eyes off that flower, it was so beautiful. I suddenly noticed that my mother had stopped laughing. When she nudged me, I looked at her and she pointed at something in front of me. I was overjoyed with one orchid, but seeing hundreds of them in front of me was a truly astonishing sight. I dropped the pot, which landed on the big toe of my left foot, making me see stars as well as orchids.

The tears stopped running down my cheeks. I bent down and took my shoe off. I held my toe because it was hurting so much – the pot was made out of heavy clay. When I looked at my foot, I saw that my toe was swelling up a bit but it was okay. Nonetheless, the pain calmed me down. When I finally looked at the orchid on the ground, I was relieved to see that its pot wasn't broken.

My mother had gone a little way away and sat down on a chair. I went over and sat next to her. She put her hand on my cheek and we both remained silent. This was my way of trying to show her my gratitude. Seeing that I wasn't going to move, she asked me to go and look at all the other orchids. I kissed her hand and went over to them. It was like being in a dream until I touched them. There were all kinds of orchids growing there. As they were extremely delicate flowers, I was very careful not to damage them.

At that moment I understood why Christian's mother loved orchids so much.

I felt my mother's hand on my shoulder. She said, "Don't waste the joy of this surprise; go and get your friend so that you can enjoy them with him."

As my mother ended her sentence, I stood up and sprinted off. After a few steps, I stopped and glanced back at her: she looked so peacefully happy. I returned to her side and after telling her that I loved her very much, I made off again at full pelt.

I ran past my father so fast that I had no intention of breaking my step until I heard him say, "Where's my little lightning going?"

I stopped and replied, "Your little lightning's running to strike someone," and continued my sprint. He laughed loudly and called me back, so I returned. He handed me my diary. With a sad expression on his face, he told me never to leave it lying around, and that I should treat it as a holy book.

Without a word, I grabbed my diary and ran off again. I was so happy that I wished I could fly. I sang as I ran. I stopped when I reached the forest. Looking into its depths, I felt profoundly anxious, but I managed to put my feelings aside and took the plunge. Hearing the rustle of the leaves and the birds singing made me feel like a prince of nature.

While totally immersed in the beauty and smells of my surroundings, the sound of whimpering brought me back to reality. It was as if someone was weeping, but it wasn't human crying. I stopped and listened; and as I couldn't see anything, I started moving towards the sound. Sadness replaced my happiness.

I realised that the sound was coming from somewhere nearby, so I stopped again and looked around. When I saw where it was coming from, I felt that my soul would leave my body. A squirrel was nudging the lifeless body of another that was lying on the ground motionless. One glance told me that it was dead. The other couldn't revive it, and that was why it was making that heartrending sound.

After giving the squirrel some time to realise that there was nothing it could do, I moved slowly closer. The one that was crying climbed a tree and sat on a branch, and continued to mourn while I bent down next to the dead squirrel. Carefully, I took it in my hands and stroked its fur.

I placed the dead squirrel in the hole, and after moving away to let the other squirrel have one last look, I came back and covered it with earth. As I was just about to leave, I noticed some water droplets on my hand; the other squirrel was crying just like a human. I couldn't bear to hear it anymore, so I hurried away from that place without once looking back.

I'd buried the squirrel. I'd had no other choice; I couldn't give it its life back. I didn't want to dwell on this anymore, so I tried to bring happier thoughts to my head.

Then I saw Christian's house in front of me. It was the biggest house I had ever seen, and it gave me the shivers. A voice inside me told me to hide my diary. The closer I got, the more I trembled; I didn't understand why I was so frightened.

Very slowly, I approached the steps leading up to the front door. I could feel my legs becoming heavier, so much so that I had to push them forward. I couldn't answer the many questions I was asking myself either. I finally managed to reach the front door and rang the bell. No one answered so I pressed it again.

I still had my finger on the doorbell when a servant opened the door. Smiling, I told her that I wanted to see Christian. With a frozen smile on her face, she told me that I couldn't, and slammed the door in my face. This angered me, so I kept on pressing the bell until she reopened it. But she only repeated what she had said before and asked me to leave immediately, this time slamming the door even harder. Not to be put off, I rang it yet again; and I continued ringing the bell until the door was opened by a big blond man.

With a menacing look, he grabbed me by the arms and pulled me towards the steps. He then tried to throw me down them. I held on to a huge pot of flowers and started screaming, but he still managed to throw me down the steps. I landed on the ground like a football with some earth in my hand. After three or four forward rolls, I stood up and found a stone, and threw it at the big blond man. It hit him on the head and he fell down. And while he was dazed, I ran as fast as I could back up the steps and into the house, pushing the maid aside.

Moments later, the man was there too. He was bleeding and looking at me as a bull looks at a red rag. As he lifted his arm to hit me, I cowered on the floor and covered my head with my hands. I waited for him to strike. The terror had made me stop crying.

However, the man wasn't granted his wish; a voice stopped him. When I lifted my head towards the voice, I saw that it was Christian's father. The man left my side but I remained in the same position. All I could think was that I might never be able to see my friend again. Then Christian's father came and gave me a handkerchief and pointed to a chair. I started to cry as I sat down and couldn't look at him. He ordered me to cease weeping and didn't resume talking until I had stopped completely.

When I finally did and all was silent he said, "I will tell you a story: One father louse told his son that he always had to live in dirt. His son believed him and thought that he could turn anything into dirt in order to live in it. One day, he found a clean place and settled down and waited for it to become dirty; but it remained clean. Before long, he died.

"I like the friendship you have with my son and it pleases me that you are crying for him."

As he finished his story, Christian appeared. His father told him to go with me wherever I wanted to take him, as he had business to attend to. I tried to give him his handkerchief back, but my friend grabbed it first and threw it in the bin. After smiling at his father, Christian asked me to wait outside.

Trying to make sense of what had just taken place, I went outside and sat down on the steps. Although I was very intelligent, some things took years for me to understand, to make sense of everything that happened and every story I was told. But whatever these things meant, like Christian, I was grateful.

I was deep in thought, but the sound of truck engines brought me back to reality. I stood up slowly and went down the steps but I still couldn't see anything. I had started walking towards the noise when Christian suddenly grabbed me and pulled me onto the path.

Looking as surprised as I was, he said, "So, because of you, my father gave me my freedom."

But when the trucks turned into the drive, my friend's face went pale. He pulled me behind a huge bush. Eight trucks preceded by a car had stopped in front of the house. Christian's father opened the door of the car.

"This is the second time in my life I've seen him this happy," said my friend. "The first was when he took the orchid and stamped on it." His mother had died not long after; it wasn't a good sign.

Four middle-aged men got out of the car. It was obvious that they knew Christian's father very well from the way they embraced each other. One of them waved in our direction but my friend stopped me as I was about to wave back. The others noticed this and they all started to laugh at us. As he was talking to them, Christian's father pointed at us and they all laughed again.

As they began moving towards us, I suddenly became frightened. Now that the engines of the trucks had stopped, we could hear dogs barking inside. Worried, we looked at each other and my fear increased: there wasn't just one dog but a whole pack of them.

As the trucks were opened, men poured out of them, each person leading two dogs. The animals started playing and barking loudly. Seeing how frightened I was, Christian tugged my hand, making to leave. At that point, I made eye contact with his father, who smiled at me. I shuddered and followed my friend.

We were just about to run for it, when I remembered that I didn't have my diary with me. I pulled up and whispered, "My diary, my diary," to myself. I had completely forgotten where I had hidden it. I started wandering around, looking under the fallen leaves. But when I couldn't find it, I started to cry.

Christian didn't know what I was looking for, so I told him. Hearing that I had started a diary made him very happy. He jumped up and down saying, "One day everyone will know of my mother and her love for orchids."

My friend told me to get on my knees and pray that we wouldn't lose such a special diary. His words had an effect on me; I stopped crying and knelt down. I was just about to start praying when I felt the wind; it was such a warm breeze that it felt as if my soul was leaving my body.

I opened my eyes when I heard Christian say, "Your diary's over there," but when I looked in the direction he was pointing, I couldn't see it. I stood up and walked towards the place my friend was indicating and finally saw my diary under a tree.

I picked it up and ran back to Christian, who said, "I know you've forgotten everything my mother taught me and I passed on to you. Yet, whatever you allow yourself to forget, never forget to pray. On your saddest, happiest, or most peaceful day, always remember to pray just like you remember to breathe.

"Just now, you witnessed it yourself: you were about to start praying and seeing that you had remembered Him, God helped you."

My friend was absolutely right and I felt ashamed of myself. As soon as he'd finished, with my head still a little bent, I grabbed his hand and we started to run in the direction of my house. As I couldn't say anything, and seeing me breathing with difficulty, he reminded me that it had been a long time since we had been for a run or a cold shower. I mutely nodded, pointing at my diary.

Seeing that I was out of shape, Christian made us take a longer way round. As we ran, he asked me for details from my diary, which I was finally able to gasp out to him.

Suddenly, I realised that we were running in a completely different direction to my home, so I stopped. I told my friend that we had to go to my house because I had a surprise for him. He was so pleased that saying he knew a short cut, he immediately sprinted away. I only just managed to keep up with him; I never could outrun him. He was right again: very soon, we were near my house. Even though I had been born and bred around there, I'd had no idea this short cut existed.

We stopped when we arrived in front of my house. I turned towards Christian and saw that he was very excited. He wanted to know what the surprise was, but I just smiled and produced my handkerchief. He immediately understood what I intended to do.

My friend became very serious, bending his head and saying, "My promise is stronger than the handkerchief you're holding." Then he looked straight at me and continued, "I'll close my eyes and I won't open them until you tell me too."

I became embarrassed and put the handkerchief back in my pocket. After Christian had closed his eyes, I held his hand and we proceeded towards the house. I stopped when we reached the back garden where the orchids were. Eyes still closed, I saw that he was smiling and his lips were moving. I knew he was silently thanking God for the surprise he was going to have.

I was just about to tell my friend that he could open his eyes, when I sensed my parents' presence. They pointed at him and asked me to hurry up, so I quickly told him that he could open his eyes. The moment he saw the orchids, he burst into tears. He couldn't believe his eyes. Talking to himself and circling around the flowers, he exclaimed, "Am I in paradise? Am I in paradise?" Then he slowly knelt down and started to caress them.

After a while, Christian looked up at me with tears in his eyes. Then he stood up and came over. Holding my hands in his, he tried to speak, but he couldn't; his words wouldn't come out. Overcome with happiness, he just wept. I was very happy for him.

My friend was just about to hug me, when he saw my parents. He went to them and started mumbling his gratitude, but he kept stopping in mid-sentence, for he was simply overwhelmed by the orchids. He'd never been happier in his life, but he'd started to stammer; I could barely understand what he was trying to say. His tears of happiness had also managed to make my mother cry as well.

Christian knelt down again, so my father knelt down beside him and said, "I appreciate your happiness. I have never felt that happy in my life, but I am so glad for you. And I am glad that you are my son's friend.

"Go quickly to your mother's grave and cover it with some of these orchids so that she will be happy as well. But even if they are tears of joy, do not cry there. If you smile, you will feel your mother's joy too!"

After hearing my father's words, my friend calmed down. He started to talk more fluently to my parents, saying that he didn't know how to thank them. He hugged and kissed them both, and then came over to me. My parents immediately left us. When he realised that we were on our own, he knelt down beside the orchids again, and I joined him to hear better what he was saying.

"When she was seven, my mother became very ill," Christian began. "The doctors didn't expect her to live. A very close friend of my grandmother's heard this, and travelled a long way to console my mother and bring her a present. My grandmother was very happy and relieved to see her friend. The present was an orchid.

"My mother was so ill that she couldn't even lift her head, but she managed to look at the orchid. When she saw it, she pointed at the flower and asked to hold it.

Seeing her daughter caress the flower, my grandmother was amazed by this miracle. Looking at that orchid every day cured my mother; her love of orchids saved her life.

"When she was finally better, her mother's friend told her, 'I've been nurturing this flower for many years, so our souls are dependent on each other. When I fall ill, it too begins to wilt; when I get better, it thrives again. We can't live without each other.

"'I'm very old now, but I don't want this flower to grow old as well. I knew you loved it from the way you perked up as soon as you saw it. Perhaps this flower will love you back and continue to live with you like it did with me, but perhaps it won't. So if one day it wilts and shrivels up, then you will know that I've died.' With these words, she briefly caressed the flower and left.

"From that moment onwards, my mother could never be separated from her orchid.

"Years later, the orchid wilted and died. Although my mother loved it, it couldn't get used to her. When she saw that the flower had died, she cried and cried, and felt that her soul itself had shrivelled up. Then she remembered what the lady had said and convinced herself that the flower was loved more by someone else.

"After caressing it one last time, she buried it. That night she had a dream about the old lady: smiling, she gave her another orchid. This calmed her down; and since then, she never imagined a day without an orchid in it."

As Christian finished his story, I started, "Yes but why then...?"

My friend knew what I was about to ask, and so he continued, "I'll tell you that too. You want to know why my father hates orchids. I often think very hard and wonder if my mother was unfair to him in any way. All I know is that my abiding memory of her has always been the same: she always loved *me*; that has never changed.

Chapter 15

"My mother also loved the opera," Christian began, "so when she was eighteen, her mother treated her to a trip to Vienna, including a concert at the Opera House. My mother managed to find a seat close to the front. On her left, sat a very handsome man – the man who was to become my father. Throughout the whole performance, he looked at my mother rather than the stage. She was so engrossed in the opera, that only at the end of the show did she notice his stares. She gave him a smile and left.

"She was delighted to be in Vienna, with its spectacular architecture. After the performance, she went for a stroll and suddenly found herself in front of a flower shop. There were a great many orchids on display, but as the shop was closed, all she could do was touch the glass. Sighing heavily, she walked back to her hotel.

"Seeing so many orchids had excited her so much that she couldn't sleep. She couldn't afford to buy any, but all she wanted was go into that shop and touch them. That whole night, she fantasised about orchids, her sole desire being to caress them. Finally, she fell asleep with the sunrise and woke up very late.

"She hurried back to the shop, but was very disappointed to find that there wasn't a single orchid left. The shopkeeper told her that someone had bought them all. She became very sad and almost lost the will to go on. Feeling extremely miserable, she returned to her hotel. But when she went into her room, she was shocked to find that orchids were everywhere.

"There was an envelope on a small table. Impatiently, she tore it open and found an invitation to dinner. Although there was no name with it, she had an idea who might have sent her the invitation. She was so happy that she felt like an angel amongst all the orchids; she would have flown if she'd had any wings.

"When the time came, my father picked her up from the hotel in his beautiful chauffeur-driven car and took her to an expensive restaurant. My father was very rich. He delighted her so much with his sparkling conversation that by the end of dinner, my mother had fallen in love with him.

"He then produced a ring from his pocket. Thinking that her life would always be filled with orchids, my mother was extremely tempted to accept his proposal. But a voice inside her told her to say 'no'. She told him that she needed time to think.

"When she returned to her hotel room full of orchids, she knew that she was in love with my father. But whenever she made up her mind definitely to say 'yes', the same voice inside her told her again to say 'no'.

"Day after day, my father sent her orchids. It was becoming impossible to find a little place or corner in the room without an orchid in it.

"One cloudy day, she opened the window and looked at the sky, and said out loud, 'My God, Thou knowest that the voice inside me says 'no' to this marriage. But I want to marry this young man. Please do not stop me.'

"A few seconds later, the sky turned blue and the sun shone. Taking this as a sign, my mother accepted my father's proposal.

"That was her first wrong decision. I don't remember many more wrong decisions though. Perhaps she didn't have time to make any more. For not long afterwards, because of that decision, she became part of the earth.

"My grandmother took one look at my father and begged my mother not to marry him. But my mother convinced her after telling her that God, too, had told her not to marry him; but He had relented.

"On the first night of their marriage, my mother filled every corner of the room with the orchids my father had bought her. She was so preoccupied with them that she forgot my father was in the room. Of course, she didn't love them more than my father, but he suddenly got the impression that she had married him because of the orchids; and at that point, he began to hate the flowers.

"He was in love with my mother's physical beauty but didn't understand her inner feelings. Yet, her love of orchids continued to increase over the years along with my father's hatred of them. In the end, he became jealous of them.

"Years later, after we had moved here, not only did he forbid orchids in the house, but we weren't even allowed to mention the flower's name. My mother then realised that many years ago, in that hotel room, she should have listened to her inner voice. But now it was too late.

"She prayed for forgiveness. And soon after those prayers, she began to see into the future. She took the gift that she had been given as a sign that He had forgiven her. Understanding more, my mother started to prepare me for the trials to come.

"One of the premonitions she had was about you; she saw you and described you to me in detail. She taught me all her wisdom. After that, just like an orchid that has reached the peak of its bloom, day by day, she started to lose her beauty, and never found it again. She wilted away. When I was six, she stopped educating me. She hardly left her bedroom. Not long after that, we buried her.

"Although many years have passed since then, my father still detests orchids; he even hates the memory of my mother. And he has started to hate me, too, because he has just an inkling of how deeply she loved me. I remind him of her and she reminds him of orchids. He says that if he hugged me, it would be like hugging my mother; and if he caressed me, it would be like caressing an orchid."

★ ★ ★

I had no words of consolation for my friend. My head bent, I tried to work out who was right and who was wrong; but I couldn't decide; I had no power to judge these things.

Hearing Christian chatting about the orchids brought me back to reality. Smiling, he asked me to bring him the wheelbarrow, which I did. When it became apparent that I wasn't going to help him load it, he asked me what my objection to the job was. I said that it would be better if his odour alone were on them, as they were going to be put on his mother's grave. He thought about that for a bit, and then started to push the wheelbarrow as I walked along beside him.

On the way, my friend didn't take his eyes off the orchids for a single moment. I stopped him when we reached level ground in order to show him my diary. But as I leaned in closer, he suddenly sprinted away with the wheelbarrow. I too ran a few steps behind him. He sang snatches of nursery songs his mother had taught him.

Christian's happiness lasted until we arrived at the cemetery. Then tears springing to his eyes, he stopped. Remembering my father's words, I tried to console him and wipe away his tears. He looked up at the sky, smiled, and approached his mother's grave. Whenever we talked about his mother or were at her graveside, he would cut himself off from reality. This time was no different. He knelt down, put his face on the ground, and fingered the grave.

Smiling again my friend whispered, "My mother, I can still smell you; I can still hear your heartbeat, and even feel your breath. When I touch this sacred ground,

I feel as if I were caressing your face. My dearest mother, you never left my side.

"Look what I've brought you: lots of orchids; they will cover the whole of your grave. I also bring you my promise that your grave will never be bare of them. Seeing all these orchids makes me feel so much lighter.

"My dearest mother, I can feel your happiness. I know you have orchids in heaven, but placing them on your grave makes me feel that you are near me, and I feel alive again. No one will ever replace you in my heart; you will always be there, and your grave will always be sacred to me. I feel calmer near your grave.

"I would be free if you were with me, but I'm still happy. Seeing the orchids here reminds me of your hugs and our days together. As I haven't rebelled against God, I don't ask why He has taken you from me. But I know that when I finally complete my promise to you, my soul will join yours and we will never be separated again. As I cover your grave with these orchids, I will leave your side and leave you with them. Good bye, my dearest mother."

Christian then kissed the ground and placed the orchids on the grave. We went to the wheelbarrow again and again until we had brought all the orchids to his mother's graveside. There were so many that the whole grave was indeed covered; we even had to put some of the pots on top of each other.

When all the orchids were in place, my friend looked at me and said that as his dearest wish was to be reunited with his mother, I should pray for that. These words made me cry; I thought if he was taken away from me, I would be as heartbroken as *he* was for his mother. I told him that if he was ready to give up his life now, I was ready to do the same.

He smiled and knelt down beside me. Lifting my head, he said, "Of course, that time will come too, when you complete your diary. Read it to someone and give him the diary; and then our souls will be together.

"It's too early for you to ask for such a thing now. But as my duty here is nearly done, I have the right to ask for it. I feel the emptiness in my heart. Living without my mother kills me more and more every day. Without my mother I'm half dead anyway. Even angels would find such a life unbearable."

My tears had increased while Christian was talking. He wiped them off my face and whispered in my ear, "I'm living for you!"

My friend slowly stood up, and after telling me he'd come and see me tomorrow, and that I should now run home and have a cold shower, he sprinted off. I was crying so hard that I couldn't even lift my head to look at him. After he was gone, I felt very lonely and screamed at God, demanding how He could allow such a thing, because I couldn't bear to be separated from my friend.

I collapsed in exhaustion. I was crying still louder, when it suddenly started to rain. The huge raindrops shone like diamonds, but none of them fell on me. They formed the shape of another grave next to his mother's and remained there. I had goose pimples.

Aware of the message I was being sent, I stood up and ran. I was very much shaken, and, instead of drying my tears, I cried even more all the way home.

When my parents saw the state I was in, they were frightened. I knelt down in front of my father and told him everything. As usual, he tried to calm me but I couldn't be pacified because of the message I had received, which was clear to me.

Seeing that I was still very upset, my father said to me, "I will give you an example, my son. If I gave you two pearls, one real and the other one plastic, you would not look after the fake one as carefully as you would the real one would you? You would put the real one in a special place, and the other one you would leave out.

"But no matter how much you looked after the real one, sooner or later, you would lose it. After that, every time you thought of it, your heart would break into pieces. On the other hand, you would keep the plastic one, and it would remain where you had left it for years. Even if you lost it, you would not care, you would not feel anything.

"God takes the good ones faster because He needs them; He takes them because he loves them. The people that love them continue living with sorrow and pain, and always remember them because they are worth remembering.

"If He wants to take your friend, let Him. We are powerless in the face of His wishes. Let your heart ache because he deserves it. You will always remember him; you will never forget him."

But my father's words had no effect on me; I refused to believe that Christian could simply die and leave me alone. But my tears for him were just the beginning. I fully understood what my father had told me, but I didn't want to believe it. After a glance at my parents, still crying, I ran out of the house and went to sit under a tree in the garden.

I couldn't calm myself. I wanted to ask once more why this had to happen. As I lifted my head towards the sky, in spite of the fact that it was bright daylight, I saw a shooting star. I followed it until it disappeared. Each time I started to ask my question, another shooting star would appear. After the third one, I was calmer but still crying. For the first time in my life, I had decided to rebel against God, but He was revealing His miracles to me.

I got up to go back indoors, wiping my tears as I reached the front door. My father was sitting in his chair smiling at me. I hugged him and told him that I loved him very much, but I loved God more; that sometimes, only He could calm me. "I'm proud to have a father like you," I finished; and, before going to my room, I repeated the same things to my mother.

I took out my diary and sat on the bed. While writing, I remembered Christian's instructions about the cold showers. So I stopped and went to the bathroom. I filled the bath with cold water and prepared to get in. As soon as I put my toe in, my whole body froze. As I was contemplating how I would manage to immerse myself completely, I heard my friend telling me to pray. So I prayed the way my father had taught me and threw myself in. Of course, I immediately wanted to get out again, but Christian's voice in my head stopped me. I sat shivering in the bath for a long time. Then I got out and continued to write my diary.

* * *

Christian had said that he'd come to my house the next day, but after four days of no news I started to worry. No amount of running and cold showers could make up for his company. I didn't even feel like writing my diary anymore. When what patience I'd learnt ran out, I decided to go to my friend's house.

Until then, each time I was going to Christian's house, I'd feel very happy and look forward to enjoying the scenery on the way. But this time, I was anxious and felt as though something was trying to stop me: I could hardly move my legs and couldn't even breathe properly. This was the second time this sort of thing had happened.

I lifted my head towards the sky and begged not to be stopped from going to see the friend I loved so very much. At that moment, I felt a great sense of peace and I was grateful that my prayers had been heard. Then I started to run. The smells that reached my nostrils were as fresh as if the world had been created yesterday.

The forest appeared in front of me. I stopped and looked deep into it. Previously, it had been so silent that you could hear your heartbeat and the dry leaves scrunching underfoot, but today it was different: I could hear dogs barking and birds twittering in fear.

Feeling curious, I advanced towards the forest, but before I could set a foot in it, I heard someone telling me to stop. So I did. The person who'd asked me to stop appeared and walked towards me. He circled me with two Alsatian dogs, one on each side. They looked ferocious and frightened me to death. Soon, another three men appeared, each with two Alsatians as well. I was surrounded by dogs and was speechless with terror.

The dogs nosed around, barking at me and the men whispered amongst themselves, sometimes looking in my direction and laughing. I realised that this might go on for some time, so I started praying and telling them that all I wanted to do was visit my friend.

Suddenly, all was silent. After looking at each other, the men and their dogs all moved aside, allowing me to pass. So I moved on, but I was so terrified that not once did I look back; and I continued to pray.

As I left the forest and the barking behind me, I slowly relaxed. But suddenly, I heard it again. I froze. Shivering and whimpering, I awaited my fate. One of the Alsatians jumped on me and I fell to the ground. I lay there without moving, the dogs circling me. I thought that one little move would spell my end.

One of the dogs growled loudly and salivated over my face. Doing my utmost not to swallow it, I closed my mouth and breathed through my nose. But soon, I had so much saliva on my face that I couldn't breathe that way either.

The owners of the dogs approached me and started to laugh. One of them said that they were waiting for one more order before the dogs ripped me apart. Fortunately, it came in the form of my reprieve. Warning me never to speak to them so impertinently again, one of the men ordered the dogs off. The moment they moved away, I sprang to my feet and ran away as fast as I could.

I wept as I ran, wiping the dog's saliva off my face as best I could. As soon as I saw the river, I jumped in. After washing my face thoroughly, I felt cold and got out. I then walked home. The cold I felt didn't calm me. I couldn't make sense of it: why were these men walking their dogs in the forest?

When I got home, I didn't tell my father anything; I just said that I'd stumbled on the riverbank and fallen in. My mother swallowed the story, but from the way my father looked at me and smiled, I knew that he didn't believe it. But he didn't force me to tell him the truth either.

After I'd put some dry clothes on, I sat by the fire and came to the conclusion that I had no choice but to wait for Christian to visit me. All I could do was to be patient, wait and pray. That night, I couldn't sleep.

In the ensuing days, I spent all my time wondering when I would see my friend again. I was so preoccupied with these thoughts that I stopped running, taking cold showers, and writing my diary. I was like a crazy child, wandering around and talking to myself. At night, instead of going to bed, I prowled about the darkened house fretting all the while.

One morning, after I'd finally managed to drop off, my parents told me that they'd heard me talking in my sleep. They were very worried about me, but they let me be. My father didn't ask me what was wrong, and he didn't let my mother ask either.

Chapter 16

It felt like years since I'd seen Christian. It was early one Saturday morning and my father was getting ready to go to the synagogue. By now, I was so worried about my friend that I thought I was going to have a nervous breakdown. Seeing the condition I was in, my father didn't disturb me. He left me to sleep, but I wasn't asleep. My eyes were closed and I was thinking that this was the end of the world when, as if in a dream, I heard Christian's voice. I couldn't believe my ears.

When my father said, "Your friend is here," I was so overjoyed that he might just as well have announced that an angel had come to visit. I jumped up and opened the door.

It didn't come as a surprise to see Christian weeping; he couldn't stop. He was crying so hard that I couldn't understand what he was trying to tell me. He then went on his knees in front of me, still trying to talk. When he realised that he couldn't, he took me by the hand and started to run. I turned back to look at my father but he wasn't there.

Now both of us were crying; I had never wept so freely before, perhaps because nobody was trying to stop me. I was crying from the joy of being reunited with my friend, but I didn't know why my friend was crying until we reached his mother's grave. I was immediately silenced, for the scene in front of me was unbelievable.

The grave we had covered with orchids was totally bare except for a holy thorn tree standing next to it. I did my best to convince myself that this vision wasn't real, but when I touched the grave, I knew that it was. Christian tried to move the tree and I helped, but it was impossible. When we realised the futility of our efforts, I started crying again. We both prayed and wept. In spite of his wretchedness, instead of rebelling against God, my friend prayed to Him. Finally cried out, we lay down under the tree.

Christian took a handful of soil from the grave, kissed it, and began, "My mother used to say that the world was heaven for believers and children were the fruit of heaven. It's hard to think of a tree without fruit. It's the same with children: you can't imagine the world without them.

"To prevent the fruit from being devoured by worms, you need to look after it. It's the same with children: you need to feed them with love so they can blossom.

"I had more than enough love from my mother, but only received hatred from my father. And I continue living with that hatred. I know he doesn't love me because I look like my mother, but he forgets that his blood is also running in my veins.

"I manage to live with his bad treatment of me every day, but I can't bear the desecration he has caused to my mother's grave. If my mother hadn't willed me to live, I would have joined her long ago; this you know. Just as he killed my mother, this makes me think that it is now my turn. I'm not *sure* yet; all I know is that he planted this tree here because of the orchids.

I've had enough of his trickery. I wish he'd got rid of his hatred for my mother when she died, and let this grave be. I know he'll never do that but my patience will win out in the end."

Then, my friend began to cry even louder. All he wanted was his father's love; he was dying for it. But no one could give him that love, so I let him cry. Yet, I knew I couldn't appreciate what he was feeling.

When Christian's eyes were all swollen up from crying, he looked at me and said that he couldn't go home; he wanted to come with me. I sighed and smiled. Giving the grave a last sorrowful look, we stood up and began to walk away. After a few steps, he turned to face it and walked backwards until it disappeared from view. We never again went back to his mother's grave together.

I was relieved when my friend smiled at me as we walked away from the grave, but this didn't last long. He suddenly saw something in the distance and began to sprint. When I caught up with him, I saw that he was gazing at a spider's web with sadness. A beautiful butterfly was trapped in it and fighting for its life. He couldn't bear it; he furiously destroyed the web and freed the butterfly. It was still alive.

Christian took the butterfly in his palm and handed it to me. Then he said, "My mother was even more beautiful than this butterfly. But like the butterfly, which can no longer fly and will soon die, my mother was trapped in my father's invisible web; and once her freedom was taken away, she too died."

While my friend was talking, the butterfly died. I knew very well what his predicament was but I couldn't do anything to help him; I couldn't give him his father's love or bring his mother back. Then I remembered his grandmother's advice: she'd asked me to just listen to him because that was all he needed. Well, that was what I was doing. Even though listening to him caused me pain, I was determined to hear him out. And everything he told me became engraved in my brain.

After one last little stroke, Christian buried the butterfly under a tree. As with our departure from his mother's grave, we walked away backwards from the butterfly's resting place until it disappeared from view. Immediately after that, we started running. As usual, it was very quiet; I could hear the wind blowing in my ears as I ran.

To cheer us up, I started to laugh. My friend found that bizarre and asked me what on earth could be thought of as funny. I didn't answer and just continued to laugh. The more he asked, the more I laughed, so he finally joined in too.

We stopped laughing when we saw that there was a crowd of people in front of my house. My blood froze and I thought my heart would stop beating. Christian quickly told me to go to the tunnel in the morning before sunrise, for he had a surprise for me there. I nodded. The next time I looked in his direction, he had already gone.

Shivering, I walked up to the door. The crowd parted to let me pass, but my father stopped me from going inside. As he was smiling, I began to relax; and when I saw my mother, I almost felt happy again.

The village elders had come to our house. The others in the crowd asked me what was going on; but when I told them that I didn't know any more than they did, they started to disperse.

I then went and sat under a tree. While I was thinking, talking to myself, and waiting for the house to clear, I kept tugging at tufts of grass.

A little girl of about four came towards me. She was smiling but, from what I could gather, she was sad because while she had been feeding her kitten, it had scratched her. She showed me her hand, and after telling her how sorry I was, I caressed and kissed it better.

Feeling sorry for the little girl, I asked if she would like me to tell her a story. This was a big mistake, for, of course, she nodded – what four-year-old wouldn't want to hear a story? She then sat down in front of me and waited for me to start. I kissed her hand again and thought. I had never told a story before in my life, I gave her another kiss on her little hand and said a little prayer. Suddenly, a fly landed on my hand and I smiled for I had thought of a story.

I began, "A long time ago, a fly lived in a faraway village. He was a special fly, for he helped everyone. Whoever had a problem would go and see him, and he was loved and respected by all the flies around.

"One day while he was happily flying around, the good fly heard cries of help from a fly trapped in a spider's web. He tried to get help from other flies to free the poor trapped fly, but no one would help. Feeling very angry, the fly attacked the grinning spider but didn't manage to destroy his web.

"The spider continued to grin. So, this time the good fly grabbed a twig and attacked the spider's web just like a knight with his lance, and destroyed the web. The spider then got very angry.

"The trapped fly was now free and flew away. The helpful fly momentarily turned his back on the spider to see the freed fly's flight. Taking advantage of this, the spider attacked the good fly and pulled off one of his wings. The good fly fell to the ground, quickly realising that he would never be able to fly again.

"None of the other flies came to the good fly's assistance, so, in search of a new life, he left his birthplace on foot. But wherever he went, the flies there refused to help him or even to live near him. He became desperate and even thought about ending it all, but his religion prevented him from going that far. He knew that if he continued praying, one day his wishes would be granted. So, he continued to wander far and wide, looking for a new life.

"The good fly was becoming very tired of walking when one day, he came to a river. He was very thirsty and was just about to get a drink when he heard a lizard crying in pain. In spite of his thirst, he asked what was upsetting the lizard so. The lizard opened her mouth and showed the fly a twig stuck in her tongue. Without thinking, the fly walked into the lizard's mouth and removed the twig. After that, the lizard asked why he'd helped an enemy, laughing that now she would be able to eat him.

"The good fly replied, 'If by eating me, I will be able to do some good for you, I'd be happy to comply,' and closed his eyes! Then the lizard laughed out loud and suddenly turned into a fairy.

"The fairy said to the fly, 'Open your eyes.' The fly opened his eyes and couldn't believe what he saw.

The fairy then said, 'You have helped everyone and acted like a hero; you have always prayed as well; but most importantly, you have never given up and you have continued to help others, so I will reward you.'

"She touched him with her magic wand, giving him two new golden wings. The fly had been rewarded for doing good. He could now fly higher and faster than any other fly, and with no extra effort.

"When the good fly had quickly flown back to his own village, none of the other flies could look him in the eye, for they were all ashamed of themselves. But the good fly went back to living amongst them as if nothing had happened, and continued being as helpful as ever."

When I'd finished my story, the little girl smiled and asked me, "Will the fairy come to me, if I carry on helping others?"

I said, "Yes, the fairy will come to all those who help others." She became even happier, and stood up excitedly and ran towards her house.

I was amazed, but not because of her joy; because of my ability to tell a story.

While I was lost in thought, I noticed my father's shadow loom above me, so I stood up. He ruffled my hair and sat down under the tree. I joined him. He then told me that my sick aunt who lived abroad had died, but no one was allowed to go to her funeral, not even her close family; the state was confiscating their passports.

I had no words to console my father, who was smiling but had tears in his eyes. When they started to flow freely, he left me.

Following my friend's instructions, the next day before sunrise, I left the house without disturbing my parents. Taking careful note of my surroundings, I made my way to the tunnel. The landscape around me was spectacular in the early morning light; I was totally mesmerised by it and couldn't think of anything else. The sound of the leaves underfoot and the birdsong, including baby crows calling to their mothers, had such an effect on me that even if my life had been taken at that moment, I'd have wished my soul to remain there.

Before I had drunk my fill of this beauty, I found myself in front of the tunnel entrance and spotted

Christian. I was so excited to see him that I started jumping up and down. I was just about to let out a joyful whoop when he stopped me with a movement of his hand. I then realised where I was and walked quietly towards him.

My friend whispered that his father had put guards around the area and if they saw us, nothing that his mother had envisioned would become reality; and all his efforts would have been in vain. From now on, we had to whisper to each other. I breathed that I couldn't live without his friendship.

As we approached the tunnel entrance, Christian said, "Listen." So I listened: the sound of dripping water was like heavenly music to my ears. I had never before heard such a sound – and never did again. I was so impressed that it felt like dancing on clouds.

Nonetheless, after a while, the beautiful sound ceased. My friend pointed at the sky, whispering that since it had become lighter, the music had stopped.

Christian entered the tunnel and I followed him. To enable me to see better, he handed me a torch. I was surprised by what I saw inside: there were two big backpacks, a long thick rope, and a huge can, the last of which intrigued me the most. When I asked what was inside it, he said that it was goose fat. And when I asked why all of these things had been stored in the tunnel, his only reply was, "I did what my mother asked me to do, and I will continue to do so."

I was very surprised by what I saw, even if there wasn't a lot to see. When we felt the damp cold seeping into our bones, I switched the torch off, put it in one of the backpacks, and we went outside. It was a chilly morning, but the wind still felt warm on my face compared to the tunnel, which was so cold.

I wanted to tell Christian what my father had told me, but he wouldn't let me. He asked me to concentrate on one thing only, otherwise we wouldn't succeed. He said that I must listen to him and do what I was told, regardless of what was going on around us. He repeated that I should run and take cold showers.

My friend then hugged me and told me to run home keeping a good look out for danger. As soon as he said this, I took off, but after a while, I turned back to look at him. He had covered the tunnel entrance with branches and twigs, and was praying. I was very sad for him. I thought never in my life had I loved anyone more than I loved him, and I never would.

On my way home, I kept a good look out just as Christian had instructed. When I saw my house, I was frightened because there was a car in front of it and several men standing there with dogs. The dogs were Alsatians. The men had a malicious look in their eyes. Confused and perspiring, I walked towards them.

One of the men saw the sweat running down my face and turned to his friend saying, "The little Jew's stinking sweat makes me feel sick," and he spat on my shoes.

Grimacing as I continued to walk slowly towards my house, the other one spat at me. I remained calm and approached them still smiling. I wanted to say something but I changed my mind. I remembered that Christian had told me to focus on the one important thing and forget everything else. For a second, I stood there staring into their faces.

Then I turned my back on them and carried on walking slowly towards the house wondering why they had said such a thing and why they had spat at me. I couldn't for the life of me understand what made them hate us. In the past, we Jewish children had played together with German Christian children; we used to get on well with each other. I couldn't make any sense of this present hatred.

While I was thinking that perhaps this present climate would pass, I came to our back garden and face to face with Christian's father. I was shocked and amazed at the same time, and went pale seeing him sitting and chatting with my father. My father saw me and called me over. He told me that my friend's father had returned the rucksack I had left on the train.

I was eager to find out how my bag had ended up in his hands, but I didn't dare ask. Immediately, I started to rummage in it for the stone Christian had given me, but it wasn't there. It had been lost, or he had taken it; I had no idea but I suspected the latter. I put the rucksack on the ground and went to sit on my father's lap.

Christian's father tried to hide his feelings of hatred towards us but he couldn't because he was surrounded by orchids. There were even more of them now than before. When my father started to talk about them, the other man stood up. He was furious; he cut my father's words dead and sidestepped the orchids. His face went from pale to red. My father stood up as well and went over to the other man smiling at him.

It seemed that my friend's father couldn't bear that smile, as he said, "I shall never understand for as long as I live why people love these disgusting flowers. They make me feel sick; and, if I could, I would destroy them all.

"You will never reach your goal if you do not find something to hate," he added.

"If I gave you the choice of two places to live, one full of sunshine and the other as dark as a dungeon, which one would you choose?"

Smiling, my father moved closer to him and replied, "My father taught me to love and appreciate everything. Even if some things are disgusting to some people, everything, he said, is part of Creation.

"*I* do not think God has ever created a disgusting thing; but when people themselves become disgusted, they see even beautiful things as disgusting because of the situation they are or have been in.

"Coming back to your question, if a person lives in the light but cannot appreciate it, would he suggest that another should choose such a place? You already have a light shining within you. Do not try to turn that light off; let it shine on others.

"However, I will not refuse your invitation to dinner and I will join you with some of my neighbours; I will be proud to do so."

I nearly cried as my father ended his sentence. And I froze from the look Christian's father gave me. He didn't try to hide his feelings anymore. His eyes were bloodshot and he bit his lower lip. Suddenly, without saying another word, he turned his back on us and walked away. Soon afterwards, we heard the sound of his car moving off.

As soon as Christian's father had gone, my father asked me to leave him. I was about to go but changed my mind. I held on to his jacket; I didn't want to let him go. Smiling, he crouched down in front of me. He told me that he knew what I was feeling, and even what I was thinking, but it was too late. He ruffled my hair and stood up.

Again, my father asked me to leave and again, I held clutched his jacket. Then he grabbed me by the collar and marched me to the centre of the village. He stood me on a large rock by the roadside and said, "Come on, let us tell these people what you and I know."

His actions surprised me; he had actually read my thoughts. He couldn't get all the villagers to come over, but some of them approached us to see what we were doing. They were curious to find out what I was going to say to them, so they gathered around me. I started trembling. Luckily, my father came to my rescue and gave me courage by smiling and ruffling my hair.

Then I told everyone to leave the village as soon as they could because a terrible calamity was about to fall upon them. As soon as they heard these words, they started to laugh and mock me, asking if I was the new prophet. Without waiting to hear any more, they drifted away. I hung my head and remained standing on the stone.

My father sat down beside me. He said, "For centuries, our people have treated their prophets in the same way as they treated you today; but the true prophet does not give up. As you are not a prophet, do not repeat this mistake. Regardless of what happens to others, try to save yourself.

"Perhaps His intention is to punish our people in order to change them. Perhaps He will bring them together so they have greater strength for the future. I do not know." Then my father walked home.

Chapter 17

One afternoon, I saw my father dressed in his best clothes and I guessed rightly that he was going to dinner at Christian's father's house. When I put my diary down, he shook his head, indicating that I couldn't go with him. I went on my knees and begged, but he wouldn't change his mind. However, when I started crying, my mother, who was ill in bed, intervened and my father finally agreed. I sprang up and went to get changed. My father didn't like what I'd put on, so he helped me choose some clothes that were better suited to such an occasion.

As we were leaving, I smiled at my mother, who smiled back and then shut her eyes. I was excited and worried at the same time; but I couldn't quite put my finger on the nature of my disquiet.

As soon as we stepped out of the house, some of my father's close friends who were coming too joined us. When they saw me, they were about to say something to my father, but he stopped them by saying, "He knows the way there."

I was so happy with the prospect of seeing Christian again that I started to sing a Jewish song that my father liked, and he lifted me up and sat me on his shoulders. Yet, the real reason I was singing was to stop myself from being frightened into doing something silly. I could see from the way my father looked at me that he understood my motives and approved.

Still singing, we arrived at my friend's house. But our joy soon turned to fear, for the grounds were in complete darkness and we heard dogs growling about the premises. My father started praying quietly, but I could only distinguish the last part, where he asked for us to be saved now as Jews had previously been saved from their past enemies. When he had finished his prayer, my father put me down.

Before we could ring the bell, one of the maids opened the door. We were led into a lobby and asked to sit down. My father continued to pray; he had even forgotten my presence. The rest of our party exclaimed at the beauty of the house.

Christian's father soon joined us. He was smiling, but the expression on my father's face was different, as if to say, "My end has come."

Announcing that he wanted to introduce us to his friends, Christian's father led the way into the drawing room. As he walked next to me, I could smell alcohol on his breath and realised why he was smiling: he was drunk. He had taken an interest in our friends and forgotten all about my father. As for me, the only one who acknowledged my presence at all was my father.

Taking advantage of my apparent invisibility, I started to wander about the house looking for Christian. I soon came to a big room with beautiful paintings on the walls. As I was standing admiring them, I heard a door opening behind me. When I turned round, I was bewildered to see two soldiers with machine guns standing there. They too were surprised and hastily shut the door.

Guessing what was going to happen, I ran out of the room with tears in my eyes screaming for my father. I didn't pray, for at that moment, I had forgotten the very existence of God. Both my father and Christian had told me never to do that, even in the most difficult situations, and yet, when tested, I had failed.

I was still crying when I felt a hand around my neck. It was Christian's father. Smiling slightly, he told me that he wanted to tell me a story. Because I didn't want to hear anything from his mouth, I attempted to escape, but he gripped my neck more tightly and took me outside to sit on the steps. I had no choice but to stop crying and listen to his story.

He began, "Some sheep and their lambs lived happily together in a village. One day, one of the lambs saw a field mouse creeping slowly along. As it was the first time the lamb had ever seen such a creature, he decided to follow it. Realising that it was being pursued, the field mouse began to run and quickly reached the forest, where it disappeared under some fallen leaves.

"Once alone, the lamb noticed that he was far away from the flock. Although he was frightened, he was mesmerised by the beauty around him and went further into the forest.

"Suddenly, the lamb came face to face with a terrible scene. There were countless wolves in front of him, who were deep in discussion. Luckily, they were so engrossed in their scheming that they didn't see the lamb, who in spite of his terror, hid behind a tree and listened to the wolves' plot. They were discussing how to kill all the sheep and lambs in his flock.

"The lamb was very frightened and quietly ran away. The wolves saw him then but knew that no sheep would believe a lamb and carried on discussing their plan.

"The wolves were right: when the lamb told the sheep everything, no one believed him, not even the other lambs; even his own mother disbelieved him. So, instead of getting together and planning how to escape from the wolves, they continued grazing peacefully, each on his own plot of land.

"Realising that he was on his own, the lamb had started to think of ways in which he could save himself, when he saw the wolves coming. The rest of the flock saw the wolves too, but the sheep became so confused that they just ran round and round in the field. The wolves ceased their opportunity to kill them all.

"Finally, the wolves came to the little lamb. The leader of the pack, who was accompanied by his son, said to him: 'You are very young, but you acted well. If your friends had listened to you, they would still be alive now. You were brave and you wanted to warn them, but your words were not enough to convince them.

"'There is a secret to knowing how to make others believe your words, and I know that secret. I could teach it to you, but it is too late now. I have promised you to my son and I never break my promises.'

"His son licked his lips and, his mouth watering, killed the lamb."

I knew what message Christian's father intended to convey to me with his story. Even if I'd been stupid, I'd have understood what he wanted to tell me; but I had no desire or time to think about how he was going to achieve his goal. Then we both sensed my friend's presence behind us. Sneering at me, his father let go of my neck.

I looked at Christian's father and the solemn expression on his face froze me, so I remained rooted to the spot. He ruffled his son's hair and told him to look after me, and left with a sour expression on his face. Smiling, my friend lifted his head up and closed his eyes. He was happy because his father had shown him some affection.

Yet, it seemed that the more his father disliked him, the more Christian loved him. Still fearful, I stood up and went over to my friend. When I saw his father wiping the hand with which he had ruffled his son's hair with a handkerchief and handing it disdainfully to a servant, I realised just how much he hated him.

Christian told me that he had seen what his father had done and that it wasn't the first time. He kept his eyes shut and told me to keep smiling at his father, and let him know when the other had gone.

Before long, my friend's father went back into the house closing the door behind him. When I reported this to him, he asked me to stand up and take his hand. He then put something in it and told me not to take any notice of what I had just heard; I would soon be able to make sense of it all, but we had no time to talk now.

We walked round the house, coming to a halt at the door to a cellar. I looked at my hand to see what Christian had given me and saw that it was some dried meat. He said that we had no time to lose and couldn't afford to make any mistakes, and I should just follow him.

My friend unlocked the cellar door and gripped my hand tightly. As there was insufficient light from the narrow windows and my eyes had had no time to adjust to the semidarkness, I couldn't see anything. But Christian told me exactly where to put one foot and then the other. In this fashion, we began our decent. I counted all the stairs; we stopped at stair thirty-four, and then he opened another door. Just then, I heard growling and grabbed his hand even tighter, which made him laugh.

I was just about to turn my back on the dogs and run away, when my friend stopped me, saying that this would make them attack. It was true that all the dogs were ready to pounce, all eyes on me. Smiling, Christian asked me to get closer to him. So I put on a big smile for him and the dogs and drew nearer to my friend. Seeing me walk among them calmed the animals down.

Christian asked me to break the meat and give it to the dogs so that they would get used my scent. I had no other choice but to heed his words. As I distributed the meat, they licked my hands and began to make different noises. Being slobbered over by dogs was one of the things I hated most; my friend knew this, so he kept on grinning.

After a while, I had no more meat left; so I lifted both arms up in the air, which was a big mistake. All the dogs got to their feet and started growling at me. Both Christian and I were very frightened. He then asked me to slowly lower my arms and stroke the dogs, and not to lift them up again. His face had gone pale. As I gradually put my arms down, he asked me to sit on the ground and fondle the dogs as if they were babies.

After that, the animals calmed down and their licking didn't disgust me so much anymore. Once they were completely passive, I returned to the door, where my friend joined me. He told me to keep smiling and walk away without turning my back on the dogs, as if I were taking my leave of a king. When I had reached the second stair, he asked me to wait for him. I sighed and continued to follow his instructions.

As I waited for Christian, he told me that my face had looked so funny. I waved my hand as a joke but as soon as I did that, the dogs became wary again. Luckily, he managed to quickly calm them down, and then he joined me without turning his back on them.

Once through the door, my friend quickly shut it behind us, warning me not to flirt unnecessarily with danger. We then climbed back up the cellar stairs. After closing the other door as well, he finally took a deep breath and looked at me. He asked me to smile again, the way I had looked at the dogs, and started to laugh, saying he had never seen such a face that had both fear and a comical expression on it at the same time. That made me laugh too, so much so that we both got stitches and had to stop. We went up to a tree and sat down.

Christian took something out of his pocket and showed it to me. It was a picture of his mother. He said, "Long ago, my mother and I sat under this very tree. It was my birthday. She gave me this photo and told me that the day I laughed until I had stitches would be the day I must separate myself from this picture." He then gave it to me.

My friend stopped abruptly: there was a lot of noise coming from the house. Telling me to go and sit on the fifth step opposite to the living room and wait there no matter what happened, he hurried towards the house.

I started to run as I tried to put the little photo in my pocket without creasing it. I managed that, but forgot I was supposed to wait on the fifth cellar step; I must have slumped down somewhere further up, for I was able to see what was going on. Although I could only make out a little, what I did see made me cry.

In the living room, one of Christian's father's friends poured a bottle of wine over my father's head; that set me off crying and I wanted to go in and do something, but I remembered what my friend had told me: I wasn't to move – so I didn't. Christian's father and his friends continued to laugh and drink as they abused my father. Then there was more noise.

Suddenly, I heard Christian ordering me to stand up. I turned my head towards him as he shouted, "Stand up you fool, you filthy Jew!"

That put a stop to the commotion in the house; all the doors opened and everyone looked out. My friend then kicked me so hard in the chest that I flew down the rest of the steps. I then realised why he had told me to sit on the fifth one. As it was, if he hadn't kicked me so hard, I could have landed on one of them and broken my back. The pain I was in still made it hard to breathe.

When I managed to look at Christian, I saw that he was wearing a soldier's uniform. Then he came and planted his foot on my neck, making it even harder to inhale. After repeating that I was a filthy Jew, he took his boot away, grabbed me by my hair, and dragged me up the steps into the living room, where I sprawled on the floor. All I could do was gasp for air.

I saw my father, head held high, trying not to look at me. His lips were moving; I knew he was praying. When I'd got my breath back, I managed to get to my knees and look at Christian. He spat in my face, and took his father's revolver and put it to my head. At that point, everything swam before me and I closed my eyes.

Then I heard my friend say, "Father, I'm waiting for your command to blow this filthy Jew's brains out."

When I opened my eyes, Christian spat in my face again. His father crouched down beside me and grinned. He then asked his son if he was truly ready to carry out his order.

My friend said, "Give me the command and you will see; but I have such lovely memories of this house that it would be a shame to sully them with Jewish blood. However, if these are your orders I will carry them out."

Evidently unconvinced by his son's bravado, Christian's father continued, "What about all the time you've spent in his company?"

To which my friend replied smiling, "Wasn't it you who told me that in order to know my enemy, I must first befriend him?"

Christian's father continued to regard his son, waiting for him to shed some tears. Yet, my friend looked so much in control of himself that he even managed to scare me. Finally, his father seemed to be convinced and took the revolver away.

Christian then grabbed me and threw me out into the garden. After spitting at me again, he re-entered the house. While I was cleaning myself up, the soldiers threw my father and our neighbours out as well. Advising us to get lost fast if we knew what was good for us, they left.

My father took my hand and we hurried home. He continually caressed my head as we ran, but I surprised him by not crying. We both knew that it was our very last night together; weeping wouldn't have changed anything. My father then started to sing a song about Moses that his father had composed. It went like this:

To God, to pray,
Moses climbed a mountaintop one day,
On a branch a heartbroken raven stood bitterly
sobbing,
For the poor raven Moses was concerned,
The raven's trouble he could not discern,
What troubles you my little bird? Moses said,
The little raven came to Moses when his kind voice he
heard,
From the little raven to Moses a painful answer came,
My son died but to God thanks and praises I gave,
My body they stoned I bore the pain,
My nest they destroyed and I did not complain,
When they threw me out from the country of my birth,
The bitterness came,
The pain and the hurt

Yet, the song *did* bring tears to my father's eyes. He took me in his arms and kissed my hands as I wiped his cheeks. I had momentarily forgotten about Christian. Then I suddenly remembered something he had said months ago about me becoming separated from my father. As I clung to him, I started crying, but he said that this was the way things were fated to be.

At that moment, we heard the dogs barking. Terrified, we quickened our pace. We had no problem running but some of our older neighbours couldn't flee so fast.

My father told them, "We know what is awaiting us tonight. Let us not be fearful of the people who hate us, who are now running after us. Like us, they too are people with lives and souls. Those who break our bodies cannot break our souls, which will lead to our reincarnation one day.

"Recall your best memories. Whether you live one day or a thousand, whether you are rich or poor, the end is the same. Everyone makes mistakes, those who kill and those who are killed as well.

"He who dies is spared from making more mistakes. He who kills can never undo his mistake and cannot turn the clock back; thus, he will continue to make mistakes. Let us rid ourselves of fear and be happy instead. Let us remember Moses and prepare to meet him."

Perhaps my father should have tried to give them hope instead of reminding them of their forthcoming death. However, this would have been deceitful and he hated lies. If someone told him that he had a terminal illness, my father would immediately say to him, "We all must die one day."

After they had listened to my father, everyone wandered home like sheep without a shepherd, and we were left alone. My father stroked his chin, shook his head, and carried on walking with me still in his arms. Smiling and ruffling my hair, he didn't hurry in spite of the dogs barking nearby.

As I regarded him, I knew what he was thinking and I wept, for I knew that every step forward brought us closer to our final separation. When I caressed his face, he kissed my hand, and finally, he could no longer keep his tears back. I clung to his neck, inhaling and memorising his scent. I knew that as soon as we got home, after a short talk with my mother, I would have to go to the tunnel entrance, where I had arranged to meet Christian.

I couldn't understand why, after we had lived for so long happily side by side, these people now wanted to kill us. And why did God allow such a thing? We all lived according to His wishes. I wanted to stop believing, but I couldn't. I tried many times to lose my faith, but I just couldn't.

The closer we got to the house, the more I clung to my father. I didn't want to be separated from him. As he opened the door, I started howling. We knelt down next to my mother and I hugged her. She didn't move. She looked and felt like death, her body was so cold. Then I realised that she *was* dead. I began screaming and crying even harder. My father held my hands and prayed.

I have never forgotten his last prayer; often when I pray, his words ring in my ears:

"I have faith in Thee. I rely on Thee. I know Thou never lies and always rewards those who follow Thee. Thou never turns down those who pray to Thee in unshakable faith. I have obeyed Thee to the best of my ability all my life. All that I know I have taught my son. Thy powers are enough for us all.

"In Thy presence, I will now share the secret that I have kept from my son. As Thou knowest, his mother suffered from brain cancer for a long time. Whenever she was in extreme pain, she went to the neighbours to scream because she didn't want her son to find out and be sad. For a long time, I prayed to Thee that she would die at an appropriate moment. As I have discovered her dead tonight, I realise that Thou hast granted my prayers.

"In the same way that I prayed for her timely death, I now pray that my son might be spared. Thou did not give us any other children; if Thou takest my son, there will not be anyone left in our family to remember us or pray for us. Please have mercy on my son and help him to have a family of his own so that our line may continue to pray to Thee and become an unbreakable chain.

"Please teach my son, who will grow up motherless and fatherless, to love all people. And please help him not to hate anyone. I am begging you again, spare my son. Help him to grow up with those people who can teach him love for Thee and faith in Thee.

"And now I am entrusting my son unto Thy hands. Thou knowest the best way to care for my son. Before I entrust my own soul to Thee, I beg Thee to grant me this prayer."

Through my father's prayer, I learnt that my mother had died from cancer; but I was happy that I knew the truth. I wasn't disturbed by her corpse, although it was a terrible shock to find her like that. I was more worried about being separated from my father, who was still alive. As I drove myself frantic with these thoughts, he regarded me steadily.

Suddenly, I left my mother's side and went to hug my father. I wept again. He caressed my head and began the lullaby he used to sing to me when I was very small. Although he wasn't crying, I could feel his hands trembling. Before he could finish the lullaby, we heard the dogs barking as if they were just behind the door.

My father didn't stop singing but, still holding me, he stood up and went calmly to the window. I could see the dogs' eyes shining in the dark. He smiled, crossed to the wall, and started rolling up the carpet; then I knew that our final moments together had come. As he continued to roll, we could hear neighbours screaming, dogs barking, and the sound of gunshots. When he opened the trapdoor leading to the passage below our house, I clung to him even tighter; I didn't want to leave him behind.

"Remember my prayer," he whispered.

I let go of my father, and was just about to leave when I looked at my mother and ran to kiss her. I kissed my father and then plunged through the inky gap. Before closing the trapdoor, he smiled, "Take your father's riches with you," and gave me a little bag from his pocket. After reminding me that I only had fifteen minutes of air in the passage so I must hurry, and that he loved me very much, he closed the door. This was the last time I saw him.

I found myself in complete darkness and unable to see anything, but I knew the passage would lead to the stables. I was just about to start off, when I heard him moving the carpet again. I stood still hoping to see him descending, but I was disappointed, for he just threw my diary down and then replaced the carpet. Clutching my diary and quietly weeping, I hurried along the passage.

Before long, I emerged in the stables. When I looked out at my village, I couldn't recognise the scene. I saw soldiers enter my house and heard gunshots. I was in floods of tears; I knew they were firing at my father. I made out the sound of Christian's father laughing. When a soldier came out of my house and whispered something in his ear, he went totally mad and started shooting in the air with his automatic.

I had no desire to stay and see him kill my people. I had seen the soldiers kill and kill, and had heard the constant screams of children: that was enough for me. I knew the time had come to run to the tunnel. All I wanted was to forget about crying and do my best to bring peace to my father's soul. As I started to run, I remembered his prayer. It felt like angels were helping me; I was flying, flying with angels, without getting tired.

* * *

As I left the village behind, the air became still and silent. The sky was full of stars. When I saw the one that shone the brightest, I remembered Christian. As I ran and gazed at the stars, I thought I could hear my friend's voice.

In no time at all, I found myself at the entrance to the tunnel. I entered. Christian was there. I crouched down trying to get my breathing under control. He told me that he knew of all that had happened. But now, I had to quickly undress and spread goose fat on my body. He also told me that we had very little time because his father would soon locate the tunnel with his dogs.

I went up closer to my friend and asked him if his father had given the order, whether he would he have shot me? "Yes," he replied, "I would have killed my father first, then you, and finally myself."

I started to undress. The smell of goose fat was so overwhelming that I could hardly breathe. I vomited, holding my nose as I retched. Christian told me that he was very sorry to see me in such a state, but I had to put the goose fat on or else I wouldn't live for long; and even if I did, I would very quickly fall ill and die anyway. Then he started to spread the goose fat on my back. Knowing I had no choice, I reluctantly began to help him.

Next, my friend produced a piece of plastic sheeting and told me to wrap it around myself. He said that it would make running a bit harder, but we had no alternative. I wound the plastic around my body and got dressed. It was difficult to do the simplest thing, as I felt so heavy; but our clumsy movements didn't make us laugh.

Once I was fully dressed, Christian handed me a rucksack but I couldn't put it on by myself, so I asked for a hand. Finally laughing a little, he helped me on with it and then I returned the favour. But I couldn't bring myself to smile; all I could think of was my parents. My friend enquired where my diary was and wrapped that up in plastic as well before stowing it in my rucksack.

Christian then asked me to give him everything I had in my pockets, so I handed him the little bag my father had entrusted to me; I had nothing else. He looked inside and then hiding it carefully under some stones, told me to come and get it after some years. I asked him what was inside the bag. He was surprised that I didn't know. He said that the contents of the bag were very valuable; but now we had to get out of there and it was in my best interest not to know everything all at once.

When we were finally ready to move on, we took a last look around the tunnel entrance. It was then that we heard the dogs barking. This was quickly followed by my friend's father's voice. Christian grabbed my hand, sat me down, and handed me some dried meat. He then whispered into my ear that whatever his father did, I wasn't to react or move. He also breathed that I mustn't budge unless he told me to. Hand in hand, we stared at the entrance and waited.

Before long, we heard my friend's father's raised voice and laughter much closer now. He stopped at the tunnel entrance and ordered his men to go in. Some made unsuccessful attempts. He then ordered one of them to remove his kitbag and try again. He still couldn't manage; so he told the others to push him in.

As the soldiers huffed and puffed in their efforts to squeeze their comrade through the narrow entrance, he shouted in pain, which made us laugh. Although we were being as quiet as could be, Christian's father heard us and told his men to pull the other out; but he was by now stuck and screaming in agony. By the time they had finally managed to extract him, we were doubled up with laughter, which only increased his father's anger.

My friend's father snapped, "I always thought you were as smart as me, but as innocent as your mother. I was wrong, for you are not only as smart but also as cunning as me.

"I have been an unbeliever for years, but now I am tempted to convert. Shall I tell you why? Because I have started to believe in the devil; for you have managed to fool me. When you asked me to order you to kill the filthy Jew, you did not shed a tear. So I asked myself what you would have done had I ordered you to shoot. I will tell you: you would have shot me, and then you would have shot the Jew, and finally yourself; am I right?

"All these things convince me of the existence of the devil, but not in the existence of God; for if He did exist, He would have helped me; not one Jew would have escaped from the village.

"You know I have always hated you, but now I am disgusted by you as well. I am ashamed to have you as a son for the same reasons I was ashamed to have your mother as my wife.

"Now you are quiet in there; you are probably listening to everything I have to say. You think you are safe because you are smart but my dogs can smell you. I know that nothing I say can make you surrender, but my dogs cannot wait to go in and bring both your corpses out." Then he released two Alsatians.

I was shivering with terror. Christian told me to let them sniff me and remain calm. The dogs came in barking. As they approached, they stopped and smelt us. I gave them the meat but instead of taking it, they went over to my friend. After smelling him, they started licking his face. Then they came back and began to lick my face; I liked them licking my face.

Outside, Christian's father realised that the dogs had remained calm and went berserk. He angrily called them and they ran out. My friend took my hand and asked me to stand up, so I did. We saw his father shouting at the dogs before shooting both of them.

Christian shouted, "Run!" So I sprinted. Then he told me to turn to the right and I did. As soon as his father saw us running, he ordered the soldiers to shoot but we were already out of sight.

My friend then asked me to lie down, which, again, I did, lodging my head between two stones. There was a lot of noise when the bullets hit the inside of the tunnel and ricocheted all around the place. If we hadn't been lying flat we would have been hit and killed. They kept on shooting into the tunnel for a long time, but were finally ordered to stop. Christian threw a big stone at his father, which elicited a grim laugh.

My friend's father shouted, "You are telling me that you are alive. Okay, fine, but this tunnel has an exit. You can run but I will find that exit and wait for you there; and I bet it is not as narrow as the entrance.

"Go on, you run with your faith and I will find you with my intelligence! We will see who wins in the end

– you and your religion, or me and my intelligence – we shall see. Go on; run so that you do not waste my time!"

When Christian's father ordered his men to move, my friend rummaged in the bottom of my rucksack, and got my torch out and gave it to me. Then he told me to get going fast or his father might get there before us. So I started to run, but the plastic sheeting made it hard. It was very cold and dark; all we could hear was our footfalls.

I have no idea how long we ran, but when breathing became difficult, I knew that it had been for a long, long time; even my friend was having trouble. Apart from that, all I was aware of was the cold and the all-enveloping smell of goose fat.

I turned my head to see what Christian was doing but he suddenly grabbed my hand, really scaring me, and I started sobbing. He nodded as if to show me something in front of him. I shone my torch on the ground and could hardly believe what I saw. It was water; we'd come to the end of the tunnel. He saw the terror on my face, but before I could say anything, he smiled and reassured me that this wasn't the end. He then asked me to find the long thick rope he had in his rucksack.

I wanted to see if the water was cold but my friend wouldn't let me. "If you put your hand in this water, you'll never be able to dive in." he said, "Just when you need to," he added.

I was still contemplating the water uneasily when Christian turned his back so that I could get the rope. When I'd given it to him, he told me that he'd go first: he would tie the rope around his waist and swim to the other side with it; then I had to tie the other end around my own waist and plunge into the water after him. Finally, I was supposed to follow the rope to the other side.

My friend smiled, took a deep breath, and dived in. At that moment, I was filled with anxiety and started to cry, but the tears froze on my face. As soon as I'd tied the rope around my middle, he gave a pull on it. I signalled that I was ready by giving a few tugs in return. Then I took a deep breath. Suddenly, I remembered what he'd said about swimming under water for a couple of minutes. I took an even deeper breath and dived in.

The water was so cold that I fainted. As I sunk into its icy depths, I saw a vision of my parents: they both had sad expressions on their faces. I opened my mouth to call, "Father!" But as soon as I did, I got a mouthful of water and came round. At that instant, I felt a pull on the rope so I started to swim.

When I no longer had any air left in my lungs, I burst to the surface and was overjoyed to find that I'd come up right next to Christian.

He started to cry, for he thought I'd drowned. He then hugged me and helped me out of the water. He told me that I could now remove the plastic sheeting, which I happily did; I thought I might finally get rid of the stench of goose fat. But I was mistaken: in spite of all my efforts to wipe the fat off my body, the smell lingered, although, fortunately, it wasn't as strong.

Once I'd changed into dry clothes, my friend said, "Each step you take will bring you closer to your future. The real run starts here, for I knew how to get this far, but I don't know what lies ahead of us. All I do know is that your freedom starts here. I also know that you'll never forget this run."

At the time, I didn't realise – and because of that, I still believe that I'm a bit stupid – but Christian used the singular: "*your* future" rather than "our future;" "*your* freedom" and not "our freedom." Finally, he said, "*You* will never forget."

Many years later, I found the answers to all my questions from that time, but in that tunnel, I wished that I had them there and then. However, had I managed to get the answers at the time, perhaps I would've taken my own life, for I didn't want to live without Christian. As my father always said, "When you think of something you want for yourself, God always provides better than your own desire."

Chapter 18

I was highly agitated. I removed the torch from my rucksack, and was just about to put it back on, when Christian said that I didn't need it anymore. "Anyway," he added, "both rucksacks are now sodden and heavy."

All we needed, my friend said, were the torches, the rope, and some dried meat; anything that would have slowed us down had to be discarded. The only personal possessions I kept were my diary and Christian's mother's photo. I looked at him and told him I was ready.

We set off at a steady jog. After a few steps, I was just about to ask something, when my friend said, "Talking wastes energy," and that we had to concentrate on our running. So I stopped speaking, but I couldn't stop thinking. I had mixed memories of the tunnel, some good and others bad, and I didn't know which to dwell on. I was confused. Should I think about my unknown future, just putting one foot in front of the other, the freezing tunnel, or something else entirely? But our laboured breathing constantly reminded me of the bad days.

Lost in thought, I slipped and fell heavily on the little stones underfoot. When my head hit them, I saw stars. Christian was also on the ground for he had slipped too. But he didn't make a sound and neither did he move. Quickly, I tried to get to my feet, but I slipped again, badly punishing the bruise I already had on my head. This time, I saw all the planets as well as stars, and let out a loud scream.

I then felt my friend's hand on my head and held on to his arm. This time, he slipped again and it was he who yelled and fell to the ground. He was in a lot of pain, but I didn't know how to help him. My head throbbing, I bent down to pick up the torch and saw that he was holding his arm. When I looked at it, I wished I had never been born: his arm was blue and bleeding profusely.

While I was waiting for Christian's pain to ease, he said, "We must run; I don't want us to die of cold." We moved around a bit but we couldn't stand up. Crawling like babies, we succeeded in crossing the slippery patch, but we had lost a lot of time, which meant that his father was gaining on us.

As soon as we managed to stand up, I tore some material from my shirtsleeve and bandaged my friend's arm; I'd seen my mother do this to a cat when it had injured its leg. I wept as I was doing this because he was in a lot of pain. We were just about to set off again, when he took a handkerchief from his pocket and gave it to me to wipe away the blood running from my head. Then we started to run again.

As we ran, all I could think of was the pain; we couldn't even go very fast because of our injuries. But suddenly, we were faced with a scene that stopped us altogether. We forgot our cuts and bruises and just stared. Christian looked extremely frightened.

Thinking that our end had come, I pointed at the sight and asked him if he had any idea what was going on.

My friend laughed and said, "I don't but God does; we'll ask Him. I've told you several times to ask Him whenever you find yourself in difficulty, but you've never got used to it, have you? He's brought us all the way here; do you think He'll abandon us now?" Christian went on his knees. I knelt too and listened to his prayer.

In front of us was a large open space with eight passages leading off it. It was enough to frighten anyone and make him forget to pray, as I had. But Christian didn't; his mother had taught him too well for that.

My friend's prayer was short and simple: "Thou knowest our need. When we open our eyes, please show us the right path. We love you with all our hearts.

Amen. "When we opened our eyes, we started to laugh because we were immediately shown the right way: there was a squirrel staring at us from the entrance to the fifth passage. Happily, we ran to it. But when we got there, I realised that what we had taken for a squirrel was actually a stone. When I pointed this out to my friend, he smiled and patted my head.

We resumed running, even though I was frightened of slipping and falling again. Christian was very happy and only occasionally groaned from the pain of his injured arm. I had no idea how far we had come or whether it was night or day outside.

I didn't even think about my parents; all I could think of was our freedom and the fact that we would surely now have the chance to live out our lives. Of course, I was daydreaming; I couldn't or wouldn't see the reality of the situation. Perhaps this was for the best; the not knowing actually prolonged my life. Even years later, I still didn't want to know. Knowing made me grow old much quicker.

My friend was in such pain that he could finally no longer run and asked me to slow to a fast walk instead. But he wouldn't let me help. Every time I looked, my heart bled for him.

Suddenly, I felt what seemed to be a creature moving on the back of my neck and stood still. I asked Christian to have a look. I was scared and could see that he was too. As he examined my neck, he grew pale and asked for the handkerchief he'd given me. He tied it round my head to stop the bleeding, remarking that I should be relieved to learn that there wasn't a creature there. I breathed more easily again.

Smiling, my friend started off again but before I could join him, he stopped. I was instantly fearful once more, for I could see the end of the tunnel. That should have made me happy, for a few steps ahead of us there was a way out; but stones blocked it and we couldn't see any light.

Without realising it, I knelt down to pray like a Christian. This made my friend laugh: "Why don't you pray like a Jew, I'm the one who's a Christian not you. You should pray the way your father taught you.

"I know in the past, we've prayed together, but now you're praying on your own so you should pray like a Jew.

"Use your hands and feel if the ground is soft; otherwise, we'll have no air and we'll pass out," he added.

That made me laugh, for given the circumstances, most people would have prayed without worrying if it was like a Christian, or a Buddhist, or anyone else.

I started feeling the ground and found a soft spot of earth before Christian did. I was very excited when I told him that I'd found one but in reply, he hissed urgently, "Don't push anymore; get away!" I started shivering with terror and jumped back.

My friend took a deep breath and asked me if I'd intended to keep pushing. I said, "Of course."

"If you'd come face to face with my father, how would you have greeted him then?" he laughed. "Have you forgotten why I asked you not to rush?"

I said that my father used to tell me that too, but I never learnt to be patient. Using his finger, Christian started making a hole in the spot I'd found. But his finger was too short and the soil was too hard so he didn't get very far. While I was looking around for something to help him with, I felt the little drops at the back of my neck again and, knowing what it was this time, tied the handkerchief more tightly around my head.

I couldn't find anything long and thin enough; there were some big stones but nothing else. Suddenly,

I thought of my diary, which had lots of blank pages at the back of it. I quickly removed its plastic wrapping and was just about to tear some leaves out when Christian again shouted, "Stop!"

My friend gave me such a fright that I dropped the diary and jumped back. He picked it up and, seeing the blank pages, apologised, saying that he didn't know there were leaves in it that I hadn't written on. He then tore some pages out, wrapped the diary up again, and handed it back to me.

"It's you who's always telling me to be patient, but this time, you were the one who rushed in," I muttered.

"Look after your diary as you would value the Torah; it's just as sacred, Christian replied. "You mustn't tear any more pages out of it; I didn't know it had *any* blank pages, and I apologise again," he added.

My friend then took a few leaves of paper and scrolled them tightly together, and, with this improvised tool, managed to enlarge the hole. As soon as the paper hit empty space, he withdrew it and we both saw daylight.

We were frustrated that we had no idea how long we had been running for; it might have been the whole night or longer: we simply didn't know. But it wasn't dark and that disappointed Christian. Sitting down on the ground, he told me that we had to wait for nightfall.

Taking some dried meat, my friend started to eat and I did the same. He said that by sitting and waiting we were giving his father time to catch up. Perhaps he was a long way off yet, but if he was nearby, he'd have no trouble catching us in daylight. That angered Christian.

I wanted to look at my friend's arm, which was blue from his shoulder down. My head was swollen like a balloon and still bleeding a bit although I wasn't in much pain. When I looked across at Christian I saw that he had fallen asleep with a piece of meat in his mouth. In spite of my resistance, I fell asleep too.

I had no idea how long I'd slept, but I woke up with my friend rubbing my back to warm it up. He said that we should leave as soon as possible. I felt dizzy but finally woke up properly when he let some air and rain in.

As we peered through the hole, we saw that it overlooked a precipice. Christian was so agitated that he frightened me; this was the first time I'd seen him in such a hurry.

With the rope in his hand, my friend constantly wandered about the tunnel talking to himself. He repeated over and over that his father would find us. I was desperate to find a place where we could tie the rope.

Having lost all his strength, Christian sat down and started to cry. Then I saw two huge stones at his side. I took the rope from him, tied a knot in one end, and secured it between the two stones. I put lot of smaller stones on top of the knot and then let the rope drop over the precipice; luckily, it was long enough to reach the ground below.

My friend was crying so much that he hadn't noticed what I was doing. I told him to stand up and get ready to lower himself down. I startled him and he was surprised to see what I had done. Then he tested the strength of the rope. I was just about to put my plan into action when he stopped me. He said that he was going first to test it; if it wasn't strong enough, I could retie it. If that were the case, he would have just fallen and been dashed to pieces on the rocks below, but that thought didn't seem to have occurred to him. Would I have survived on my own after that? I couldn't tell.

Although I had doubts about the feasibility of Christian's plan, I gave him all the help I could as began his slow decent. He was only using one arm and screaming in pain. I was silently weeping. I could no longer feel the cold.

Before long, my friend called up to me that he had reached the ground safely and it was now my turn to come down. Without realising, I knelt down and prayed. I suggested to Him that if the rope wasn't strong enough, perhaps His angels could help me. I stood up and looked at the sky, and ended my prayer with a hasty, "I know you will accept prayers in any way offered," and slid down the rope. Perhaps the knot wouldn't be secure enough, but the prayer had enabled me to forget that it might fail.

Finally, I reached the ground and smiled at Christian. He didn't reciprocate; instead, he grabbed my hand and started to run. It was so cold that the raindrops turned to ice on our skin. All I could think of was that at any moment we might come face to face with his father. I was terrified, but I didn't dare mention this to my friend. I was afraid that he would collapse altogether and we wouldn't be able to go any further. Every now and then, I smiled at him but he never returned it. Oblivious to my presence, he just continued to talk to himself, but I could see he was terrified too.

Suddenly, my friend came to a standstill, stopping me as well. We moved forward slowly, and then he asked me if I had heard anything. I strained my ears for the slightest sound but couldn't discern anything. He kept repeating, "Listen, listen." We started running again, but this time not so quickly. We came to the top of a hillock and stopped; we were both shocked at the sight before us. Then we looked at each other and simultaneously exclaimed, "A river!" It was wide and running very fast.

I lifted my head and protested about this obstacle. I knew that it was wrong of me to complain to Him but no other thought came to mind at that time. I had acted exactly like someone who has given up all hope; it is the sceptic who always bemoans his fate when he has no one else to blame for his misfortune. I had done exactly that.

Christian smiled and went to the riverbank, inviting me to join him. He pointed to the forest on the other side and said, "Your freedom starts there."

Again, he said '*your*'.

Then my friend addressed the river: "I do not have a stick as Moses did, but like him, I have my belief and

I have my prayers. Just as the Red Sea was parted to help Moses escape the Pharaoh, He will help us to cross Thee." Then he took my hand.

I rejoiced at hearing Moses' name for my father loved Moses. Then Christian asked me to jump in; so we both jumped, but it wasn't as deep as we'd thought. My friend's plan had been to swim across, but this was thwarted when we found ourselves stuck up to our knees in mud. While wondering what to do next, we couldn't help laughing; events were unfolding thick and fast.

I dared not move, but as the mud was soft, I started to sink deeper anyway, and it was soon impossible to budge at all. We had no idea how to get out. We looked around but couldn't see anything until a smile finally lit Christian's face. He pointed to a tree trunk being swept along in the current and swiftly coming our way.

My friend shouted, "Dive under when the tree reaches us! Wait until it passes a little, then come up and grab it!"

I did as I was told but the branch I took hold of snapped off the trunk, so I immediately transferred my grip to Christian's leg, and was free. We constantly tacked first to the left and then to the right, but gradually advanced towards the far bank.

I realised that what I'd thought was a branch in my hand was actually the tail of a dead cow. My friend clung to the cow's leg screaming in pain because I was hanging on to him. That was too much for him, but if he'd released his grip on the cow we would have doubtless drowned, for we had no strength to swim.

The current carried us a long way. It took the cow to the other side, then Christian let go of the cow, and I let go of him. The bank we'd fetched up on was stony rather than muddy.

Instead of resting a little, my friend insisted that we keep running, but he didn't know which way to go. He slumped down and started to cry.

I spotted a squirrel and told Christian that we should run in the direction that the animal was headed. He looked at me and laughed because I was still holding on to the cow's tail. I let go of it, chuckling as well.

My friend looked at the squirrel and his face shone. We ran towards it but when we got closer, we realised that it was only a piece of wood. He picked it up, and giving it to me, suggested I keep it as a souvenir. Smiling, I was just about to put it in my pocket when he said that he'd been joking.

The rain turned to snow but neither of us could feel the cold. Christian's face suddenly lit up when he saw the forest ahead of us and beyond that, he was certain, Switzerland. He started running as fast as he could and I followed him.

"You see, my mother never lied to me. I'm finally managing to fulfil my destiny," my friend said.

When we were deep inside the forest, we stopped to catch our breath. Christian sat on a tree stump repeating exultantly, "We've done it! We've done it!"

We had a good rest and then began to walk towards the sunlight. But after a few steps, hearing his father's voice, my friend froze. His expression frightened me and I tugged at his sleeve, but he wouldn't budge although I kept gesturing "no" with my head. He quickly explained which way I should go and then turned his back on me.

I started to cry so loudly that Christian's father heard me. "You have saved the Jew haven't you? he laughed. "Well, that is what you think, for I am about to come and get him. The entrance to a forest is not like the entrance to a tunnel."

As we stood listening to his father's voice, my friend implored me to run and cross the border, saying that he'd keep his father occupied, but I refused. Christian then made a move towards his father, but I screamed, "No!" and grabbed his leg so tightly that he couldn't move.

When my friend realised that he couldn't release himself, he crouched down and said that he'd promised his mother that he would save me, but not that he would *go* with me. I kept repeating, "No, no."

However, Christian just patted my head and then began to pray, "I have been true to my word, and now it is your turn to keep the bargain and release my foot, Amen."

The moment my friend had finished his short prayer, I felt a heaviness come over me and I slumped to the ground powerless. He then withdrew his foot.

After kissing the top of my head, he called to his father, "I'm coming!"

No matter how hard I tried, I couldn't move and all my prayers were in vain: Christian's was stronger. When I managed to move my head a little, I could see him approaching his father and my tears flowed even more profusely, although I was prevented from uttering a single word. My friend strode closer and closer to his father, repeating all the while that he loved him.

When Christian emerged from the trees and they came face to face, he extended his arms to his father and began "Fath…"

But the other slapped him so hard that he flew through the air and then slid for some way across the snow before a tree brought him to an abrupt halt. He let out an ear-piercing scream as his injured arm slammed into the wood, yet he immediately raised his head, smiling at his father.

I still couldn't move. I had no choice but to look on impotently. Christian stood up and returned to his father, who made no comment. He then handed his son a book, saying to him, "Here is your mother's diary. It is full of disgusting things, such as how God told her to look after you.

"Why didn't you show this to me before? You were afraid, weren't you? But you left it in my bedroom when you fled. If you had shown it to me earlier, He would have still helped you wouldn't He?

"But why would your God worry about a Jew anyway, and why did He choose your mother to assist him? If He has such powers, why wouldn't He give wings to that Jew?

"You know, if I had not picked her up from the roadside…"

My friend screamed at him to stop, before resuming evenly, "Enough of all this; enough of rebelling; and enough of betraying my mother. The way you behave is no different to the way the devil behaves. My mother was like an innocent child, like an orchid."

Then in spite of his acute pain, Christian grabbed his father's hand and continued, "You know, my dearest father, my mother was born on this day and died on this day too; happy birth- and death-day to my dear mother."

Then my friend pressed something into his father's hand and began to laugh. When the other saw what it was, he became wild, screaming, "An orchid! An orchid! Disgusting flower!" and threw it on the ground, and crushed it. Then he began to pace up and down.

It was the 27th of December: Christian's mother had been born on that day and had also died on that day.

His father began to circle his son with even strides. Wiping his hands on the snow because he had touched an orchid, he remained silent for a time.

My friend closed his eyes and lifted his head towards the sky, which frightened me terribly. I tried my hardest to stand but was still rooted to the spot; all I could do was weep.

His father glanced towards the forest and then back at his son; then he quickly brought his left hand to his waist, withdrew his revolver, and placed it to his son's head.

"It is time for you to join your mother," he said, and pulled the trigger.

As Christian's lifeless body fell on the snow, his blood soon turned it scarlet. I saw a bright star fall from the sky; and the heaviness upon me lifted. I felt as if it was all a dream, but *knew* that I saw the truth. It wasn't a dream; I couldn't believe he'd actually shot his own son, but it was true: my friend was lying dead on the snow. But I couldn't even cry anymore because I didn't want to believe it.

I made an effort to stumble towards Christian's father but I couldn't; it was as if someone was holding me around the neck. I heard his father giving orders to shoot and I heard return gunshots coming from somewhere, and then I fainted. I don't remember anything else.

Chapter 19

When I opened my eyes, I was in hospital. The adults and children around me looked dazed; they were all injured as well. Then I remembered what had happened to Christian and started to cry. The doctors came to try and calm me down but they couldn't. In the end, they gave me something to sedate me and I fell asleep again. This must have happened several times.

One day, a lady noticed how the doctors were trying to stop me crying and said to them, "Let him cry; if you try to stop him every time he cries, you'll never succeed in curing him. Let him cry."

The doctors looked at her and then looked at me, and decided to do as she suggested: they let me cry. This lasted for weeks. I couldn't stop because wherever I looked, I saw my friend. I disturbed the other patients so much that I had to be moved to a good size room of my own in a remote ward of the hospital.

Another day, I awoke with the sun shining on my face. I was just about to shield my eyes with the blanket when I saw a beautiful bird singing on the windowsill. I got up and went to the window, but the bird had flown away. I looked out of the window. Yet, I immediately wished I hadn't because Christian's image instantly appeared, calling out to me. I became extremely agitated for the apparition looked so real that I forgot he was dead.

Another time, I dreamt that I was in my father's house. I got dressed and went out, but Christian wasn't there. Then I woke up and remembered what had happened. I sat down and started to cry quietly.

I was interrupted by a little girl who wandered into my room with a smile on her face. As I smiled back, she came closer and wiped my tears away, murmuring, "I was sad like you, not for my father – I never knew him – but for my mother, who I lost years ago. Did you lose your mother too?"

I told her that it was my friend who I'd lost, which surprised her. Although I'd lost both parents as well, I only told her about the loss of my friend, for his death made me forget that my parents were also dead.

The little girl replied, "When I lost my mother, I hadn't had enough time with her because I was very young when she died. Now, I live with another family. Perhaps my father will look for me, and perhaps he will find me.

"I used to cry like you, but now I've stopped and started to laugh again. Do you know how I managed that? Let me tell you.

"Did you know that daisies are the most unfortunate flowers in the world? That's because careless people always walk all over them!

"Worse still, in some countries, people in love lie down on the grass and pick daisies. They take a daisy and then they pluck off its petals one by one. As they pluck each petal, they say, 'he loves me; he loves me not,' and if the last petal turns out 'not', they crush the whole flower in despair and start all over again with another daisy.

"I love daisies so much. One day, while I was crying for my mother, a large teardrop fell on a daisy and broke it, making me angry at my tears; so in order not to harm any more daisies, I stopped crying.

"The day I broke that daisy, although I stroked it tenderly, I couldn't bring it back to life because my tears had harmed it. But then I looked at the broken flower in my palm and thought it looked like the sun. As I looked more closely, I saw the face of my mother smiling at me. That frightened me, and I dropped the daisy and ran away.

"But before getting far, I turned round and went back, and picked it up again. When I looked at it, I saw my mother's face again, smiling at me as before. I ran and showed it to my adopted family, but despite careful examination, they couldn't see anything.

"Then I took it to the priest. He couldn't see anything either, but he still believed me. He told me that years ago when he'd visited the Holy Land, he'd had a vision of Jesus sitting by Jacob's Well smiling at him. His friends couldn't see anything, so they'd mocked him, but he'd carried on gazing at the vision. That's why he believed me.

"I'm telling you these things so that you too will be able to see your friend's smiling face in a daisy. This is the last time I'll come here because we're moving far away; so you won't be able to tell me if you've seen your friend's face or not, but I believe you will see him."

She handed me a freshly picked daisy and took a few steps back. Then she looked at me and asked which flower I liked the most. I smiled and said that it was the orchid. She said that of course, it was one of the most beautiful flowers in the world, but daisies were beautiful flowers as well. She gave me a big smile; I could even see her dimples. She left waving.

The little girl hadn't really understood why I was crying: I was crying because I saw Christian's face everywhere I looked, not because I couldn't see him.

At first, I didn't dare look at the daisy, but then, for her sake, I did. To begin with, I couldn't see anything at all, but by and by, as I concentrated on the delicate beauty of the flower, I saw my friend's face. He looked at me sadly, and tears rolled down my cheeks. But when I finally stopped crying, my friend smiled.

Astonished, I tried to make sense of it all. I thought of the girl. I got up and went around the ward asking if anyone had seen her, but no one had. I was very confused and thought that perhaps she too had been a vision. Yet, the flower I was holding was real enough.

As I dried the last of my tears, I fancied that I felt her hand on my shoulder. Not wanting to think any further, I regarded the daisy. This made me start crying all over again, although not one teardrop fell on the flower. However, I only stopped weeping when I saw Christian's face. It was clear that his apparition in the daisy stopped my tears from falling; then I understood why she had given it to me.

While I was still gazing at the daisy, I sensed someone nearby. It was my doctor. He pulled up a chair and sat down beside me. Then he handed me my diary with an apology for reading it. He said that while I had been insensible for the past three months, I had repeatedly called out to my friend. He had wanted to find out from my diary where this person was, but had been unable to do. So I told him.

The doctor asked me to write down everything that had happened to me. Then he stood up and said that providing I didn't burst into tears, I could ask him anything I liked, and to feel free to talk about anything I had on my mind, but for now, he would leave me. I took up my diary and ran back to my room, placing it under the bed. I was terrified of opening it.

I had no desire to stay in the room, so I went out into the hospital garden and sat down on a bench. Then I realised that I no longer had my daisy and began to scream, "Where's my daisy? Where's my daisy?" I looked everywhere but I couldn't find it.

Still screaming, I collapsed on the grass. A whole crowd of nurses came to try and lift me up but I wouldn't move. Finally, one went away and came back with a daisy. That calmed me down. As soon as I saw my friend's smiling face in the flower, I cheered up. As the other nurses drifted away, I asked the one who had brought the daisy, who was the nurse who looked after me, if she could see anything in the flower. She said she couldn't.

I then asked my nurse how I had ended up in the hospital. She said that a group of Jews who'd escaped from Germany had brought me there. When I asked what was happening in Germany, she said that it had started a war in Europe. She then left. I threw the daisy away and sat down again.

I became lost in thought once more, but disturbing visions of Christian kept appearing in my mind, so I ran back towards my room. Just as I was about to go in, I heard someone talking loudly in the room next door. I was curious as to who was staying there, so I knocked three times. The talking stopped and a dwarf opened the door. I was very surprised for it was the first time I'd ever seen such a person.

The dwarf understood my astonishment, saying, "You're not the first – and I'm sure you won't be the last – to look at me in surprise; only another dwarf wouldn't. Come in so I can surprise you some more."

I couldn't help but laugh, and went in. I then realised that he was alone and so had been talking to himself.

He continued, "I know you're a Jew because you all have big noses. You've been crying for months, and me, I've been talking to myself for months; so there's no difference between us really. I talk to myself because I've lost my loved one, and you cry a lot because you've lost your parents. Am I right?" I told him I was crying because I'd lost my best friend.

The dwarf's eyes opened wide and he said, "So you're crying because you've lost your friend? I can only guess what you've been through but obviously you've lost someone special who you loved very much.

"Let me tell you this: I've just arrived here. This is the best hospital in Switzerland – everyone gets cured here; you enter as an ill man but you don't leave as one.

"Anyway, I'll carry on with my story. I lost my beloved wife three months ago. She too was a dwarf.

"Never could I imagine crying for a friend like you, for friends can turn into your enemies in the end. I've never had a friend and wouldn't want one either. Who knows what kind of friendship you had, and I don't want to know.

"What I wanted to say was that I was like you, crying all the time and wearing myself out. Perhaps what I have to say won't help you! But I will tell you anyway. I loved my wife so much that I couldn't imagine life without her. As the saying goes: 'don't love too much because you'll lose it;' and I did: I lost her. You probably lost *your* friend because you loved him too much as well.

"Often, as I came across cemeteries, I would see people being buried, but I didn't feel any pain; I only felt compassion for those people. I understood real pain when I buried my wife. I didn't want to bury her. I would have had her mummified and kept her by my side in a rose garden, but I couldn't.

"I couldn't even commit suicide because of my beliefs. Although people laugh at me because of my size, I've never questioned why He created me this way. I thought there must be a reason and I carried on living. But I did start praying to Him to take me as well. Unfortunately, my prayers have not been accepted and I'm still here.

"After I buried my wife, I stayed at the cemetery for days, even at night. People thought I'd lost my mind, but no one came to ask me why I was behaving like that. Instead, they all avoided me. And that's why I don't want to have a friend; I don't want anyone for a friend.

"One day, as I was walking along crying, I fainted. I passed out because I hadn't been eating. Some passersby called an ambulance and they took me to hospital. There, I carried on crying and calling for my wife. This situation lasted for many months. I couldn't even sleep well.

"Then, one day, I heard someone calling, 'Dwarf! Dwarf!' It was an old lady with a bandage on her chin. She kept on calling me, 'Dwarf! Dwarf!'

"Normally, I wouldn't get annoyed but that day, I just snapped, so I retorted, 'Did your husband do that to your face, old woman? Did he send you here?' She stood up and marched over to me. I was frightened, then, thinking she was going to hit me.

"'No, it wasn't my husband,' she replied calmly, 'it was my dog. I looked after that dog like I would my own child; I fed him with the best food every day, and look what he did to me.'

"She then sat down on the edge of the bed and began to ask me about my troubles. As soon as I'd told her, she took me on her lap and started slapping me.

That startled me. After slapping me for some time, she asked, 'Do the slaps hurt as much now as when I started?'

"I replied that they didn't. She brought me a mirror and although my face was blue, I couldn't feel any pain.

"Then she said, 'You lost your wife and felt great pain, and when you cried every day, you became use to it. But if you opened your heart, you would see that it was as blue as your face.

"'Instead of crying for her, you should go to the cemetery and talk to her. That way, you will make her spirit happy. The way you're behaving now not only harms you, but it harms her spirit as well. And if that doesn't help, sit at the table and imagine she's there with you and talk to her.

"'Don't burden your heart with crying. You know that it's our most delicate organ; don't hurt it – don't hurt yourself.' Then she gently sat me on the bed and left.

"I thought I would follow her advice and started talking to myself. But they thought I was going mad and transferred me here.

"Thinking I was crazy too, the doctors here treated me differently. Finally, one of them had the common sense to ask what was troubling me and who I was talking to. After he'd heard my story, he told all the other doctors to leave me alone and said I could stay here for as long as I wanted.

"That's my story. If it's helped you in any way, once I'm dead, and providing you know where I'm buried, you can bring me a bunch of flowers."

★ ★ ★

When the dwarf had finished, I gave him a hug and went next door to my room. I locked the door so that no one could disturb me, and immediately went to check my nose in front of the mirror: it was true that I had a big nose. Laughing at the thought of that, I lay down on the bed to think. I contemplated both the little girl and the dwarf, and what they had each told me.

I had been thinking for days. When I thought of all the things that had happened to me, I cried. But every time I thought of what I'd been told by these two people, I stopped crying. Yet, I wouldn't open the door to anyone. The nurses brought my food and left it outside.

One day, when I opened the door to pick up my food as usual, I saw a big daisy on the tray. Immediately, I ran to ask a nurse who had put it there. She told me that a little girl had left it, and that she had been with an old woman.

I ran out into the hospital grounds, but there was no one there. I stood looking about me for a long time, but I couldn't see either of them. After a while, I went back to my room. I sat on the bed and held the daisy in my hand. I could see Christian's face in the daisy again, and I talked to him.

While I was getting better, the dwarf left the hospital. During the following months, whenever I felt like crying, I ran out into the garden and found a daisy. Then I talked to the vision of my friend in the flower in order to gain strength. Consequently, I started to take more of an interest in the troubles of the other patients and I told them mine as well. Since I was still young, many people gave me advice. I didn't allow myself to cry anymore, but I never forgot Christian for I could see his face in all the daisies.

★ ★ ★

I spent many months in that hospital. But one day, a Jewish family came to adopt me and we left the hospital together. They didn't have any children of their own, and throughout their lives they'd always adopted Jewish orphans; once they'd raised them and they'd left home, they adopted other one. They weren't believers, but they gave me their love. And they didn't try to make me forget Christian; I always carried a daisy with me.

★ ★ ★

Years passed. The couple who'd adopted me didn't let me leave even though I was old enough. I only lost them when they both died of old age. The war ended and Hitler's death brought joy to many. Every one celebrated Germany's defeat but I didn't. The German people had lost, but it wasn't they who'd started the war; yet they were the ones who'd suffered. I decided to continue living in Switzerland. I enjoyed living there; it was a very clean country.

I remember one day vividly. It was a Monday and I'd gone to a park where I sat watching the swans on the lake. I was thinking how unique and fragile they were, just like orchids, when I suddenly had a flashback to Christian's story about the beautiful swan. I quickly switched my attention to the ducks that were swimming with the swans; but they were taller and no matter how hard I tried, I couldn't ignore them.

I didn't mind recalling my friend, but I didn't want to cry. In order to be strong and keep the promise I'd made him, I had to have my freedom and not spend my time in hospital. So I turned my back on the lake and stared at a tree behind me.

As I was admiring the tree's splendour, I felt something moving on my hand: it was the most beautiful butterfly. It reminded me of Christian when he'd told his story about a butterfly to the opera singer on the train; actually everything reminded me of my friend. I started talking to the butterfly and it moved its legs as if it could understand what I was saying. Occasionally, it would lift its head and flutter its wings.

While I was talking to the butterfly, a little hand suddenly struck my hand, killing the beautiful creature. I had no idea what was going on but turned to see a little boy smirking at me; he even stuck his tongue out.

At that point, my tears started to flow. Why had this child killed the harmless butterfly? I thought that one always harmed the defenceless and the weak; if I'd had a wasp in my hand, the child wouldn't have been so quick to strike out. I took the beautiful lifeless body in my hand and continued talking to it while silently crying and patting the creature.

Then I heard a female voice: "Such a shame," it said, and its owner sat down next to me. Immediately, I caught the faintest scent of rose oil. "While you were talking to the butterfly, it was obvious that you were a million miles away. I couldn't hear what you were actually saying, but watching you and seeing your tears made me realise that the butterfly had reminded you of someone dear to you.

"Fortunately I've never lost anyone I loved that much, so I don't know anything about that kind of pain. I'm sure I will experience it one day, but I hope that isn't for a very long time. Your sorrow is vast; who have you lost?"

I looked at her with tears in my eyes and told her that I'd lost my best friend. She knew I was Jewish and, from the way she spoke, I knew she was Jewish too.

"Many of us have lost our loved ones," she replied sorrowfully. "Are your parents with you?"

I told her that I'd lost them too before I left Germany. She then asked if my friend had come from the same village as me. I knew she was thinking that he must have been a Jew as well. I confirmed that we'd both lived in the same village and then added, "He was a German boy."

She was surprised and stared at me. No doubt she wanted to say, "Do you know what the Germans have done to our people?" She had no idea what I'd lived through, so she was right to think like that.

She smiled and stood up. As she was about to leave, she took a piece of paper from her bag and on it she wrote her address, saying that I could visit her at any time and that her father would be pleased to meet such a person as myself. Then she was gone.

I looked at the scrap of paper in my hand and saw that she lived in a village not very far from me. She'd also written down her name and telephone number. Her name was Rebecca.

I was alone again with the dead butterfly. After stroking its beautiful wings once more, I buried it. I never went back to that park again; I even avoided passing it.

★ ★ ★

Weeks went by and I forgot all about the girl I'd met in the park. One day as I was walking along, I saw an advertisement for a bank on a bus. It read, "Don't forget to call us." I walked on; then I saw the same advertisement again, and that made me think of the girl. I went to a phone booth and called her.

When she answered the phone, I sensed that she was in a very good mood; but I didn't know if it was my call that had made her happy or whether it was something else entirely. I asked her when I could come and visit them. I held on while she consulted her father, and he made her ask when would be convenient for me. I told her that I was standing next to a bus stop and I could come right away. When she agreed, I got very excited; I was being invited to a Jewish family home for the first time since the death of my adopted parents.

On the way, I admired the cleanliness and beauty of the Swiss countryside. Before long, I arrived at the bus stop in her village. I had to ask directions from a few people, but I found the right street in the end. When I looked around, I saw that it was in a Jewish neighbourhood. Everyone greeted me warmly – probably because of the size of my nose.

I found myself in front of a door. I rang the bell and some children came to open it, which I thought was a good sign. Then an old man appeared and invited me in. I removed my shoes and followed him. I saw that they weren't poor. Indeed, I'd never met a poor Jew in my whole life. I followed the old man into the living room.

As soon as I sat down, Rebecca came in. As she said "hello" to me, she blushed. I remember thinking that it must be because of the overheated room.

Before long the place was filled with guests; they all wanted to see me and get to know me. There was even a writer who wished to record everything I had to say. But that stopped me talking freely.

Seeing my discomfort, an old man said to me, "This fellow is indeed a writer, but he never lets the general public read about our lives. Our stories will be added to the special library for our people where no one else but us has access."

So amidst my tears, I told the writer everything I could remember about what had happened to Christian and me. They all listened for hours and looked sad at the end. I promised that I would donate a copy of my diary, when I'd completed it, to their special library. When I looked at Rebecca, I knew she understood why I had such affection for my friend.

When I finally ended my story, the eldest person in the room said, "We have known for hundreds of years why we are being punished; and why all those who yet live are still being punished. As the world is rid of bad people, good ones will disappear as well, but His aim has always been to make us a pure nation."

This evaluation made me regret having told them everything, but it was too late. I remembered my father's words: "If you open the door of a bird's cage, it will not think you have released it, it will think it has found its freedom."

Rebecca's father had heard what the old man said. He hugged me and, addressing the older fellow, said, "You are wrong. Your thoughts are the same as those Jews who lived thousands of years ago. No one being was created to be superior to another. Eve was not only created in the same way as Adam but she even came from one of his ribs.

"Neither is it God's aim to make us a pure nation, for do others not suffer as well? Can we say that they are not pure? No we can't. It is only when we no longer utter His name that calamity befalls us.

"Remember Moses? Do you think God wanted to make him pure? He never made any mistakes, or forgot to be thankful, but, because of his people, he too wandered about the desert without ever setting foot in the Holy Land."

Rebecca's father's words made me feel better because they were similar to my own father's. The old man gave Rebecca's father a hug. "I'm just an old man," he said laughing.

The time had come to eat. I sat next to Rebecca's father and she was opposite me. Sometimes, she'd look up at me and smile. Her father asked me to tell him a little about myself, which I did, and this made him very happy. After blessing the food, we started eating. Although Rebecca's eyes were often on me, my attention was devoted wholly to the tasty food I was enjoying so much.

In the middle of dinner, Rebecca's father said some things that made me blush. He began, "I want to tell everyone that I really like this young man. I have six sons, but only one daughter. I would have liked at least one more daughter."

He then stole a mischievous glance at me before continuing, "Will you marry my daughter? Will you look after her? Everyone knows that she is one of the people I love most in this world; but there is one condition: I will not give you my precious pearl before you finish writing your diary."

I reddened even more deeply and nearly choked on my food. I stood up slowly and looked at him. He calmly repeated what he had just said. I looked at her and she looked at me.

Almost shouting, her father said, "I expect you here with a copy of your diary soon! Rest assured that until then, I will not give my daughter away to another, because I know you will come back."

Walking along the street after I'd finally taken my leave of this eccentric but endearing family, I saw my reflection in a shop window: it was still scarlet. The shopkeeper jokingly said that I must be in love; I could only confirm that I was. It was the first time I'd been in love, so I didn't know what to do next.

While waiting for the bus at the bus stop, I overheard someone in the phone booth saying, "I love you." The bus arrived as the call ended. Instead of getting on the bus, I darted into the booth and dialled Rebecca's number.

She answered and I asked her to put her father on. I told him, "Yes, I will marry your daughter, but I won't come back before I complete my diary and make a copy of it."

"We will wait for you," he said approvingly, "but don't rush; write down everything you remember."

I promised that I would do that and put the phone down. When the next bus arrived, as I got on, I smiled at the driver, who said, "When I was in love, I too smiled at bus drivers."

Then all the passengers began to laugh, and they kept on laughing until I got off.

As soon as I got home, I started to write my diary again. As I'd been blessed with a very good memory, I was able to recall everything as if it had happened yesterday.

* * *

I wrote for months with the utmost care. Yet, when the time came to write about Christian's death, I couldn't; each time I tried to begin, I started crying. I called Rebecca and explained the situation.

She said, "If you stop writing your diary now, you'll never be able to go back to it; you have no other choice but to carry on, as you weep if you must."

Her advice was very simple. I laughed at myself, for I wasn't expecting her to be so level-headed. That stopped me crying, and, ambitiously, I went back to my diary. The more I thought of her words, the more I wrote, and I didn't shed another tear after that. I'd been expecting her to show sympathy but if she had, I would have just continued to weep and wouldn't have been able to write at all.

After several months, I'd finally finished my account. It hadn't been easy, for I'd relived all my past trials. But the hardest part was yet to come: I had to show it to Rebecca's father if I was to marry his daughter.

When I called him to announce that I'd completed my diary and had made a copy of it, he was extremely excited. Not long after that, Rebecca and I were married. In spite of our youth, we were very happy, and we loved and respected each other. We travelled around the world and even went to Jerusalem, where my ancestors had lived. My past sunk into history and my tears were replaced by laughter. Rebecca soon became pregnant and we had an addition to our family: a baby boy. I was fully content with life.

Having a son was wonderful. But twenty-seven days after his birth, I had an unexpected dream: Christian and his mother were playing in the middle of a field. As I called their names, they turned round to look at me but carried on playing. Although I ran towards them for a long time, I never managed to reach them. I got slower and slower.

Shaking his head, my friend smiled, "You're very tired aren't you? You can't run anymore can you?" I could hardly breathe.

Suddenly it began to rain orchids. Christian said, "We haven't forgotten you. Here, take all these orchids."

He gathered up a bunch from the ground and, coming over to me, said, "Take them."

I woke up sobbing. I'd frightened my wife; then my son started crying. She didn't know who to attend to first. I asked her to go to the baby so that I could be alone for a moment.

My worst fears were confirmed: I went back to crying uncontrollably, and Rebecca couldn't stop me. She didn't know how to help. If I wasn't languishing in bed, I just sat in a corner, refusing to eat or drink anything much at all.

This situation lasted for weeks. I had constant visions of my friend with a garland of orchids around his neck. I knew nothing could be done for me, but it was worrying and disturbing for everybody.

Thinking she could cure me, Rebecca even asked her family to look after our son and devoted all her time to nursing me. After a month, she too had lost weight and had dark rings under her eyes due to the many sleepless nights. Her family could hardly recognise her. Although they felt sorry for me, their daughter's state of health worried them more.

As Rebecca couldn't help me, she cried along with me. Her family finally told her that if she put me in a mental hospital, I would stand a better chance of recovery. But she refused to take such a drastic measure, saying that she loved me very much and couldn't do that; if she did, she would end up in an institution herself. In an attempt to avoid aggravating the situation, her family virtually stopped visiting us altogether.

One day, I left the house in tears. I was alone and had no idea where I was going. I ended up at a school playground and stood watching the children. I had a vision of Christian and cheered up a bit. I was totally immersed in my daydream, when I heard the sound of bells peeling dolefully. I turned my head towards the sound and saw a huge church.

Many people were filing into it; they were in mourning and all dressed in black. Weeping again, I followed them. They all looked at me thinking I was crying for their departed. The dead person was an old woman. Everyone put flowers on her coffin.

As I had no flowers with which to pay my respects, I kissed her forehead. My lips froze: it had been like kissing a cold stone. I cried harder, which didn't shock anyone for they were all immersed in their own grief. I sat down and listened to the priest, whose words eased my sadness.

When the service was over, I knelt and prayed for hours. Suddenly, I felt a hand on my shoulder. I thought it was the priest asking me to stop praying, but there was no one there. I closed my eyes and was just about to resume praying when I felt the same touch on my shoulder again. Still, no one was there, so I carried on praying.

When I felt the touch of the hand a third time, I didn't open my eyes; I just smiled and continued praying with my eyes closed. When I ended my prayer and said "amen," I became aware of a weight on my shoulder again. I opened my eyes and this time, I saw the smiling priest.

He asked how I was and invited me to sit down; so I did. He then asked how he could help me.

I said, "Teach me to be a Christian." That reminded me of my friend's grandmother, who had told me a story about a similar religious experience.

The priest asked, "Aren't you a Christian, then?"

I replied: "No, I'm a Jew."

Frowning, he enquired, "Then why are you praying like a Christian? There are plenty of synagogues around here."

"Teach me Christianity," I repeated.

He fetched a Bible, but warned me that I shouldn't be hasty in changing my religion; yet, if I truly wished to convert, I would have to study the New Testament first. He said that I needed to work through my reasons for wanting to change my religion. More importantly, I must pray for guidance and confirmation before committing to Christianity. He promised to talk to me about it once I'd finished reading the Bible.

I took the Bible and arrived home without a tearstained face, which surprised Rebecca. But when she saw the book in my hands, she was startled, and this time, it was she who started to weep. I went to my room and started reading.

A few days later my wife returned to her family, saying that she couldn't live in a house where there was a Bible. This didn't shock me; she was devoted to her religion.

No one had visited me for months, and now I was left all on my own. Once I had finished, reading the Bible, I took the priest's advice. I knelt down and asked for confirmation and then I left the house.

Outside, a strange thing happened. I saw a bird that was singing beautifully. However, when I neared it and stopped to listen, it flew away. But it landed on a nearby branch and continued to sing, as if to say,

"Follow me."

I thought about this for a while and then decided to follow the bird. It flew very low and stopped at a graveyard, which didn't please me at all. I was just about to protest when the bird alighted on a grave.

It was like a dream: the grave was covered with orchids; I couldn't have wished for a better sign. In spite of the fact that I was obviously reminded of Christian, I didn't shed a single tear. Instead, I decided it was about time I talked to the priest. He baptised me without hesitation; I had become a Christian.

I went to see my wife and told her everything. With tears in her eyes, she told me that she couldn't live with a Christian; and even if she could, her family would disown her.

"I love my family very much," she said sorrowfully. "I love our son very much, and I love you so very much. I would have been prepared to stay by your side even if you had cried for the rest of your life; but I can't live with the fact that you've become a Christian.

"Think carefully: don't change your religion because of your beloved friend; otherwise, it will end our marriage."

I was taken completely by surprise by what she said, but I told her, "I didn't change my religion because of my friend. Even if I tried to explain why I've become a Christian it wouldn't change anything would it? But the truth is that I believe that when my soul was created, Christ the Lord saw it and touched it, and that's why I've become a Christian."

As her tears flowed, I kissed Rebecca on the forehead. After going to see our son for the last time, I told my wife that I was going back to Germany, and then I left her.

I never saw Rebecca nor heard her voice again from that day forth. Once again, I had lost a loved one and was left on my own, but I thought it was my destiny and I remained strong; those I had lost this time were at least still alive, and I was very thankful for that.

After I left my wife and son, I had to stay in Switzerland for a few more days. At night, I constantly dreamt of Christian; but the dreams didn't make me cry anymore because I had decided to return to the country of our birth.

I had one last meeting with the priest, and then left Switzerland and recrossed the border back into Germany. But this didn't cheer me, for I knew I was going to be reminded of my childhood and start crying again. I was truly going back to my past.

Chapter 20

As soon as I set foot on German soil, I could see that everything had changed. Despite the end of the war, people seemed sad. Their sorrow was obvious: there was no communication between them; everyone had lost a loved one during the war.

I had no idea who had won this war but it was clear to me who had lost it. Some had made money out of the war by writing books. Many books were written and films made about Hitler. But without realising it, they were turning him into history's unforgettable figure. They didn't consider that no one now alive had seen Hitler die. It was said that he had committed suicide and his body had burnt, and everyone believed that.

Nothing much had been done about the innocent people who had died in the war, nor for those who had survived and knew the truth. It seemed that the books and films had merely commercialised the war. However, I considered that on Judgement Day, some would get their reward and others their punishment; for those who had done bad things, and those who had done good things, everyone's turn would come.

I journeyed towards the tunnel. The natural beauty of the countryside was at least still the same. Everything was as I remembered it. I had tears in my eyes even though I didn't want them there. As I approached the tunnel entrance, I started trembling. I knew I wasn't going to be able to hold back the tears when I saw the tunnel.

But the opposite happened. I'd met Christian many years ago at a graveside while he was pouring out his heartbroken pain. Similarly now, a child of about seven was doing the same thing at the tunnel entrance. When I heard his voice, I went and sat under a tree and listened to him, just as I'd once listened to my friend so long ago.

The child was saying, "Here I am, doing exactly what you asked me to do. I don't know if my parents are alive or dead. But if they're dead, and if I knew where they were buried, I could adorn their graves instead of adorning the entrance to a tunnel. I've never seen them; I don't know what they're like. Lots of people have hugged me but I want my own parents' hugs.

"I know I'm an orphan, but why am I waiting here for a stranger to come? Instead, why don't you tell me where I should go to wait for my parents if they're alive; or tell me if they're dead, so that I can adorn their graves?

"Please, whoever is going to come let them come soon, for I don't have the strength to carry on waiting here anymore."

With tears in my eyes, I stood up and went over to him. He was frightened and ran away; he'd been deep in thought and I'd startled him. I called, "Please wait," and he stopped, and turned to face me.

I couldn't believe my eyes: he looked so much like Christian that I thought my friend had stepped out of his grave. "Don't be frightened," I said reassuringly. Then I said that I was the one my friend had told him to wait for.

Slowly, he retraced his steps. I promised him that I would look for his parents and find them whether they were alive or dead. With a smile on his face, he asked me the name of my friend, and I told him that it was Christian.

He then wanted to know my favourite flower. Hearing that it was the orchid, he began, "I live in an orphanage not far away; I was taken there when I was a baby but I don't know who brought me there. I know you will find my family; I believe you.

"From when I was very small, I've dreamt of a person who has always told me to go to this tunnel entrance and wait for his friend there; I've been coming here for such a long time.

"As your answers to my questions were right, I know it's you I've been waiting for; but why have I been waiting for you for so long?"

I said that I would tell him about the person in his dream when he was older, promising him that my friend wouldn't disturb him anymore.

As for why he'd been waiting for me here, I went up to the tunnel entrance and, gesturing towards it, said that I couldn't go in, but he could; and he should bring out a little bag that I had hidden under some stones years ago.

He went in through the small hole without difficulty, and soon emerged with the bag. We both sat down under the tree and I felt inside the bag. First, my fingers found an envelope. With trembling hands, I took it out and opened it. It contained a letter from Christian enclosing two photographs; one of his mother and the other of him. I immediately burst into tears.

The child said: "He's the one I dreamt of, and he looks so much like me, except for the ears. Mine are bigger than his; that's why I was nicknamed Elephant."

Then I showed him Christian's mother's photo. He too thought she was beautiful, and said that perhaps his mother was as pretty as this lady. He couldn't get enough of looking at the photos.

Then I read my friend's short letter.

He wrote, "Doesn't he look like me? I've included a photo of my mother and myself. When you miss me, you can look at it.

"You can put my mother's picture on her grave once it's rebuilt in marble. I have one last request: please inscribe these words on her tombstone: 'She lived for orchids but sadly never had enough of them. Her peaceful soul rests here.'"

He ended, "Your loving friend, Christian." By now I'd wept so much that my tears had soaked the letter through.

Then I felt inside the bag again and took out the five tiny pouches that it had clearly contained when my father had given it to me. When I opened the first and poured the contents out into my hand, I couldn't believe my eyes.

My father had said, "Take your father's riches with you." The child said, "Shining glass!" I said, "These pieces of *glass* are called diamonds." He had no idea what diamonds were.

I put everything back in the little bag and put the little bag in my coat pocket. I then took the child's hand and we walked towards Christian's house. On the way, I told him that he didn't have to go to the tunnel entrance anymore. With a deep sigh, he thanked me.

When we reached Christian's house, I realised that it was now the orphanage. Instead of crying, I started to laugh because there were so many children playing there.

A lady saw us approaching and came over. She smiled; the fact that a stranger was holding the hand of one of her charges didn't seem to bother her. She gave me her own hand and asked if I were a Jew. I confirmed that I was. Then the child told her that I was going to find his parents and went off to play with his friends.

The lady suddenly became sad and sat down on a chair. She was just about to tell me something when I interrupted, asking if she would mind listening to me first. She readily agreed.

I told her more or less everything, a story that lasted several hours and one that was punctuated by both our tears. I ended by telling her the reason for my return to Germany and who had lived in this house previously.

When I'd finished, in her gentle way, she said that I had a very moving life story, but she didn't think I should have made such a promise to the little boy because she knew his parents had died during the war. Some people had found him by the roadside and taken him to a hospital. He was so ill that they had simply waited for him to die. However, a miracle had happened and he'd got a reprieve.

"But we're still waiting for him to die," she concluded. There's no cure for his illness, so I won't attempt to describe it. We just try to make sure he's happy.

"For a long time now, he's been going to that tunnel. We've always known because we made sure that he was always followed; we even knew when he met you. You've given him hope but, as hard as it is, my advice would be to stay away from him so that he can forget all about you and your promise.

"He's already on strong medication, and if, in addition to that, he's led to believe that you're going to find his parents, he'll suffer even more in the long run.

"He's always saying, 'If only I knew where their graves were,' but we try not raise his hopes; and you shouldn't either. In fact, I think it would best if you didn't come here again."

Suddenly, our attention was drawn to the sound of screaming nearby. She ran towards it and I followed. There was a crowd ahead of us. Once we'd managed to get through it, all we saw was the child looking very ill and lying almost lifeless on the ground.

She looked at me bewildered while I bent down and kissed the child's hand. After murmuring, "I've kept my promise," he drew his last breath.

I turned my back on the dead child and walked away.

★ ★ ★

As soon as I'd found a place to stay, I hurried to Christian's mother's grave and uprooted the thorn tree. In its place, I beautified the gravesite with white marble. When the inscription that Christian had specified should be engraved on the stone had been finished, I fixed his mother's photo above it, adding an engraving of an orchid. I then put pots and pots of orchids around the grave, ensuring that they were replaced often with fresh ones.

My next job was to find out where Christian was buried, but I had no idea how. Yet, I knew that I first had to go to the place where his father had shot him, which was going to be emotionally difficult. It wasn't the way there I was worried about, for I wasn't going to journey through the tunnel this time, but I had reservations about recalling this aspect of the past and felt weak again.

Nonetheless, after crying and then praying on my knees for hours, I set off, paying someone to take me there by car. As soon as I saw the place, I burst into tears and asked to be dropped off further along the road – in fact, much further along.

Realising that I was a Jew, the driver asked if my family had died there. When I replied that they hadn't, it had been my friend, he said,

"Poor Jew!"

But when I corrected, "Poor German!" he became very cool and left.

It all came back. I was even able to recognise the spot where he'd fallen dead. I bent down and touched the soil and kissed it, all the while crying and praying.

My prayer was short: "I am grateful for the life Thou hast given me and I am grateful for the life of my friend. In spite of so much pain and sorrow, I have lived to grow older. And I am still faithful to Thee.

"But I made a promise to Thee that I have not yet been able to keep. I have not forgotten it, but if Thou dost not help me, I cannot keep it. I need Thy help: where is the dead body of my friend?"

As I finished my prayer, I heard Christian's voice calling me. I stopped crying when he came and took my hand. We started to run. I knew it was in my imagination but it felt so real. We ran together and at that moment my happiness was indescribable. I haven't written it down and I can't even put into spoken words how I felt then.

We ran for a long time. We finally reached a big field and he let go of my hand, and started to move away from me. When I began to cry, he shook his head as if to say, "Don't!" I wiped my tears and watched him walk on. When he stopped, I saw his mother appear next to him and they both smiled at me. For a while, they both stood there smiling. Then his mother took his hand and they were gone.

Seeing him so vividly was painful, but, although I knew he was dead, parting from him was even worse. However, this was the last time he appeared to me and the last time I shed tears for him; and henceforth, my sleep was untroubled by dreams about him.

I placed two stones to mark the spot where I'd last seen the vision of my friend, and then went to find the owner of the field. When I offered him a lot of money for it, he laughed, wanting to know why I was prepared to give such a large amount for a useless field that was as barren as a desert.

I quickly told him a very much shortened version of my life story. He still didn't really understand – but he did sell me the field. I built a beautiful grave there, making sure that it was always adorned with orchids. I also planted a hazelnut tree nearby.

Once I'd accomplished this part of my mission, it was time to visit my old neighbourhood. When I got there, it looked very different. Everything had changed and there wasn't a single Jew to be seen. It hardly looked like a village anymore. There was a newly built house where I had once lived: I just stared at it. I couldn't locate the whereabouts of my parents' bodies either, so I had no other choice but to carry on remembering them as they were.

There's a saying about God being full of miracles isn't there? That saying is true. One day, while I was wandering around the neighbourhood, I went into an antique shop. On the second floor, I found the chair I'm sitting in now; it was in a corner covered in dust, but it had been in my father's family for generations and I recognised it straightaway. Tears sprang to my eyes when I saw it and went to touch it. The owner came up smiling and said, "The chair has found its owner."

I told him my story, but he couldn't remember how the chair had come to be in his shop. He gave it to me for free.

Although I hadn't been shown where my parents were buried, He had given me as a present the chair my father had sat in for years, and my mother had polished and cherished. I couldn't expect any more from Him.

* * *

Many years later, very early in the morning, I saw someone lying on my friend's grave. Curious, I approached to see who it was. I called out but there was no reply. Once I had reached it, I couldn't believe my eyes. The person on the grave was dead. He was holding an orchid in one hand and a letter in the other. I recognised him immediately: it was Christian's father.

I took the letter and read it: "You disgusting Jew, I have no idea how you discovered where my son was buried. The fact that you found this place convinced me to start believing, but this does not mean I am about to start like disgusting Jews; I enjoyed killing every single Jew I dispatched during the war.

"If it were not for you, stinking Jew, my son would still be alive today. If his mother had not been so fond of these repulsive flowers, we could have been a very happy family.

"I have one thing to ask you: bury me next to my son. If you want, you can report me to the state and they will reward you, for I exterminated many Jews during the war. Perhaps they will mummify me and place me in a museum; those Jews who still live know me very well. But it is up to you; I would prefer to be buried next to my son."

I had no words, but I was still happy that, thanks to me, a person like him had become a believer, even if it was in his own twisted way.

His horrible letter had no effect on me; without thinking, I dug a hole alongside Christian's grave and buried his father next to him. I even placed my friend's hand into his father's. I never told anyone that he was buried there. I've spent much of my riches on orphans.

This is my life story; the story of why I abandoned you, my son.

★ ★ ★

Silence reigned in the room. While I had been reading my story, one by one, all my grandchildren had fallen asleep. I turned towards my son with tears in my eyes and asked him for his forgiveness.

He hugged me and said, "You've never done anything wrong in your whole life; what is there to forgive?" and started to cry.

I couldn't stop either. I kept calling him "My son" and he "Dear father." After a while, I noticed that there was no one else with us in the room.

My son said, "The time has come for you to read the letter my mother wrote to you," and after kissing my forehead, he too left.

I closed my diary and then turned my attention to the letter from my beloved wife, and read: "My Darling Jacob, by the time you read this letter, my soul will have already gone to heaven. I have sent our son to you and sprinkled rose oil on this letter; perhaps the smell will still be on it when you get it.

"My handwriting is a bit shaky, as I am writing to you from my hospital bed. I am also sending you my ring and handkerchief. I cannot take them with me; the only thing I can take with me is my memory of our time together.

"I cannot tell you how much I love you. My family insisted that I remarry, but I refused over and over again because I could not vow that my love for God was greater than my love for you. I still cannot express the love I feel for you, for it is too great.

"I have lived in the hope that one day, you would realise the mistake you made about your religion. I always thought you changed your religion because of your friend. But before my soul has left my body, I have come to understand that I was wrong and that you sincerely believe in your religion. My only worry is that when you die, your soul will not be with me.

"I love you; I have always loved you. I have missed you since the moment you left us. I would have gone crazy if you had left me before we had our son. When he started talking, he used to ask about you; I told him that you worked far away and always came to see him when he was fast asleep, and that you never failed to kiss him before leaving again. I often bought him toys, telling him they were from you.

"I have received all your letters, but I could not reply to them. There was no way that I could have lived with a Christian. If I had answered, I would have given you hope, which I did not want to do, as it would have been very cruel of me.

"I do not know how to tell you in words how much I have missed you, and how much I have loved you and will always love you. I have put on lipstick to kiss this letter for you. I will continue loving you through all eternity.

"It is hard to stop writing this letter, which I am sending billions of kisses with, and again, my darling, I love you. Your loving wife, Rebecca."

To let her soul know that I too had never stopped loving her, I touched my lips to the letter. I also made a promise to myself that one day I would take to her grave the most beautiful flowers on this earth.

I have no reason to worry about anything anymore. I'm grateful to my God that He sent my son to replace me so that the promise I made to my friend will be kept.

There will always be orchids on the two graves.

THE END